Happy Ch~~ T~~ !

ORGAN FAILURE

The 9th Bernie Fazakerley Mystery

Judy

JUDY FORD

Bernie Fazakerley Publications

ORGAN FAILURE

Published by Bernie Fazakerley Publications

Copyright © 2018 Judy Ford

All rights reserved.

This book is a work of fiction. Any references to real people, events, establishments, organisations or locales are intended only to provide a sense of authenticity and are used fictitiously. All of the characters and events are entirely invented by the author. Any resemblances to persons living or dead are purely coincidental.

No part of this book may be used, transmitted, stored or reproduced in any manner whatsoever without the author's written permission.

ISBN: 1-91-108338-4
ISBN-13: 978-1-911083-38-2

DEDICATION

Dedicated to the congregation of St Luke's Church,
Dunham-on-the-Hill, in memory of their organ restoration
appeal and the anxious time of waiting while the repairs
were carried out!

New Road Baptist Church, Oxford

CONTENTS

ACKNOWLEDGEMENTS

I would like to thank the authors of a wide range of internet resources, which have been invaluable for researching the background to this book. These include (among others):

- Spinal Injuries Association
  (http://www.spinal.co.uk/page/living-with-sci)
- Wikipedia (https://en.wikipedia.org/)
- Google Maps (https://www.google.co.uk/maps)
- Police Oracle (https://www.policeoracle.com)
- The Disabled Police Association
  (http://www.disabledpolice.info/)
- The Roman Catholic Diocese of Westminster
  (http://rcdow.org.uk/), Diocese of Lancaster
  (http://www.lancasterdiocese.org.uk/wp-content/uploads/2015/05/Celebrating-the-Sacrament-of-Confirmation-Jan2016-1.pdf),
  Archdiocese of Birmingham
  (https://www.birminghamdiocese.org.uk/) and
  Archdiocese of Cardiff (https://rcadc.org/year-of-mercy/confession-the-sacrament-of-mercy/).
- The Institute of British Organ builders
  (www.ibo.co.uk)
- The Royal School of Church Music
  (http://www.rscm.com)
- The Sentencing Council for England and Wales
  (https://www.sentencingcouncil.org.uk/)
- The Crown Prosecution Service
  (https://www.cps.gov.uk)

I am indebted to FutureLearn
(https://www.futurelearn.com) for its excellent online courses in forensic science and the UK judicial system.

Members of the *Pesky Methodists* Facebook group provided valuable opinions on churches and organs. I am particularly grateful to group member Andy Stoker, who suggested the title for this book.

Members of the *Apostrophe Protection Society* Facebook group gave useful advice on grammar.

I would like to give particular thanks to Gillian Gilbert for reading the manuscript, giving helpful comments and pointing out typographical errors.

Every effort has been made to trace copyright holders. The publishers will be glad to rectify in future editions any errors or omissions brought to their attention.

GLOSSARY OF UK POLICE RANKS

Uniformed police

Chief Constable (CC) – Has overall charge of a regional police force, such as Thames Valley Police, which covers Oxford and a large surrounding area.

Deputy Chief Constable (DCC) – The senior discipline authority for each force. 2nd in command to the CC.

Assistant Chief Constable (ACC) – 4 in the Thames Valley Police Service, each responsible for a policy area.

Chief Superintendent ('Chief Super') – Head of a policing area or department.

Police Superintendent – Responsible for a local area within a police force.

Chief Inspector (CI) – Responsible for overseeing a team in a local area.

Police Inspector – Senior operational officer overseeing officers on duty 24/7.

Police Sergeant – Supervises a team of officers.

Police Constable (PC) – 'Bobby on the beat'. Likely to be the first to arrive in response to an emergency call.

Crime Investigation Department (CID) – Plain clothes officers

Detective Superintendent (DS) – Responsible for crime investigation in a local area.

Detective Chief Inspector (DCI) – Responsible for overseeing a crime investigation team in a local area. May be the Senior Investigating Officer heading up a criminal investigation.

Detective Inspector (DI) – Oversees crime investigation 24/7. May be the Senior Investigating Officer heading up a criminal investigation.

Detective Sergeant (DS) – Supervises a team of CID officers.

Detective Constable (DC) – One of a team of officers investigating crimes.

These descriptions are based on information from the following sources:

[1] Mental Health Cop blog, by Inspector Michael Brown, Mental Health co-ordinator, College of Policing. https://mentalhealthcop.wordpress.com/, accessed 31st March 2017.

[2] Thames Valley Police website, https://www.thamesvalley.police.uk , accessed 31st March 2017.

PLAN OF ST CYPRIAN'S CHURCH AND GROUNDS

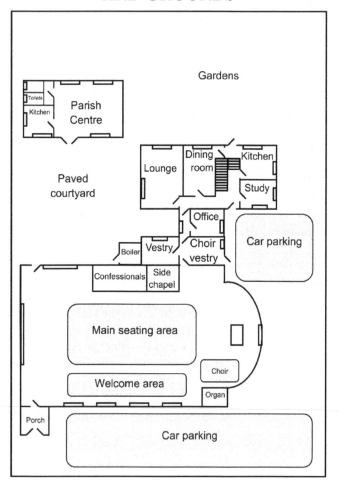

1 EMERGENCY ROOM

'And then I lead the way into the church, carrying the Paschal Candle, and-,' Father Damien broke off at the sound of a knock on the door of his study. He looked up from the leather-bound missal that lay open on the round meeting table in front of him. Who could that be? There was nobody in the house to answer the front door, so whoever it was must have come through the interconnecting passage from the church. There was work going on in there to fix problems caused by a recent roof leak. Please God this was not more bad news about the fabric of the building. It was going to be touch and go whether the current renovation work would be completed in time for the Easter Vigil, as it was. The knocking came again, louder this time.

'Come in!'

The door opened a few inches and a man's face appeared round it. Fr. Damien's heart sank as he recognised Keith Boswell, the organ builder who was restoring the pipe organ. His expression made it clear that he had not come to report good news.

'I'm sorry to disturb you, Father, but ...,' he paused as

if reluctant to go on.

'That's alright,' Fr. Damien assured him. 'What can I do for you?'

'There's – we've found – there's something you ought to see.'

'Could it wait just a few minutes?' Fr. Damien inclined his head towards his confirmation candidate, who was sitting in silence a little further round the table.

'I – I think – I'd rather you came now. Arthur's all shook up about it. I really think you ought to see it right away.'

'Alright.'

The priest got to his feet. What could have happened to cause such disquiet in the usually placid organ builder? Numerous setbacks and mishaps had left him completely unperturbed up to this point. He had brushed away Father Damien's anxious enquiries as to whether the organ would be ready in time for the Easter Masses with calm equanimity. No need to worry: the replacement parts would arrive; the damage was more extensive than he had thought, but there was no question of the instrument being beyond repair; the job was taking longer than expected, but there was plenty of time.

There must be something seriously wrong to turn Keith Boswell's round, red-cheeked face so grey and make his speech so faltering.

Father Damien crossed the room, turning back as he got to the door, to address the tall man with fading red hair who was still sitting patiently at the table.

'Sorry about this, Peter. I'd better go and see what this is all about. Carry on looking through the liturgy. I don't suppose I'll be long.'

The organ builder led the way at a brisk walk, along the passageway from the presbytery, through the door into the vestry, and out into the church.

'You remember there's this wooden platform that the organ's on?' he said, speaking rapidly and in a rather breathless voice.

Father Damien nodded. 'Mmm?'

'The rain must've rotted the boards. Arthur was on it, fixing a new panel ready for getting the tracker action and the console back up there. He stepped back and his foot went right through.'

'That shouldn't be too much of a problem, should it?' Father Damien asked, relieved that the hitch seemed to be a relatively simple one. 'I'll get on to the builder right away and get him to replace the boards.'

'It's not the boards I'm worried about. It's what's under them.'

'Oh?'

'We didn't know how bad the rot was, so we ripped up a couple of the boards and then we saw it.'

'What? What did you see?'

They crossed the chancel to reach the organ – or rather the place where the organ should have been. The disastrous leak in the roof above where it had stood had necessitated it being stripped down and rebuilt, a process that had been predicted to take three weeks and which was now threatening to exceed three months. Indeed, in his darker moments, Father Damien was beginning to worry that it might extend to three years!

Arthur, Keith's son and assistant, was sitting on a chair in the area on the south side of the church where the pews had been removed and replaced with comfortable chairs and small tables to facilitate socialising after the Sunday Mass. Fr Damien looked at him anxiously. Was he ill? His face was very white and he kept moistening his lips and running his fingers through his hair.

'Come and have a look for yourself,' Keith continued, stepping up on to the platform and taking a small torch out of his pocket. Father Damien clambered up beside him and they both crouched down next to a jagged hole in the floorboards.

'There!' Keith said, 'shining the torch down into the

hole and pointing with his other hand. 'Is that what I think it is?'

Peter Johns dutifully studied the rubric of the Easter Vigil. After nearly forty years as a police officer, he found it hard not to be distracted by thinking about the safety implications of the rituals. Who would be responsible for the fire that was to be set alight, outside in the small courtyard at the back of the church? Once it had been used to light the Easter candle, and the congregation had gone inside, would the bonfire be left there to burn out unattended? With the church in complete darkness as they all trooped in, how would they avoid trips and falls? Was it really wise to allow up to a hundred or more people, including a good number of children from the church's associated Primary School, to carry lighted candles in procession?

Peter told himself sternly that none of this was his concern and that he should be concentrating on the symbolism of the rites. This was all part of *a brief service of light*, according to the book. The whole point was that they would begin in complete darkness and then the lights would go on as a sign of the resurrection. Nevertheless, he hoped that those children would be well supervised and that there would be safe holders where they would deposit their candles once they had reached their places.

After that came something called *the liturgy of the word*. Father Damien had asked Peter to read one of the Bible passages. Perhaps he had better check that it didn't contain any unpronounceable names or tricky sentence constructions. He did not want to make a fool of himself in front of what Father Damien had assured him would be the largest congregation of the year. Disconcertingly, he was himself expected to be a big draw: they did not often have adult converts at St Cyprian's.

The mobile phone in his pocket vibrated. He pulled it

out and looked down at the screen. It was Father Damien. What could he want? And why had he chosen to telephone instead of coming back to speak to Peter in person?

'Peter? Can you come through to the church? I think we need to call the police, but I'd like your opinion first.'

What had happened? A break-in perhaps? Had some of the church valuables gone missing?

'OK. I'll come right away.' Peter slipped the phone back into his pocket and headed for the door.

When he got into the church, he saw Father Damien and Keith Boswell sitting on a raised area beyond the choir stalls. Two broken floor boards lay next to them, overhanging the platform. Peter hastened across to join the others. Father Damien handed him the torch and pointed to the hole in the floor.

'Have a look down there and tell us what you think.'

Peter did as he was told. For a few moments, he could see nothing but splinters of wood, cobwebs and dust. He moved the torch, rotating the beam slowly, trying to work out what it was that he was supposed to be looking at. There was a dead mouse and several spiders, but those could hardly be causing the others so much concern. Then the light from the torch picked out something smooth and brown. Peter gasped as he moved the beam slightly and bent lower to get a better view.

'It is, isn't it?' the organ builder said from behind him.

'I think so, but I don't understand. This part of the church has been undisturbed for ... how long?'

'Since the organ was installed,' Father Damien told him. 'That's thirty – thirty-five years ago.

'So I would have expected decomposition to have been ... well, pretty much complete. And yet ...,' Peter sat back on his heels and looked round at Keith and Damien. 'It looks almost as if he's asleep, doesn't it? Well, apart from all the dust and spiders' webs all over his face.'

'You don't think it could be ...? I mean, could it just be a dummy?' Father Damien suggested hopefully.

'I don't *think* so. The teeth look too real, somehow. I mean – they're not perfect enough for a dummy. And the hair – a dummy would have much better hair, and it wouldn't have gone that strange dull brown colour ... or at least I don't think it would.' Peter put his head back down the hole and shone the torch around again. 'The whole body seems to be intact, but I can't be sure because there's so much dust and debris down there.'

So what do we do now?' Father Damien asked. 'Should I call the police?'

'I'll do that,' Peter volunteered, settling down with his legs over the edge of the platform and fumbling in his pocket for his phone. 'I think maybe you ought to see if you can do anything for the lad over there. He's looking a bit shaken up.'

2 ISOLATION WARD

A police patrol car drew up outside the church and a tall uniformed officer got out. Peter, who was waiting at the door, recognised the sparse figure topped with rusty brown hair as PC Malcolm Appleton. He stepped forward to meet the young man.

'Hello sir!' Appleton evidently remembered him from before Peter's retirement some six years previously. 'I got a call to say that someone has found human remains inside the church. Do you know anything about it?'

'Come inside. Yes. By pure fluke, I happened to be here when they made the discovery.' Peter opened the outer door and led the way through the porch and then, through a second door, into the church. 'I gather congratulations are in order,' he continued conversationally. 'DCI Porter tells me that you've passed your sergeant's exams.'

'Yes. I finally got up the courage to have a go, and they weren't nearly as bad as I was expecting.'

'I always knew you could do it. Now, let me introduce you.' Peter stopped next to one of the small tables in the South section of the church. Father Damien and the two organ builders were sitting round it, drinking mugs of tea. 'This is Father Damien Rowland. He's the Parish Priest here at St Cyprian's; and this is Mr Keith Boswell, who's restoring the organ, and his son, Arthur. It was the Boswells who found the body.'

'I see. And where exactly is it?' Appleton asked, looking round the church for signs of where a corpse might be concealed.

'I'll show you,' Peter said. 'Follow me.'

He continued down the aisle, pointing towards the organ platform. Appleton followed, gazing about him at the unfamiliar surroundings. Along the wall to his right, behind the tables and chairs, there was a line of tall, rectangular windows, each portraying a different stained-glass saint. Each figure had a scroll entwined about its feet, bearing a name: St. Christopher, St. Anthony, St. Francis of Assisi, St. Mary Magdalen. The bright spring sunshine slanting in through the coloured glass dappled the tiled floor with spangles of light.

Part of the "Welcome Area" where Father Damien and the Boswells were sitting, was fenced off by a low wooden rail, forming a large playpen affair. Inside there were a range of toys suitable for the under-fives and a shelf of books for rather older children.

In between the windows, the white-painted walls were adorned with square paintings, hanging at about head-height, each featuring a scene containing people dressed in the sorts of clothes that he had seen in a children's Bible belonging to his mother. At the bottom of each picture was a number in Roman numerals and a short caption. Looking across the rows of wooden benches on his left, he saw, hanging on a pillar, another painting. It depicted a red heart, with what looked like barbed wire entwined about it. There was a flame emanating from the top of the heart, with a cross inside it. The combination of wire and candle flame reminded him of the *Amnesty International* logo. On one side of the heart, there was a spear or arrowhead sticking into the flesh. Drops of blood were oozing out of the wound and dripping abundantly. It seemed a very strange thing to have in a building where children evidently came.

'What's all that?' Appleton asked, pointing towards a complicated arrangement of rods and wires on a wooden frame, which stood blocking their way.

'It's the innards of an organ,' Peter told him, squeezing past between the strange contraption and a concrete pillar supporting the arched ceiling. 'They were supposed to be putting it back on its stand today, but then they found this. Come and see.'

He climbed up on to the platform and knelt down by the hole. Appleton followed suit, peering into the gloom, with Peter directing the light beam to pick out the skull.

'It's weird,' he said, sitting back on his haunches and looking Peter in the face. 'It sort of looks like a skull, and then again, it almost looks like it's still alive. Have you ever seen anything like this before?'

Peter shook his head. 'No. In my experience, once a body's been dead a day or two the flesh starts to decay and flies get in and you get maggots growing, and the skin turns a green colour and starts to-'

Appleton shuddered at Peter's graphic description. 'But in this case,' he cut in to halt the flow, 'it's almost as if the body has just sort of shrunk away, so that the skin is tight on the skeleton. Is it just a head? Or is there a whole body down there?'

'I think it's probably a complete skeleton,' Peter told him. 'I can't be sure, because I didn't want to disturb the scene any more than we had to, but it looks like it.'

'I suppose I'd better have a look myself.'

Peter passed over the torch, and Appleton lay down on his front and put his head and shoulders down inside the hole in the floorboards. After a minute or two he emerged again, scrambled to his feet and started brushing himself down. He handed the torch back to Peter.

'You're right,' he agreed. 'It looks like a whole body wrapped in some sort of cloth, which looks like it's been chewed almost to bits by mice or rats or something. I'd better secure the scene and get on to CID and Scenes of Crime – unless you'd like to do that, sir?'

'I'm retired, remember. It's your call. Don't worry – you're doing fine.'

'Thanks, sir. Well, could you just explain to your friends that they need to keep away from the scene and not disturb anything?'

While PC Appleton went outside to call for assistance and to get tape from his car to secure the crime scene, Peter imparted the unwelcome news to Father Damien and the organ builders.

'How long to do you think it will be?' Father Damien asked anxiously.

'Difficult to tell,' Peter said cautiously, trying to lower expectations without giving the impression that the police were unconcerned about the inconvenience that was being caused. 'For a start, it may be a while before we can get a forensics team out here. There have been a lot of cutbacks recently and I know they're stretched to the limit. And then, the Crime Scene Manager may want to leave the body in situ until we can get an expert in to look at it, and that could take some time. That may not be necessary,' he added hastily, seeing the consternation on Father Damien's face. 'Usually, once they've taken photographs and done an initial assessment, they can take the body away and do a full examination in the mortuary. I'm just a bit … well, I've never seen a corpse quite like this one. They may need to get in a forensic archaeologist or someone else who specialises in this sort of thing.'

'But are we talking hours or days or …?' Father Damien left his question hanging, fearful of voicing the possibility that the work on the organ might have to be suspended for a matter of weeks or even more. 'As you know, we were banking on having the organ back in time for the Easter Vigil. And, even if *that's* not possible, we can't keep people out of the church at the most important festival of the year.'

'I'd guess it'll take a day or two. I certainly don't think you can expect them to be able to start work again today. Maybe tomorrow. They may decide that, once they've got photographs of the scene and removed the body, it's OK for you to replace the boards and install the organ. It rather depends what else they find down there.'

'What sort of thing *might* they find?' Father Damien asked nervously. 'You don't think there might be more than just the one body, do you?'

'Who can tell?' Peter shrugged. 'But I was thinking more that there might be evidence of *how* whoever it is died.'

'The murder weapon, do you mean?'

'Possibly. Of course, just because the body has been hidden, we shouldn't assume that it must have been a *murder*. Sometimes people do very odd things with dead bodies, even when they die of natural causes.'

'Well, it looks like we might as well go home,' Keith Boswell said, getting to his feet. 'No point us hanging around here all day doing nothing.'

'Isn't there anything more you can be getting on with while the organ's still where it is?' Father Damien asked, anxious to avoid any delay or to allow the organ builders to move on to another job, in case they did not return. 'Didn't you say that you still had some work to do on the casing? New varnish or something?'

'Be better to wait until it's in place,' Keith replied. 'You never know what damage may get done during the installation.'

'I'm afraid that you must both wait here until the Senior Investigating Officer arrives,' Peter told them. 'They'll need to interview you about finding the body. And they may need to ask you about the organ and how long it's been off the platform and so on.'

11

'You mean the body could have been put there recently?' Father Damien asked in surprise. 'I thought it must have been there since before the organ was built.'

'I expect you're right,' Peter agreed, 'but, until it's been properly investigated, we can't be sure that someone couldn't have somehow taken up the floorboards and put it in there in the last week or two.'

'But what about all the dust and stuff down there?' Arthur asked, speaking for the first time. 'It looked like nobody had been down there for years.'

'Yes. That's how it looked to me too,' Father Damien backed him up.

'I know. I agree, but we need to wait until the experts have had a look at it.'

PC Appleton returned with a roll of blue-and-white police tape. Peter helped him to cordon off the crime scene by tying it to four chairs, arranged in a square around the organ platform.

'Would you like us to move the action and console out of the way to give you more room?' Keith asked, as Peter squeezed past the naked organ.

'No. We must leave everything exactly as it was when you found the body,' Peter told him. 'The Crime Scene Manager will let you know when it can be moved.'

The older Boswell slumped back down into his chair, put his elbows on the table in front of him and rested his chin on his hands.

'I'll go and make us all another cup of tea,' Father Damien said, gathering up the mugs and escaping through the vestry door.

3 PHYSICAL EXAMINATION

'I hear you have a dead body that you'd like me to take a look at! Where are you hiding it?'

At the sound of Mike Carson's familiar cheery brogue, Peter turned from his conversation with one of the Scenes of Crime Officers and looked towards the main entrance of the church. The burly pathologist advanced down the aisle, escorted by Malcolm Appleton, who had positioned himself by the door to intercept newcomers. When he drew level with Peter, he stopped.

'Peter! What brings you here? Are they so short-handed that they've had to bring you out of retirement?'

'No. I just happened to be paying a call on Father Damien when they found the body.' Peter tried to make it sound as if this were a simple courtesy call, such as one might make on any neighbour. He felt unaccountably shy of admitting the purpose of his visit and perhaps facing questions about his conversion on some future occasion. 'It's underneath where the organ used to be.'

'Any idea who it is?' Mike asked. 'The choir master set upon by the choristers, perhaps? Or the organist done away with for refusing to play the right tune to-'

'No,' Peter cut in, seeing Father Damien approaching and wishing to prevent him from hearing Mike's facetious comments. He knew that Mike took his job extremely seriously and that this jocular style was his way of coping with the reality of dealing with death on a daily basis, but to strangers he often appeared callous and irreverent. 'It's nobody anyone knows and, to be honest, I'm not sure it's going to be easy to identify. As far as we can make out, it must have been there for more than thirty years.'

'Whew!' Mike whistled through his teeth. 'I'm not sure I'm going to be the right person to deal with it at that rate. There can't be much more than a skeleton left.'

'That's just it,' Peter told him. 'It looks like no corpse I've ever seen before in my life. But there's no point me trying to describe it. Come and have a look for yourself. But first I'd better introduce you to Father Damien,' he added, seeing the priest hovering expectantly at his side. 'Father, this is Dr Mike Carson. He's a Home Office approved forensic pathologist.'

'Dr Carson.' Father Damien held out his hand towards Mike, who shook it heartily, while smiling a little nervously.

'Father.'

Like many of his fellow-countrymen, Mike was a lapsed Catholic. The presence of a priest always had a tendency to provoke feelings of guilt and an irrational desire to admit that it was he-knew-not-how-many years since his last confession.

'Well, I'd better get on. No doubt you'd like me to get this finished as soon as possible.'

'Yes. Yes, I certainly would,' Father Damien agreed. 'Yes. Please do carry on.'

'I'll show you,' said Luke Gray, the senior Scenes of Crime Officer, who had been updating Peter with their progress when Mike arrived. 'The remains are underneath that wooden platform over there. The organ builders found them when they fell through the rotten boards.

We've photographed the remains through the hole, but we need to take up the boards in order to get a proper view. Do you want to see the scene as it is, or are you OK for us to go ahead and open it up?'

'If you've got everything that you need, then carry on. I'd far rather do my assessment in the daylight than peering down into some dark hole.'

'Good. Thanks. OK Simon! Get those boards up!' Luke called to one of his assistants. 'And Jan – get ready to photograph everything as he does it.'

'Right you are!'

While Mike donned his protective suit and latex gloves, in readiness for entering the crime scene, the SOCOs worked systematically, levering up the boards, one by one, inspecting them each for any signs that they had been raised before and recording where each had been. Soon the entire surface of the organ platform had been removed and the boards stacked neatly at the side of the church, within the police cordon.

Peter lifted the tape to allow Mike to pass under it. He stood for several minutes gazing down at the newly-revealed crime scene. Essentially, he was looking at an open wooden box, about ten feet by eight and about two feet high. It was built into the outer walls of the church on two sides. To the left, shallow red-tiled steps led up to the chancel, which was at the same level as the top of the organ platform. There were beams fixed from the front to the back of the box, to support the boards upon which the organ had stood. Lying in the direction of these beams, and between two of them, was an unmistakeable human form. The torso and legs were wrapped in some greyish-greenish material, the remains of which also clung to the area of the head above the left ear and to part of the right cheek. Otherwise, the face was exposed. Mike stared at the smooth, brown skin, which seemed to be stretched taut over the bones beneath. The corpse had an unusual appearance to say the least.

He swung his leg over the side of the box, selecting a place from where he could reach the body without having to climb over any of the beams. He walked gingerly across to it and crouched down to look more closely at the face of this strange cadaver. He put out his gloved hand and touched the face, gently at first, then more firmly. It had a leathery feel and appearance. He looked up and motioned to the photographer to step inside the box and take more pictures of the corpse.

Once she had done so, he cautiously took hold of the fabric that encased the body and slowly unwrapped it. The figure was fully clothed, in trousers and a sweatshirt, both in dark colours, and with brown suede shoes on its feet. Like the cloth wrapping, the garments had holes in them suggestive of the teeth of small rodents. Mike looked it up and down, measuring it with his eye. It was a man of about average height or maybe a little over. The hands, which were lying crossed over on his chest, were the same dark brown colour as his face and their skin had the same leathery appearance.

Mike stepped back to allow the photographer to take pictures of the exposed corpse from a number of angles. Then he bent down closer, using a small pocket torch to search for any signs of trauma to the body, which might indicate the cause of death.

He was still engrossed in this examination when the door from the church porch opened again and Malcolm Appleton came back in. Peter turned to see two very familiar figures: DCI Jonah Porter, in his electric wheelchair, and his Personal Assistant (who was also Peter's own wife) Bernie Fazakerley.

'Hi there, Peter!' Jonah greeted him. 'I heard it was you who reported this find, so I thought I'd better come over in person and see what's what. Tell me what happened.'

'They've been having the organ repaired,' Peter told him, hastening up the aisle to meet the new arrivals. 'It stands on a sort of dais, made of wood, which, it turns out, had rotted. One of the organ builders fell through and they found this strange body underneath. It must have been there for years – ever since the organ was installed. Mike's having a look at it now.'

'Good afternoon.' Father Damien, seeing Jonah in his wheelchair came over to speak to him. 'I'm Father Damien Rowland. Is there anything I can do for you?'

'DCI Jonah Porter. I'm the Senior Investigating Officer for this case. I think you know Bernie, my PA.' Jonah inclined his head towards her and Father Damien nodded assent. 'I'll need to ask you a few questions in a minute – just as soon as I've had a word with the pathologist – if you could just sit yourself down on one of these chairs, I'll be with you in two ticks.'

He glided off in the direction of the organ platform. Bernie hurried after him to lift the tape and allow him into the cordoned-off area.

'Mike! What can you tell me?'

The doctor straightened up and looked towards the sound of Jonah's voice. Then he made his way to the edge of the box and climbed out, peeling off his gloves as he did so.

'It's an interesting case,' he remarked, 'a very interesting case. In fact, I don't recall coming across anything quite like this before.'

'In what way, exactly?' Jonah enquired.

'The body is completely mummified,' Mike told him.

'Like the ancient Egyptians, you mean?' Peter asked, coming up behind Jonah.

'Similarly preserved,' Mike agreed, 'but in this case, it presumably happened naturally, rather than being done deliberately. Essentially, the body has just dried out, instead of decomposing. It's usually associated with places that have a hot, dry climate. This body must have been kept in those conditions for some time immediately after death, so that desiccation occurred before the normal processes of decay could become established.'

'How hot?' Jonah asked. 'Would the heating in this building be sufficient?'

'Not judging by the temperature at Midnight Mass last Christmas!' Bernie interjected. 'I wished I'd worn my thermals then!'

'I'm not an expert in that area,' Mike answered, 'so I'd have to look it up, but I'm sure that ordinary central heating wouldn't be enough – not unless the body was lying right up against one of the radiators, perhaps.'

'Do any of the heating pipes run close to where the body was found?' Jonah asked.

'Nope!' Mike shook his head. 'You can see them there. They've been routed around the outside of this box thing. Presumably the heating was installed after it had already been built and had the organ put on top of it.'

'OK. And what can you tell me about the body – apart from its unusual condition?'

'Male, average height – I'll get you an exact figure when we get it back to the mortuary – youngish, I think, but not that easy to tell.'

'Any idea how he died?'

'No obvious signs of trauma – except possibly some damage to the neck – but it's not easy to be sure with the body in the condition it's in. Again, I may be able to tell you more after I've had a better look at it back at the mortuary. Don't hold your breath though: I think I may need to get an expert in with more experience of mummified remains.'

Jonah left Mike to continue with the task of removing the corpse from its resting place, sealing it into a body bag and wheeling it out to begin its journey to the mortuary. His interest now switched to the witnesses who had made the grisly discovery. Peter made the introductions.

'This is Mr Keith Boswell, and this is Mr Arthur Boswell. They've been restoring the organ. They were in the process of putting it back on its stand when they found the body.'

'Good afternoon,' Jonah greeted the two Boswells. 'I'm DCI Jonah Porter. I'm in charge of this investigation. And this is my assistant, Dr Bernie Fazakerley. She'll be taking notes for me, while I ask you a few questions.'

Bernie sat down at the next table and set up a laptop computer, which she had taken out from a storage space at the back of Jonah's wheelchair. Jonah positioned his chair where he could look both men in the face. The two Boswells stared at him with expressions of incredulity and suspicion on their faces.

'You're a policeman?' Arthur asked sceptically, looking down at the wheelchair and at Jonah's limp right arm lying uselessly in his lap.

'Yes. That's right.' Jonah smiled calmly round at them both. He was well-used by now to people's surprise. 'A bullet in my neck a few years back put me in this thing, but it didn't affect my mind. I just need Bernie here to help me with a few things. Now, first of all,' he continued, 'I need you to tell me exactly what happened.'

'It was Arthur who found it,' Mr Boswell senior volunteered, after a brief pause. 'Like Mr Johns said, we were about to lift the action and console on to the platform when two of the boards just gave way under him.'

'And you fell through into the space underneath?' Jonah turned to Arthur for confirmation.

'That's right. Dad helped me out and then we thought we'd better check how many of the boards were rotten. So we both got down and had a look with the torch that we use for seeing inside the action, and ...'

'Yes – go on. You looked under the floor and you saw ... what, exactly?'

'It gave me a right turn,' Arthur shuddered. 'There was this horrible face staring up at me.'

'Not literally staring,' his father intervened. 'The eyes were closed like. But it was a nasty thing to find when you weren't expecting it.'

'Yes. I'm sure it was. And what did you do then?'

'Arthur was looking white as a sheet, so I made him sit down on one of these chairs and then I went and got Father Rowland.'

'I see.' Jonah looked towards the priest. 'And you were, where?'

'In my study, in the presbytery. There's a door through from the vestry. Keith came through and got me and we came back here together.'

'And what time was this?'

'I'm not sure,' Father Damien thought for a few moments. 'About one thirty-five, maybe quarter to two. Peter came just before half past, and we hadn't got far before ... so it can't have been any later than, say, one forty-five.'

'That's fine. It probably doesn't matter. I just like to have everything as clear as possible in my notes, that's all. So, you both went back and had another look down the hole – is that right?'

'Yes,' Father Damien confirmed. 'And then, when I saw what it was, I rang Peter's mobile and he came and had a look too.'

'And then he rang the police,' Jonah acknowledged, 'in a call that was logged at three minutes past two. OK. Now tell me a bit more about the place where the body was found. When was the last time anyone went underneath those boards?'

Father Damien and the two organ builders looked round blankly.

'I don't think anyone ever has before,' Father Damien said, after a brief pause. 'I mean, they've had the organ there on top of them ever since ...'

'Since when?'

'The platform was built when the organ was installed,' Father Damien explained. 'And then, there was no way anyone could get underneath without dismantling the organ.'

'I see. And when was that?'

'There's a plaque on the console, says 1982,' Keith said.

'We've got a leaflet which tells you the history of the organ,' Father Damien added, eager to help. 'One of our members is a bit of a local historian. He did it to help raise money for the restoration work. There are some copies at the back of church. I'll get you one.'

He bustled off and was soon back, holding out a small A5 booklet with a colour photograph of a pipe organ on the front.

'Just give it to Bernie, please. I'll have a look at it later.'

Bernie leaned forward, took the booklet and put it into a plastic document wallet.

'Are you saying that – that – that dead body has been lying there for ...,' Arthur paused to work out the years on his fingers, 'thirty-five years? It looked like he could've died yesterday!'

'According to the pathologist, the body hasn't decayed,' Jonah told him. 'It's just dried out and mummified. That's why it looks so strange. He said that it must have been in very warm, dry conditions.'

'But that doesn't make sense!' Keith protested. 'You'd never allow that around an organ. The temperature and humidity have to be carefully controlled to prevent the wood from shrinking and cracking.'

'Is that why the pipes go round the outside of the organ platform, instead of underneath it?'

'I suppose so,' Father Damien said. 'I always thought it was so they were easier to get at, but ...'

'And was the heating installed before or after the organ?'

'Before, I think. I believe that the heating has been there ever since the church was built.'

'Which was?'

'I'd have to check. Not long after the War. Nineteen-fifties, I think. We've got a little history of the church I could look out for you or I think it's on the website.'

For a few minutes, Jonah was silent, with his eyes cast down concentrating on a small computer screen attached to his chair as the first two fingers of his left hand manipulated a small keypad.

'Ah!' he said at last. 'Yes. Here it is: "The building was completed in 1951." And you say that the heating was installed then?'

'That's right.'

'And it hasn't been modified since?'

Father Damien shook his head, with a puzzled expression on his face.

'I was just wondering if it was possible that the pipes used to go under the organ and they were re-routed later.'

'Wouldn't that have meant taking up the floorboards?' Peter asked. 'If your idea is that the body was lying on hot pipes that were later removed, why wasn't it discovered then?'

'I thought it might have been possible to disconnect them at both ends and pull them out without going inside the box.'

'Wouldn't you just cut them off and seal them inside?' Bernie said sceptically. 'And wouldn't pulling pipes out from underneath the body have disturbed it? It looked as if it was just lying where it had been laid, however many years ago.'

'OK. Let's leave that for the time being,' Jonah said briskly, turning back to Father Damien. 'Presumably you don't have any idea who it could have been? There aren't any stories of people going missing back in the eighties?'

'No.' the priest shook his head. 'But that's way before my time. I only came here in 2008. My predecessor might know. That's Father Daniel Callaghan. I think he came here in the eighties. It may even have been before that. He's retired now and in a nursing home, but I think he's still alive. I could probably find the address for you, if you want it.'

'Yes please. And is there anyone else who might

remember the organ being installed? Some of the older members of the congregation perhaps?'

'I'm not sure,' Father Damien answered hesitantly. 'It's a long time ago. I can't really imagine any of them would remember anything significant.'

'What about the people who installed the organ? Do you know who they were? And did they make the platform as well, or was that someone different – a builder perhaps?'

'I can't tell you off-hand, but we've got records going back to the year dot in the Church Office. If you give me a day or two, I could probably find you the original invoices for the work.'

'Excellent! And there's no need for you to hunt them out. If you just show me where everything is, I can get one of our officers to go through the records.' He turned back to the Boswells. 'You dismantled the organ and took it off the platform – is that right?'

'Yes,' Keith answered.

'And when was this? When did the work start?'

'January.'

'That's right,' Father Damien confirmed. 'We had trouble with the organ at the Christmas services and it gave up completely in the New Year. I called Keith in to look at it at the beginning of January – and that was when we realised that the problem was a leak in the roof, which had made bits of the organ swell. We got a builder in to fix the roof and repair the damage that the water had done to the interior of the building, and Keith and Arthur took the organ apart and started on renovating it. That must've been around the middle of January, I suppose. We anticipated that the organ would be out of action for a few weeks, but …, well, as you see, we were only just putting it all back together now. I just hope your investigation doesn't delay things too long. We've been managing with an electronic keyboard, which is all very well during Lent, but we really need to have the organ back in time for the big services at Easter.'

'We'll do our best,' Jonah assured him. 'But it is important to go over the area carefully to make sure we don't miss anything that might help us to work out what happened. It could be a couple of days before the Crime Scene Investigators are finished.'

'What about Mass tomorrow?' Father Damien asked anxiously, suddenly realising that the interlopers might still be there when the small congregation that attended the weekday services gathered the following morning. 'We have Morning Prayer followed by Mass every day at nine-thirty.'

'That shouldn't be a problem, provided you make sure that nobody crosses the police tape. I'll tell our people not to come back until … what time will your service finish?'

'Ten fifteen probably, certainly not later than ten thirty.'

'OK. I'll tell them to come in at half past ten.'

Jonah looked round, surveying the scene. Two men in protective suits came past wheeling a trolley bearing a black body bag. Mike followed behind it.

'I'll be getting back,' he told Jonah as he passed. 'I'll let you know the results of the PM when I have them.'

'Good.' Jonah nodded. Then he turned back to the three men sitting around the table in front of him. 'I think that's all I need to ask you at the moment. If you could look out that address for me and be ready for us to sift through the parish records, I'll be back at ten thirty tomorrow.'

4 FAMILIAL DISORDER

Peter bent down to pick up the pile of envelopes that were impeding the motion of the door as he tried to open it. The post had come while he had been out at St Cyprian's. He shuffled them together and put the stack down on the hall-stand, while he took off his waterproof jacket and hung it on one of the hooks that were ranged in a row on the wall.

Then he picked up the letters and walked with them into the kitchen, sorting them as he went. There were two matching envelopes for him and Bernie – bank statements, he deduced. A brown envelope from the local authority addressed to Bernie probably contained news of the Council Tax for the following financial year. That white window envelope looked like a credit card bill for Jonah, and he also had a postcard with a picture of a beach on Lanzarote from his son and daughter-in-law. Then, there was a brochure about retirement homes addressed to Peter himself – the penalty you paid for being over sixty-five – and, what was this?

Peter placed the mail in three neat piles on the table and stood staring down at the last envelope, turning it over in his hand, trying to work out what it might be and who might have sent it. It was a creamy colour and made of high quality paper. The name and address were handwritten in blue ballpoint. It had a first class stamp, over which the smudged postmark indicated that it had been posted the day before in … What did it say? Stockton? Stockwell? He did not know anyone in either of those places. There was no sender's address on the back and the handwriting was unfamiliar. And yet it was clearly addressed to *Detective Inspector Peter Johns*, and at his home address, so not some old acquaintance from his police days.

Peter sat down on one of the wooden chairs, which were arranged around the table, and prised open the flap on the envelope slowly and carefully. It was of good quality and did not tear. He slid out the contents and studied them. It was a notelet, of the type made by folding a large piece of paper twice. On the front was a watercolour of an imposing building, designed in the classical style with pillars and porticos and a very grandiose clock tower. Beneath it the caption read, 'The Town Hall, Stockport'.

Stockport? Who would be writing to him from Stockport? He hardly even knew where it was. He had only ever been there that once, back in 2007 when … Oh no! It couldn't be! Peter opened the card and hunted for a signature. There was an address at the top – somewhere in a place called Hazel Grove – and then yesterday's date followed by a lot of writing, beginning *Dear Peter*. He continued to scan down the page. The script broke off in mid-sentence after filling the interior of the notelet. It must continue somewhere else. Peter turned to the back, but that only contained information about the artist and the copyright holder of the card.

Of course! She must have written more inside. He unfolded the paper from which the notelet had been made and, sure enough, the reverse was covered with the same handwriting. And, there at the bottom, it finished: 'with love from your sister Jane.'

How dare she? They had agreed! After ten years, what could she want with him now? Without reading it, Peter crumpled up the letter in his hand and stuffed it into his pocket. He turned back to attend to the rest of his mail. He tore off the plastic wrapping around the brochure and put it in the bin. Then he took out the bank statement and scanned the lines to check that it contained nothing unexpected. Leaving it on the table, he crossed the kitchen and deposited the brochure and both envelopes in the recycling bin. He reached into his pocket and pulled out the screwed-up notelet, hesitating for a moment before tossing it in after them.

He returned to the table, picked up the bank statement and carried it upstairs to the filing cabinet in Bernie's study where they kept such things. Why had that wretched woman written to him now? Could she really have failed to get the message that they were nothing – less than nothing – to one another? He stuffed the statement into the hanger and slammed the drawer closed. She was as bad as her mother! Why couldn't they stop persecuting him?

Peter slouched back downstairs and returned to the kitchen. He looked at his watch. Time was getting on. Lucy would be home soon, and he had planned to clean the kitchen floor while everyone was out. He set to, putting the chairs up on the table out of the way and sweeping up crumbs and dust with a broom. Occupied though he was, he could not prevent thoughts of the letter nagging at his mind. Perhaps he was being a bit hard on Jane. After all, it wasn't her fault that her mother had been a bigoted racist with a mind about as open as a high security jail.

He put away the broom and took the mop bucket to the sink to fill it. Perhaps she had some family news that she felt compelled to tell him, despite his having made it abundantly clear that, as far as he was concerned, her family was no concern of his? Whatever it was, he did not want to know.

He put the full bucket down on the floor and soaked the mop. He began cleaning the floor, working methodically from the far side so as to finish at the back door. As he passed the recycling bin, he hesitated. It was no good! He couldn't just ignore that stupid letter. She had no business writing to him, but now he had it, he would have to find out what it contained. He opened the bin and took out the crumpled paper, stuffing it back into his pocket before resuming the mopping. He would read it later when he was less busy.

As he stepped backwards through the door and lifted the bucket out into the garden, he almost collided with his stepdaughter, who had arrived back from school and was coming indoors after leaving her bicycle in the shed.

'Hi Lucy! Do you mind taking your shoes off before you go in? The floor's still wet and I'd rather you didn't tread mud all over it.'

'OK.' Lucy put down her school bag and bent down to untie her shoelaces. 'There are two police cars outside St Cyprian's and what looks like a SOCO van. It looks as if something must've happened there.'

'They've found human remains under where the organ used to be,' Peter told her, emptying the mop bucket into the drain beneath the outlet from the kitchen sink.

'Human remains? You mean bones?'

'More than that. According to Mike Carson, it's a whole body that's sort of dried out and become mummified.'

'What would make that happen?' Lucy asked with interest, picking up her shoes and bag, but making no move to go indoors.

'Mike thinks it must have been lying somewhere hot and dry for a period immediately after death.'

'Not there in St Cyprian's then. It's always cold in there whatever the weather outside.'

'That's what your mam said. She's been there, with Jonah. He's the SIO[1].'

'I didn't see our car there.'

'No. They went back to get a team together to work on tracking down who the victim might be.'

Peter took off his own shoes, picked them up and carried both shoes and bucket back inside the house. Lucy followed, and they both padded across the kitchen and into the hall. Lucy dropped her bag and shoes on the floor, took off her fluorescent cycling jacket and hung it up next to Peter's coat. Peter meanwhile stowed the mop and bucket in the under-stairs cupboard. Then he sat down on the bottom step and pulled on his shoes.

'I reckon the body must have been kept somewhere else and then moved.' Seventeen-year-old Lucy's major ambition in life was to become a forensic pathologist herself and she did not wish to miss this opportunity to learn more about this interesting case. 'Is that what Mike thinks?'

She sat down beside Peter and started putting on her shoes.

'You know what Mike's like. He never likes to express an opinion about anything until he's done umpteen tests. This time he's talking about getting in some other expert to have a look at the body – a forensic archaeologist or anthropologist or something.'

'So won't Mike be doing the post mortem himself?'

'I'm not sure. It won't be the normal sort of PM, whoever does it. Like I told you, the body is more like something you'd find in an archaeological dig – or like those bodies you see on the news sometimes that have been found in a peat bog somewhere. It was this strange brown colour and it was like skin stretched over bones. At least, I only saw the head. The rest of the body may have

---

[1] Senior Investigating Officer: the police officer in charge of an enquiry.

had more to it.'

'You've seen the body?' Lucy was suddenly struck with the thought that, now that her stepfather was no longer a serving police officer, it was strange that he should have been present at the crime scene. 'What were you doing there?'

'I was with Father Damien when they found the body.' Peter finished tying his laces and stood up. 'Neither he nor the guys who found it knew what to do. So they asked me to take a look and then I called the police.'

'And now Jonah's in charge of the investigation. That's good. He'll be able to tell me all about it when he gets home.'

'Talking of which, I'd better start thinking about what we're going to have to eat this evening.'

'And I've got a stack of Biology homework to do,' Lucy nodded, picking up her bag and starting up the stairs to her room.

Peter went back into the kitchen and started taking down the chairs from the table. Then he went into the large walk-in larder and brought out potatoes for their evening meal. He put them in the sink and turned on the tap.

As he peeled them, he pondered on the events of the day. Who could that man be, who had been concealed for so long within inches of all those people who had come to worship in the church over the years? Who had killed him and why had they chosen such a bizarre hiding place? What would happen when the press got hold of the story? There would be speculation and the church was likely to come under suspicion. People would say that the strange corpse must be a victim of clergy abuse – and perhaps they would be right! And yet, whatever had happened was far back in the past, nothing to do with poor Father Damien and his current congregation.

But you could never get away from the past, could you? It was the same with that wretched letter from Jane. For more than fifty years, Peter had been content with knowing that his mother had put him into the hands of the National Children's Home when he was only a few weeks old, presumably for some good reason. Then, out of the blue, she had turned up demanding to meet him, expecting him to be equally pleased to see her, and, worst of all, hoping to become a grandmother to Peter's two children. Foolishly, and much against his better judgement, he had agreed to a meeting – and now, here was his half-sister, unbelievably in view of what had happened, pestering him again to renew their acquaintance!

He cut up the potatoes and put them into a pan of water, which he placed on the hob. He lit the gas and stood watching, waiting for the water to come to the boil. He sighed. Oh well! He might as well see what it was that she wanted.

He put his hand into his pocket and pulled out the crumpled paper.

'Dear Peter,' he read, 'I realise that you will be surprised to receive this and I understand that it will not be a pleasant surprise.'

If she knew that, then why did she still carry on and write the blessed letter?

'But something has happened that I want you to know about.'

Here it comes! Don't say she's found some other long-lost relative who wanted to meet him!

'And I want to ask you a massive favour.'

What on earth! What more could she want from him? He had already handed over to her the entire legacy, which their mother, so inexplicably, had left divided between the two of them.

The water hissed as it boiled over and nearly put the gas out. Peter hastily forced the letter back into his pocket and turned it down. Then he turned his attention to preparing the meat and onions for the base of the cottage pie that he was making. What a nerve that woman had!

What made her think that she had any right to ask for favours from him, after the way her mother had behaved?

He had just put the pie in the oven when Bernie and Jonah arrived home. He put down the oven gloves and went out into the hall to meet them.

'Tea will be ready in about half an hour,' he informed them.

'Good.' Bernie smiled at Peter and then turned to Jonah. 'That gives us just nice time to get you changed into something more comfortable.'

'I'll do that,' Lucy volunteered, appearing at the top of the stairs. 'You go and sit down, Mam. I'll take over.'

'I thought you had homework to do,' Peter reminded her.

'It's done. Now I want to hear all about this body in St Cyprian's.'

'Alright,' Bernie agreed. 'You can have him!'

Lucy ran softly down the stairs and greeted Jonah by putting her arms around his shoulders and kissing him lightly on the cheek. Jonah smiled up at her briefly, before turning his wheelchair and heading for his ground floor bedroom. The automatic doors opened to let him through as he approached. Lucy followed, but then she turned back.

'Oh! I nearly forgot. Dom messaged me on Facebook. He's wondering if he could come and stay over Easter. He says he wants to see "Uncle Peter" *done*. What shall I tell him?'

Peter and Bernie exchanged glances. Dominic Fazakerley was Lucy's second cousin – the youngest of Bernie's cousin Joey's children. He and Lucy had met for the first time about eighteen months previously when Bernie had made a rare trip back to her home city of Liverpool. He was currently training to be a teacher, after having completed a degree in English Literature and Religious Studies.

'He's welcome to come,' Bernie answered. 'The spare

room is always free. How long was he planning to stay?'

'He said the school he's in breaks up on Friday and he thought he'd come down on Saturday and stay until Easter Monday, if that's OK with us.'

'Tell him that's fine – if he doesn't think he'll get bored, with us being at work all day.'

Bernie and Peter returned to the kitchen together. Bernie chopped carrots while Peter prepared a fruit salad.

'Do you think Dominic realises that Oxford schools don't break up until Maundy Thursday?' Peter asked.

'More to the point,' Bernie smiled back at him, 'do you think he realises that Lucy might well have been less keen on him being here for so long if she wasn't going to be at school for a good part of his visit?'

5 CASE NOTES

'This is Detective Sergeant Lepage,' Jonah told Father Damien. 'He's going to go through those parish records that you mentioned.'

'Yes, of course.' Father Damien smiled round at them both, taking great care not to stare at the sergeant's brown skin and frizzy black hair, and berating himself inwardly for having been taken aback at seeing a black police officer. It was remarkable how difficult it was to rid yourself of the stereotypes that you had been brought up with. 'I've sorted through them a bit,' he added, as he led the way through the presbytery to the church office, 'and I think I've found all the financial records relating to the installation of the organ.'

He opened the door and ushered them in. Jonah looked round. One wall of the room was lined with filing cabinets, the drawers each labelled in neat script. On top of them were balanced several dozen box files, similarly labelled. Jonah noticed that there was a gap near the centre of the row, where one of them had been removed. There was a desk under the window, on which lay a pile of manila document wallets and a black box file. Presumably, that accounted for the gap in the row on top of the filing cabinets. On the opposite wall, there was another desk with a desktop computer on it. Next to that, a colour printer and a photocopier lay side-by-side on a heavy wooden table. Under the table, Jonah could see boxes of paper and spare toner cartridges stacked neatly, while on the wall above there hung a wooden crucifix.

'This used to be the study for the assistant priest,' Father Damien told them, 'back in the days when St Cyprian's had two clergy. Now that we only have one, it's been converted into an office. We have a number of lay people who take care of administration that would once have been done by the priests.'

He crossed the room and pulled out a drawer in one of the filing cabinets.

'This contains the invoices and receipts for 1982, the year the organ was built. There's a hanger for each month from January 1981 to December 1983. In the drawer below, you'll find all the bank statements for a similar period. This file,' he continued, going over to the desk and putting his hand on the box file, 'has correspondence for 1981 and '82, including some discussion about commissioning the organ and disposing of the old harmonium. And these other folders have an assortment of press cuttings and photographs and stuff relating to the fundraising and the dedication service and so on.'

'Thank you. That's all very helpful,' Jonah said. 'Will it be alright for Sergeant Lepage to work in here – rather than taking all this away?'

'Yes, of course. He can use this desk. He won't be disturbed today, but if he hasn't finished by tomorrow, I hope he won't mind if one of our volunteers comes in to print the weekly newsletter?'

'No problem!' Andy Lepage spoke for the first time. 'I'm used to having people working around me. Will it be alright for me to look through these other files?' he added, running his eye over the labels on the filing cabinet drawers. There's nothing confidential in there that I shouldn't see?'

'Oh no,' Father Damien assured him. 'Anything personal I keep locked away in my study. Feel free to browse – if you think it'll do you any good. My predecessors appear to have been great hoarders of paper, I'm afraid, and a lot of this probably ought to be thrown out, but I never manage to get up the energy to sort through it all.'

'That's probably all to the good,' Jonah observed. 'The more we can find out about what was going on here back when that organ platform was built the better. Alright Andy, we'll leave you to it. I'm going into the church now to have another look at the place where the body was found.'

'I've got the names of the two priests who were here back in 1982.' Father Damien picked up a piece of paper from the desk and held it out towards Jonah. 'One of them actually died at about the same time that the organ was completed, but his assistant, Father Joseph Carey, is still alive. He's in a parish in Reading now. I've got his address here. I found it on the diocese website. I also found the name and address of the priest who replaced Father O'Leary after he died. He wasn't there when the organ was installed, but he may know more about what went on then than I do.'

'Thanks. That's very helpful. Give them to Bernie will you? She's in the church, seeing how the SOCOs are getting on.'

'Do you think they'll be finished soon?' Father Damien asked anxiously. 'It's only ten days before the Easter Vigil and we were banking on having the organ ready by then. We've been rigging up an electronic keyboard every Sunday, but for the big Easter services …'

'We'll be as quick as we can,' Jonah assured him.

They made their way through the choir vestry and out into the church. Jonah paused and looked around. The altar to his left was covered with a purple cloth embroidered in gold and white. The sun was streaming in through a large stained-glass window above it, picking out the gilding around the pictures arranged in a line along the wall opposite him and creating coloured patterns on the white plaster of the wall around them. There seemed to be images everywhere: statues of saints and pictures of Bible stories.

'Are all Roman Catholic churches like this?' Jonah asked in a low voice. 'Full of pictures and statues, I mean? And that ceiling ...?'

Father Damien followed Jonah's gaze up to where the white of the walls gradually changed to a deep blue as they curved inwards to form an arched ceiling, where golden angels smiled out from behind puffy white clouds. To their left, over the sanctuary, the blue of the ceiling became gradually lighter, changing to purple, pink, and then finally to yellow above the main altar.

'Oh that ceiling is rather unique, I believe,' Father Damien replied. 'A local artist designed it and the youth group painted it, back in the seventies, I think it was. As for the rest ...? Well, our people do tend to like to give things for the church, often in memory of a loved-one. And St Cyprian's was fortunate in having a rich benefactor who was a great patron of the arts. Sir Brian Monkton: you may have heard of him.'

'I read about him in that history of the church that you have on your website,' Jonah told him. 'It said that he owned a string of hotels all across the south of England back in the forties and fifties – a sort of up-market Billy Butlin[2]. I gather he more or less paid for this church to be built.'

'Yes. I believe he did. And the architect was the same

---

[2] Billy Butlin pioneered Holiday Camps, which provided cheap accommodation and entertainment for families, opening his first in 1936 and expanding his empire after the end of world War II.

one that he used for designing his hotels. His family used to live in a big house close by here. It's been pulled down now and re-developed. After he died, the family sold the hotels to one of the big chains. That was all before my time. There are none of them living here now. See that window over there?'

Jonah followed Father Damien's pointing finger with his eyes and saw a large stained-glass window, almost filling the wall at the back of the church. It portrayed the story of Noah's Ark. A large wooden boat stood grounded on a mountainside. Animals were emerging from an open doorway in its side. Arching across the sky above, there was a bright rainbow, which disappeared behind hills in the background.

'Sir Brian had that made in memory of his youngest daughter. She died in a road accident when she was only about seven, I believe. Apparently, she was very fond of animals. That's her pet rabbit down in the bottom right-hand corner – or so people tell me.'

They headed across the church towards the cordoned-off area where the Scenes of Crime Officers were working. Jonah paused by a life-size statue of a young woman in a blue gown and headdress holding a baby in her arms. The skin of both figures was caramel-coloured and their eyes were deep brown. The woman's hair was hidden beneath her headdress, but it would presumably have had the same black curls as those that stood out like a halo around her child's head.

'Is this the statue that talks to old Peter?' he asked.

'This is a statue of Our Lady and the infant Jesus,' Father Damien told him seriously. 'However, as I'm sure you are aware, statues never speak to anyone.'

'No, of course not,' Jonah experienced the unusual (for him) sensation of feeling rather foolish. 'But this is what he means when he says that he promised her that he'd become a Catholic?'

'Hello Father!' Bernie's voice interrupted their

conversation. 'You'll be pleased to know that the Crime Scene Manager says they're packing up now and they'll be out of your hair by the end of the morning. I see you've found Mary,' she added to Jonah. 'What do you think of her? The Christ-child is the absolute spitting image of Eddie when he was a baby.'

'I was thinking it looked a bit like Ricky,' Jonah replied, 'but I suppose that's probably much the same thing.'

Eddie and Ricky were Peter's son and grandson respectively.

'DCI Porter asked me to give you this,' Father Damien held out the paper to Bernie. 'It's the name and address of the Assistant Priest who was at St Cyprian's when the organ was originally installed. Oh! And I've also written down the details of Father Callaghan, who became Parish Priest here in 1983 – that's the year after. He wasn't there at the time, but he was a lot closer to it than I am and he may know more about it than I do. He was still here when I came in 2008, until he retired in the following year. He only stayed to show me the ropes and see to it that I didn't upset anyone. After twenty-five years, he was a bit protective of his flock and didn't really trust a young upstart like me!'

'I remember him,' Bernie said with a smile. 'He wasn't very impressed at the way I used to bring Lucy along to special occasions, but didn't show any sign of coming back into the Catholic fold on a permanent basis. I have to admit, I waited until he'd handed over all the children's work to you before I encouraged Lucy to do the preparation for her first communion.'

'It was a bit of an ordeal by fire for me, having her in my first batch of kids, I must say!' Father Damien laughed. 'She certainly kept me on my toes with all her questions.'

'Yes. But I rather fancy Father Callaghan would have thought she was being cheeky, rather than just interested to know the answers.'

'I'm afraid you may be right,' Father Damien agreed.

'He was of the old school, from the days when the people looked up to priests with unquestioning respect. I'm rather glad things are different now. It makes me feel less guilty about not being perfect myself. But we mustn't keep you talking like this,' he added turning to Jonah. 'I'm sure you've got lots of work to do. Is there anything else you need from me, or shall I leave you to it?'

'No. I don't think we need you any more for the time being – not until Lepage has had a chance to go through those records of yours. Thank you for your help.'

'And the organ? Can I ring the organ builders and tell them they can come back and get on with putting it back in its place?'

'Yes. Go ahead. Tell them they can get started this afternoon.'

6 CASE CONFERENCE

The room fell silent as Jonah entered, accompanied by a tall woman in jeans. They walked past the desks where CID officers were busily working – or chatting over cups of coffee – to take up a position in front of a large screen. Bernie closed the door behind them before sitting down in an unobtrusive position at the back of the room.

'This is Dr Penelope Black,' Jonah introduced his companion. 'She's a forensic anthropologist from the university. She's been having a look at our unidentified body.'

All eyes turned to look at the stranger. She had short dark hair and brown eyes behind large glasses. Above her rather faded jeans, she was wearing a blue tee-shirt with a skull and cross bones on it. As they watched, she slipped a small rucksack off her back and took a laptop computer out from inside it.

'Dr Black is going to talk us through what she and the forensics team have been able to find out from examining the body,' Jonah continued.

'Call me Penny, please. Now, is there somewhere I can plug this in?'

Andy Lepage stepped forward to help her to connect the laptop to the screen and to adjust the display so that she could show them photographs of the crime scene and the body. In the short interval while they sorted out the technology, one of the officers seated near the back of the room whispered to her neighbour: 'Did you hear that? Her name's Penny Black!'

'Do you think her parents didn't realise?' whispered back DC Alice Ray. 'Or could they have done it deliberately?'

'Surely they must have done,' DS Monica Philipson replied. 'I mean, people always shorten Penelope to Penny, don't they?'

'At least she doesn't seem to be embarrassed about …,' Alice's voice trailed off as she caught Jonah's eye looking at her.

'I think we're ready to start now,' he said authoritatively. 'Penny?'

'This is the crime scene as it was when the SOCOs arrived,' Penny said, displaying a photograph of the hole in the floorboards and the face of the victim beneath them. 'The body was lying on a solid concrete floor with quarry tiles on its surface. It was wrapped in something that at first I thought might have been a curtain. It was two pieces of textile fabric sewn together – like the front and lining of a curtain – the outer layer being a heavy woven cloth with gold-coloured embroidery on it, and the inner one being a typical lining material. However,' she paused to move on to a picture of the wrappings lying on a laboratory bench.

'When we unwrapped the body and took the cloth away for lab tests, we realised that it was something else. Once we had cleaned it up to remove the growth of mould, the colours became much clearer. The front was a rich green colour and the gold-coloured silk used for the embroidery was of remarkably high quality.'

Everyone peered at the screen, trying to make out the dirty yellow design, which was just visible on the even dirtier, greyish-green fabric. Penny paused for a few moments to allow them to look, before moving on to a new picture in which the colours were much more vivid.

'As you can see here, the item is far more complicated than a flat curtain. It has suffered considerable damage from damp and from the depredation of rodents, but you can still see that it comprises five panels joined together to make an elaborate covering for some sort of rectangular box. That, combined with the religious nature of the embroidered designs,' she pointed to the remains of a Celtic cross, now showing clearly in gold against a shiny green background, 'and the location where it was found, led me to suspect-'

'It's an altar frontal,' Bernie could not resist saying, becoming impatient with Penny's measured pace of delivering her findings.

'-that it was a hanging for an altar,' Penny continued, unperturbed. 'We've taken samples for analysis, to determine its composition, age and possibly where it was manufactured.'

She clicked a button to display another picture.

'The body was fully-clothed, including socks and brown suede shoes. The shoes are being investigated further, but I can tell you that there was a name distinguishable inside. It was a brand of cheap pigskin shoes from Poland, which was popular in the seventies and eighties.'

'That would fit in with the date that we think the body must have been put there,' Jonah commented. 'The platform under which it was found was constructed between March and May 1982. But sorry – I interrupted you – carry on.'

'One interesting feature is the state of the soles,' Penny continued. 'They show signs of deformation, as if they had been heated to a high temperature and the synthetic rubber has started to melt.'

'Looks like someone held his feet to the fire,' Detective

Sergeant Monica Philipson whispered again to Alice.

'Yes,' Alice grinned back, 'but I thought the usual practice was to take the victim's shoes and socks off first!'

'Like the altar cloth, the trousers and sweatshirt have been damaged by mice and had significant surface mould growth,' Penny went on,' displaying more pictures of the garments both on the body and on the laboratory bench at various stages of the cleaning process. 'However, enough of the material of both is left for us to be hopeful of establishing their origin. There are people working on that at the moment.'

Penny paused and looked round the room to check that she had the full attention of everyone present, before moving on to her next slide.

'As a forensic anthropologist, my main interest is in the body itself,' she said, waving her arm in the direction of the screen, where there was now displayed a photograph of the naked corpse lying on a stainless steel surface. 'It is immediately apparent that the body has undergone a process of mummification.'

She shone a laser pointer on to the screen.

'The skin on the face and hands is particularly striking. This brown leathery appearance is typical of a situation where a body has lain in conditions of high temperature and low humidity for a period of time immediately after death. For example, bodies have been found buried in sand in the desert, where the hot, dry environment has preserved them intact. There's a famous collection of naturally mummified bodies in Guanajuato in Mexico. The process has been known to take as little as a few days.'

'Hang on a minute,' Jonah said, as Penny paused to allow her words to sink in. 'A moment ago you told us that the clothes had mould growing on them. Doesn't that imply damp conditions? And now you're saying that the body must have been kept somewhere exceptionally warm and dry. Are you suggesting that it was moved?'

'Either that or the environmental conditions changed

after this mummification process was complete,' Penny confirmed.

'OK. Carry on.'

'The body is that of a young adult male. I estimate that his height was approximately one-point-eight metres. That's five foot eleven. The skin and soft tissue have been damaged by rodents, but the face remains largely intact. My examination of the skull suggests that he was of Indo-European origin. That means either white, middle-eastern or from the Indian subcontinent. We've taken samples for DNA testing, which may narrow that down some more.'

'Presumably you'll also check it against the police database?' Monica called out from the back of the room.

'That's not my remit, but it will certainly be checked,' Penny confirmed. She pointed with her laser pen towards the mummified head displayed on the screen. 'Most of the hair was gone – probably another example of rodent depredation – but we were able to recover a sample. It appears to be dark brown, although it's possible that some discolouration may have occurred. That's about all I can tell you at the moment about what he looked like. Do you have any questions on what I've said so far?'

She paused, looking round expectantly at the rows of faces in front of her. After a moment or two, Andy Lepage raised his arm.

'What I don't get,' he said, when Penny nodded to him to speak, 'is how come nobody smelled anything. We had a rat got into our house and died under the floorboards and it stank the house out.'

'The mummification process wouldn't produce any odours,' Penny told him. 'You see, what happens is that the tissues dry out before the decomposition process has a chance to begin. The smell that you get from a dead body is a result of gasses being produced as the tissues break down during autolysis[3] and putrefaction[4].'

---

[3] The destruction of cells or tissues by their own enzymes

'Oh! I see. Thanks.' Andy felt rather foolish at not knowing this and made a mental note to look up *autolysis* after the briefing was over.

'We haven't been able to establish how he died,' Penny resumed. 'The cervical vertebrae show some signs of damage and misalignment, but whether that was caused by trauma before death – hanging, for example – or if it happened after death or was a symptom of osteoporosis, we can't be sure. I've arranged for the bone density to be measured, which may rule out the latter hypothesis.'

She clicked the remote control button again and a new slide appeared.

'There is evidence of perimortem injury to the right forearm. Here you can see a fracture to the distal radius. The break has clean, sharp edges, indicating that it took place before death, but there is no sign of healing. My guess is that it occurred no more than a few hours before death.'

'And what might cause that type of fracture?' asked Jonah.

'The most likely cause would be a hard blow to the wrist.'

'During a fight, perhaps?' Jonah suggested, 'or by someone attacking him?'

'Yes. It looks as if he was hit with something hard, such as a baseball bat or a metal bar,' Penny agreed. She turned back to the screen, indicating the other end of the bone with her laser pointer. 'There is also evidence of a radial head fracture. However, this is completely healed, indicating that it took place some considerable time before death. This would typically have been caused by the subject falling and putting out his hand to save himself.'

'So probably just some earlier accident and nothing to do with his death,' Jonah commented.

---

[4] The decomposition of organic matter by bacterial or fungal digestion.

'Yes.' Penny clicked the button and a view of the victim's exposed rib-cage appeared. 'Here we have more perimortem injuries. There are several broken ribs, all unhealed and the majority exhibiting signs of having occurred before death.'

'So, you're saying that it looks as if he was attacked shortly before he died, and whoever it was hit him hard enough to break his arm and crack some of his ribs – is that right?'

'Yes. There's no definitive evidence, but the most obvious narrative would be that he was set upon by one or more people, who hit him with a blunt instrument and went on to kill him, possibly by strangulation, using a method, such as hanging, that crushed some of the vertebrae in his neck.'

'Thank you.' Jonah turned to face the room. 'Now, Philipson and Ray have been having a look at the Missing Persons records for 1982. Would you come up and tell us what you've found?'

Penny sat down on a chair at the front of the room and Monica got up and walked forward. Then she turned and addressed her colleagues.

'We started with reports of adult males who went missing in the Oxford area between January and May 1982, which are the months leading up to the last date when the body could have been put in the location where it was found. We found one promising candidate. His name is Patrick Doughty, an unemployed labourer who was living in a council flat in Headington at the time. His sister reported him missing in April 1982. Officers from the Dog Section searched the area around the flats and there was a house-to-house done and notices in the local paper, but he was never found. He was twenty-two, six foot tall with fair hair and blue eyes.'

'Would that description fit our unknown man?' Jonah asked Penny.

'Could be,' she replied. 'The shrinkage caused by the

47

mummification means that I could only estimate the height, based on the lengths of the long bones, so six foot is about right. As for hair and eye colour,' she shrugged, 'we really can't be sure.'

'It looks as if it would be worth looking into Patrick Doughty a bit further,' Jonah said. 'It should be straightforward to ascertain whether he is our mystery man. Presumably he'll have dental records that we could use.'

'I'll get on to that,' Monica volunteered. 'We found a few other possibles as well – when we widened the search to cover the whole of southern England. Do you want me to get theirs too, or shall we wait until we've eliminated Doughty?'

'Let's start with Doughty. But meanwhile, go through your list and check their details against the description that Penny's just given us. Then, if it isn't him, you'll know which of the others are worth following up.'

'Right you are, sir.'

'Good.' Jonah turned his head to look at a small man with sandy coloured hair and square-framed glasses who was sitting at the front of the room next to Penny. 'Now Luke is going to fill us in on what the SOCOs found when they examined the crime scene.'

Senior Scenes of Crime Officer, Luke Gray, got to his feet, a spiral-bound notebook in his hand. He looked slowly round the room, checking that he had the full attention of his audience. Then he glanced down at his notes and began his report.

'As you know, the victim was found underneath a raised platform constructed from wooden boards on a wooden frame. The area under the platform is enclosed on two sides by the wall of the church and on the other two sides by wood panelling. We examined the boards for any signs that they had been raised at any time after they were initially laid. There was absolutely no evidence of any disturbance prior to the discovery of the body two days ago. The same goes for the wood panelling on the sides.'

'So it's safe to assume that the body must have been placed there at the time that the platform was completed?' Jonah asked.

'As far as we can tell,' Luke replied cautiously. 'You also asked us to look for any signs that there was a source of heat under the platform at some earlier stage – the central heating pipes, for example. We did find vestiges of fixings for pipes along the stone walls beneath the platform, which suggest that the central heating pipes did, indeed, run along there *before* the platform was erected. However, there were no filled holes in the panelling on the side of the platform to suggest that the re-routing of the pipes had been done after the platform was in place.'

'Couldn't the panels have been replaced?' Monica asked from the back of the room.

'Unlikely,' Luke told her. 'Not without leaving traces on the wooden framework to which they're attached.'

'I've got the architect's drawings,' Andy Lepage chipped in. 'They include the re-routing of the pipes around the outside of the platform. And there's a receipted invoice for the plumbing work, dated May 1982.'

'Good,' Jonah said. 'It looks as if we can safely assume that the body was placed under the platform while it was still under construction in April or May 1982. But it looks as if he must have died some time earlier and been stored elsewhere for long enough for his body to dry out and mummify.' He turned to Penny. 'How long would that take, exactly?'

'I'm afraid I can't say,' Penny shrugged. 'Anything from a few days to a few weeks, depending on the conditions.'

'OK.' Jonah looked towards Luke again. 'Did you find anything else?'

'Nope!' Luke shook his head. 'We did a fingertip search of the area under the platform, but there was nothing there apart from a lot of dust, dead mice and spiders.'

'OK. Now Andy, will you tell us what you found in

those documents you were looking through in the church office?'

Andy got to his feet and looked round nervously. Although he had been in the CID for ten years now, he still felt uncomfortable being the centre of attention.

'The installation of the new organ began in April 1982,' he reported, glancing down at his notes. 'I've seen copies of the weekly newsletter that give a commentary on progress. The platform over where the body was found was started on 23rd January. The original aim was that the new organ would be ready for Easter, which was on 11th April that year. However, early January was exceptionally cold that year, with heavy snowfalls and record low temperatures, which made them decide not to do the re-routing of the central heating until later in the year when it wouldn't matter having it off for some time while the work was done. So they made do with the old harmonium for a bit longer and put off installing the organ until the second half of April.'

'So, when are you saying the body must have been put there?' Monica asked.

'As far as I can see, it could've been any time from early February, when the platform was substantially finished, until sometime during the week beginning 12th April, which was when the central heating pipes were removed and the platform was finally boxed in on its sides. The way it was built was: they made the framework first and covered it with floorboards, leaving the sides open so that they could still get in to remove the old central heating pipes. That means that someone could have got in through the sides and hidden the body in there at any point within that time window.'

'But it would've been a bit risky, wouldn't it?' Monica commented. 'What if the heating engineer found it?'

'Whoever did it might not have known about the plan to move the heating pipes,' Alice suggested.

'Or could they have assumed that the body wouldn't be

noticed?' added DC Joshua Pitchfork, an earnest young officer who had only recently been assigned to Jonah's team. He had been studying the plan of the crime scene. 'It was right in the middle of the platform. The central heating people would be working round the edge, where the pipes went. And there was a framework of supports for the platform between them and it – with extra vertical supports in the middle where the organ was going to go. In the dark down there under the floor, they probably wouldn't notice there was anything there.'

'It would take a very cool murderer to rely on that,' Jonah observed. 'If they were trying to prevent the body being found, then I'd say it's more likely that they were expecting the platform to be boxed in right away. That might either be because they didn't know about the plumbing work or because they didn't put it there until after it was finished.'

'Which was probably the fourteenth or fifteenth of April,' Andy added. 'The invoice for the completed building work was dated the sixteenth.'

'And then the organ builders came in after that?' Jonah queried.

'No. They were in and out of the church from round about the beginning of March, as far as I can tell. They were able to start installing the organ on the platform before the sides were put on.'

'So they are potential witnesses,' Jonah said with interest.

'Yes. I've got the name of the firm: Henry Chandler, Organ Builders. It isn't trading any longer and I haven't been able to track down anyone who worked there, but I'll keep at it and I'm sure we'll find them.'

'Good. You do that.' Jonah nodded to Andy to indicate that he could sit down. 'And there are a few other potential witnesses that we could do with finding. Unfortunately, the Parish Priest at the time suffered a fatal heart attack in April 1982, which is a real pity, because he would probably be the person best placed to tell us about who had access to the church and what sort of relationship – if any – Doughty had with them. However, we do have the name and address of his assistant. I've got an appointment to talk with him in his new parish on Friday. And Father Damien, the current Parish Priest, has suggested that we also talk to the priest who took over in 1983. Obviously he can't give us any first-hand information, but he may have heard gossip about things that went on the year before or be able to give us the names of people who were there at the time.'

'Perhaps the murderer will have confessed to him,' Monica suggested facetiously.

'If they did, I am quite sure that Father Callaghan won't be prepared to tell us,' Jonah said coldly. He looked round the room, studying the faces of all the officers present. 'Now, I think that's all for now. Monica – I want you and Alice to get hold of Doughty's dental records so that we can check them against our victim. And, at the same time, go through your list of other missing persons and whittle it down based on the description that Penny's given us. Andy – carry on tracing that organ builder. Josh – I've opened an Incident on HOLMES 2[5]. I want you to enter up the information that Penny's just given us and create a record for Patrick Doughty. You should be able to populate it with information from the 1982 Missing Persons record. The rest of you – familiarise yourselves with the layout of the crime scene and the evidence so far. If we're lucky, we'll get confirmation that the body is Doughty by the end of the day, and then we'll be able to concentrate on how he got there. If not … well, we may have to open up a whole lot of old missing persons cases

---

[5] HOLMES 2 (Home Office Large Major Enquiry System) is an Information Technology system used by police forces across the UK to collate and manage data relating to criminal investigations.

and follow them all over the country. OK. Off you go!'

He turned back to Penny, who was putting her laptop away and preparing to leave.

'I'm thinking that, if it *isn't* Doughty, we may have some trouble finding out who it is. We may need to make a public appeal. In which case, we'll need a picture of the victim that's going to be recognisable by people who knew him when he was alive.'

'How soon do you want it? I could arrange for a full facial reconstruction, but that would take time, or a computerised image would be a bit quicker. Either way, you'd need to allocate resources, which would be wasted if the dental records prove that it's Doughty.'

'Yes. I think we'll have to wait until he's been eliminated, but could you have your people on stand-by, so they can get started right away, if it isn't him?'

'Right you are!' Penny fastened her rucksack and swung it on to her shoulders. 'In fact, we've got a Masters student with an art degree, who's interested in that sort of thing and might like to have a go in any case. It would be a valuable exercise for her, even if it turns out to be your Patrick Doughty, because she could compare her model with your photograph from the missing persons file. I'll get a cast made of the skull and then we can take things from there.'

7 CASE HISTORY

'I know this is way before your time,' Jonah said to Father Damien, turning the computer screen attached to his chair so that the priest could see the photograph displayed there. 'But I just wondered if you might have heard about this young man. His name is Patrick Doughty. Apparently, he used to attend St Cyprian's occasionally, back in the early eighties. He went missing in April 1982 and was never found.'

'And you're wondering if he could be the body under the organ?'

'Yes. We're currently seeking out his dental records, which is proving more difficult than we expected. With any luck, it won't be long before we know for certain whether it is him. Meanwhile, I was hoping you might have heard of him or know someone who knew him.'

'It's not a name I've come across,' Father Damien said slowly. 'But then, why would I? You'd do better asking Father Carey. He may remember him.'

'Yes, I've got an appointment to see him tomorrow, but I was hoping not to have to wait. Impatience is one of my besetting sins, I'm afraid.'

The door of the church office opened and a smartly-dressed woman entered carrying a USB data stick. She stopped short when she saw Jonah and looked toward Father Damien.

'I'm sorry. I was hoping to print out the newsletter. Will you be long? I can come back later.'

'No, no,' Jonah reassured her. 'Just carry on.'

'Actually, Kathleen,' Father Damien said, looking towards the woman, 'you might be able to help the police. You've been coming to St Cyprian's for a long time. Do you happen to remember an Irish labourer called Patrick Doughty?'

'This is his picture here,' Jonah added, swivelling the screen so that the woman could see the photograph. 'He was reported missing back in April 1982, and nobody has seen him since.'

Kathleen Powell peered carefully at the computer screen, pursing her lips and nodding her head slowly.

'Ye-es,' she said slowly. 'I remember him. He lived in one of the tower blocks on the other side of the by-pass. I think he fell out with the priest at Corpus Christi.' She sniffed in a way that suggested to Jonah that she regretted that someone of Doughty's class had chosen to worship at St Cyprian's. 'Why do you want to know?'

'We were wondering if he could be the body that the organ builders discovered the other day,' Jonah told her. 'His disappearance fits in with the time when we think it must have been put under the organ.'

'Are you suggesting that someone from St Cyprian's killed him?' Mrs Powell asked suspiciously.

'Not necessarily, but whoever put him there – and that may not be the same as whoever killed him – must have had access to the church.'

'We always used to leave the church open day and night, in those days,' she told him, 'in case anyone wanted to come and pray in front of the blessed sacrament.'

'But we had a few things stolen,' Father Damien

explained, 'so now I open the church in the morning and lock it at the end of vespers.'

'I see. So, you're saying that anyone could have wandered in and put the body under the organ platform – including at night after everyone else had gone?'

'Yes,' Mrs Powell replied perfunctorily. Jonah gained the impression that she was intent on distancing members of the church from the mysterious corpse.

'Can you remember anything else about Patrick Doughty? Jonah asked. 'Was he well-liked? Were you aware of him falling out with anyone?'

'He was a layabout,' came Mrs Powell's verdict. 'Father O'Leary used to give him handouts from parish funds.' She sniffed again. 'I *told* him it was only encouraging idleness, but he wouldn't listen. All the scroungers in the parish saw him as a soft touch – especially the Irish ones.'

'That's interesting,' Jonah said, encouragingly. 'Do you think that Doughty might have come to the church at night to see Father O'Leary?'

'What are you getting at?' Mrs Powell asked suspiciously.

'I was just thinking that he could, maybe, have disturbed someone who was stealing from the church,' Jonah replied, carefully avoiding any suggestion that the murderer might be one of the St Cyprian's flock. 'They could have killed him and hidden him under the organ and then run off, without taking anything after all.'

'I suppose so,' Mrs Powell agreed reluctantly.

The door opened again and another woman came in. She was wearing a floral-patterned overall and a purple headscarf. She, too, stopped suddenly when she saw such a large group of people.

'I just came to get the hoover,' she explained apologetically, pointing towards an ancient-looking upright vacuum cleaner, which was standing in a corner of the room.

'Come and have a look at this, Madge,' Kathleen

Powell said, gesturing towards the computer screen. 'This policeman is asking about Patrick Doughty. Do you remember him? He was always hanging around, trying to sponge off Father O'Leary.'

Margaret Kenny took hold of a pair of spectacles, which was hanging around her neck and put them on to her beak-like nose. Then she approached Jonah's chair and peered closely at the screen.

'Yes,' she nodded, 'I remember him alright. A wastrel if ever there was one! The one I felt sorry for was his sister. He was always cadging money off her and spending it on booze or horses. I can't say I was sorry when he took himself off.'

'You think that he left of his own volition?' Jonah asked sharply. 'You don't think someone could have taken against him and done him some injury?'

'The police think that *he's* the corpse that the organ builders found under the organ,' Kathleen Powell told her. 'They reckon he went missing while the organ was being put in and someone hid his body underneath it.'

'If you're interested in mysterious disappearances while the organ was being built, you ought to be looking at that Henry Chandler,' Margaret Kenny said, with a contemptuous snort. 'He had words with that assistant of his one afternoon when I was cleaning the brasses, and then he never came again. Henry finished the organ on his own after that.'

'Really?' Jonah said excitedly. 'That's very interesting. Do you know the name of this assistant? And do you know what it was they quarrelled about?'

'Hmmm,' Margaret Kenny pursed her lips in thought. 'He had a strange surname. What was it now? Potter? Pilkington? Something beginning with P, I'm sure.'

'It was Stamp,' Kathleen told her. 'Giles Stamp.'

'Yes! That's right,' Margaret nodded her agreement. 'You're right; it was Stamp. I'm not so sure about the *Giles*, though. That sounds wrong to me.'

'And the argument?' Jonah asked again.

'I don't know. All I know is, I was in the vestry polishing the candlesticks and I could hear them going at it hammer and tongs.'

'That's very interesting,' Jonah said, 'very interesting indeed. Thank you. Now I'd better be getting back to the station. If either of you think of anything else that might help us, please let me know.'

Bernie handed one of Jonah's business cards to each of the women. As they both turned to go, the mobile phone attachment on Jonah's wheelchair rang out. He hastened out of the office, followed by Father Damien and Bernie, who closed the door firmly behind them.

'Monica!' Jonah said into the microphone, 'what's new?'

'I've tracked down Doughty's dental records and sent them over to the mortuary,' Monica's voice sounded through the loudspeaker, 'and Andy's got an address for the organ builder – or at least, for his widow and daughter. They're living together in an old people's flat in Banbury.'

'Excellent!' Jonah purred with satisfaction. 'And I've just been hearing about how Henry Chandler fell out with his assistant while he was working on installing the organ at St Cyprian's, and that assistant was never seen again. So, if our unknown corpse turns out not to be Doughty, there's a possibility that he's Chandler's assistant. Either way, we could do with getting over to Banbury to interview the wife and daughter and see if they remember Henry saying anything that could give us a clue about what happened.'

'I'll get on to that right away,' Monica volunteered eagerly. 'I'll take Alice with me. Two women living alone will probably feel more comfortable being interviewed by female officers.'

'OK. You do that. But tread carefully. It's possible that Henry Chandler killed his sidekick, who goes by the name of Giles Stamp according to a couple of people who remember them, but we don't want his widow and daughter to know that we suspect him. As far as they're concerned, we think the body is Patrick Doughty and we're interested in knowing whether Henry saw anything that might tell us how it happened. And we'd like to track down Giles Stamp, because he was there too. Have you got that?'

'Yes, sir. I'll be the soul of discretion,' Monica assured him.

Jonah ended the call and turned to speak to Father Damien.

'Now, I'm going to be meeting Father Carey tomorrow morning. What can you tell me about him?'

'Not a lot. I've never met him. Some of the congregation remember him fondly and a friend of mine served under him as a deacon and said that he was very caring and a hard worker. Why do you ask?'

'I'm not saying he was responsible for killing Doughty, or whoever it is,' Jonah said carefully, 'but you have to understand that we can't rule out the possibility that either he or Father O'Leary put that body under the organ. Who else was better placed to know that work under the organ platform was complete and there was no danger of anyone discovering it? Who had better access to the church by day and night?'

'And who else might have a motive for wanting to get rid of a young man who had become the protégé of Father O'Leary?' Father Damien suggested wryly.

'Yes,' Jonah agreed. 'I can see that you've worked out what people will start thinking if it turns out that it is Doughty lying in the mortuary at this moment.'

8 DIAGNOSTIC PROCEDURES

Peter spread the crumpled paper on the table in front of him and re-read it – again.

'I expect you remember that I have been divorced for a number of years,' the neat, rounded script said, 'after my husband threw me over for a woman who was able to fulfil his desire for children. After living alone for so long, it never occurred to me that I might ever meet someone else. So nobody was more surprised than me I to find love again quite by chance. Jude is a widower with two grown-up children. He's been living alone ever since his younger daughter got married seven years ago. Both of his girls are delightful and very pleased to welcome me into the family. We are both looking forward very much to our wedding which is scheduled for-'

Seeing the back door opening, Peter hastily stuffed the letter back into his pocket and got to his feet. Lucy entered, taking off her bicycle helmet as she did so and striding across the room to hang her jacket up in the hall.

'Hi Lucy!' Peter greeted her, snatching up a saucepan and hastening across to the sink to fill it with water. 'How did the match go?'

'We won, three-two,' she told him. 'Mind you, we were lucky to get the last goal, and our defence was all over the place so it's amazing they didn't absolutely thrash us. We're going to have to work on that if we're going to have any chance in the final.'

Lucy was Captain of her girls' soccer team and took her responsibilities for coaching her team-mates very seriously.

'Did *you* score?' Peter asked, putting the pan on the hob and running water into the sink ready to wash the vegetables.

'I scored two of the goals and Annabel scored the other one.' Lucy paused briefly, before continuing out of the door into the hall. 'I'd better get changed. Mam and Jonah'll be back soon.'

'Yes.' Peter looked at his watch. 'I'd better get on too. I hadn't noticed the time.'

A few minutes later, he heard the sound of the front door opening and Bernie's voice calling out that they were home. He wiped his wet hands on the kitchen towel and went out to greet them.

'Tea in about forty minutes,' he said, seeing Jonah advancing down the hall in his wheelchair.

'Just enough time for your physio,' Bernie declared, pushing open a door on her right and holding it for Jonah to go into the room, which had once been the dining room and now served as his study and private sitting room. He glided across the carpet, pressing a button on the controller attached to the arm of his chair to open another door and allow them both into the adjacent bedroom. They fell into the familiar routine of preparing him for functional electrical stimulation[6], which enabled him to exercise his muscles despite being unable to move them himself. Bernie carefully took off his business suit and

---

[6] Functional Electrical Stimulation (FES) is a technique that uses low-energy electrical pulses to stimulate movement in the muscles of people who have been paralysed.

replaced it with a loose-fitting tracksuit, before using a hoist to lift him on to a strange machine, reminiscent of an exercise bicycle, and attaching electrodes to his skin, which would stimulate the muscles in his legs. Lucy came in and sat on the edge of the bed, watching.

'Have you found out who your mysterious corpse is?' she asked eagerly.

'We've got a couple of ideas,' Jonah told her. 'If the first one is right, we'll probably know tomorrow, when they've had a look at the dental records. I can't think what's taking them so long, to be honest. Monica Philipson sent them across before lunch.'

'I expect they had other jobs to do,' Bernie reminded him. 'You can't expect everyone to drop everything just because you're too impatient to wait.'

'If it turns out it's not him,' Jonah went on, ignoring her intervention, 'it'll probably take a bit longer.'

'That's only the start of it, though,' Bernie added. 'The big question, whoever he is, is: who killed him and why?'

'Who are the two people that you think it might be?' Lucy asked.

'There's an unemployed labourer who went missing in 1982,' Jonah told her. 'He used to attend St Cyprian's occasionally and did odd jobs for them sometimes. He seems a good bet to me, but we won't know until we hear from the forensic team whether the dental records match.'

'And the other one?'

'Aahh! That's promising in a different way, because we've no evidence – yet – that this one ever went missing in the first place. According to a couple of women who remember the organ being built, the two organ builders fell out while they were working on it and they never saw the younger one of them again.'

'So, you think the older one could've killed the younger one and hidden him under the organ?' Lucy asked excitedly.

'It's not impossible. That does provide some sort of

motive, which is more than you can say about the labourer.'

'And the forensic archaeologist seemed to think that the body must have been kept somewhere else for at least a few days before it was stowed under the organ,' Bernie added, 'which would fit in with the death occurring away from the church – back at the organ builders' workshop, say – and the body being brought there just before the area under the organ was sealed.'

'The organ builder, unfortunately, is dead,' Jonah went on. 'Philipson and Ray went to see his widow and daughter this afternoon and they confirmed that he used to have an assistant, whom he dismissed sometime in the early eighties. The women from St Cyprian's had got his name wrong, but I'm pretty sure it must be the same one.'

'And did they know where he'd got to after that?' Lucy asked.

'No.' Jonah shook his head. 'According to them, he just upped sticks and vanished. And they couldn't tell us what the quarrel was about either.'

'Monica Philipson suspected that it could have been something to do with his daughter,' Bernie contributed. 'Her theory is that Julian Stamp – the assistant organ builder – was sniffing round Henry Chandler's daughter, Belinda. Henry didn't like the idea and told Julian to sling his hook.'

'Henry's the organ builder, right?'

'Yes,' Jonah confirmed. 'I wish I'd gone over to interview them myself now. I don't know how much credence to give to Monica's hunch. She didn't really have anything to go on except a vague feeling that there was some uneasiness on Belinda's part when they mentioned Julian.'

'Well, she also said that Mrs Chandler told her that Julian was a waster and Henry was well shot of him,' Bernie added. 'So she may have a point.'

Peter put his head round the door with a five-minute-warning that the tea would be ready. Bernie and Lucy began the job of detaching the electrodes from Jonah's body and unstrapping him from the FES machine. Soon he was back in his wheelchair and leading the way to the kitchen, where Peter was dishing up a chicken and vegetable risotto. Jonah positioned his chair at the end of the table and Lucy sat down to his right, ready to feed him. She had undertaken this task ever since he had come to live with them, on the death of his wife, nearly four years previously.

'Any news on our mysterious mummy?' Peter asked, once they were all seated around the table, tucking in to the food.

'Nothing definite,' Jonah answered. 'We've got a couple of leads, but we won't know anything definite until forensics get their finger out and look at the dental records of our number one Missing Person.'

'If it *isn't* him,' Lucy added, relishing the opportunity to discuss a real-life police investigation, 'it looks as if it might be a case of some mysterious feud over who gets to court the organ builder's lovely daughter!'

'Oh?' Peter looked towards Jonah.

'One theory is that the organ builder's assistant was making unwelcome advances towards his daughter, Belinda, and the organ builder did away with him to put an end to the affair,' he explained.

'Unwelcome by whom?' Peter asked. 'I mean: the daughter or her father?'

'Now you're asking!' Jonah dodged a spoonful of food, which Lucy was holding up to his mouth. 'I wasn't there, so we only have Monica Philipson's account of the interview, but according to her, the daughter looked sheepish and the mother was hostile, and neither of them said anything outright. They both *said* that they had no idea what the quarrel was about, but Monica thinks they were lying.'

'And the organ builder himself?'

'Is dead, unfortunately.'

They finished the risotto and Bernie cleared the plates while Peter fetched a fruit salad from the fridge. He waited until they were all eating again before resuming his questions, anxious to know whether there was likely to be bad publicity for the church of which he was about to become a member.

'And if the body is your *number one*, what then?'

'Then we have to try to work out who killed him and who put him under the organ and why?'

'It was definitely murder then?' Peter asked. 'No chance of an accident or natural causes?'

'As you know,' Jonah said drily, 'pathologists never say anything *definitely*, but they say that there's evidence of injuries inflicted just before he died which are, in their parlance, *consistent with a sustained attack by one or more persons.*'

'And there are injuries to the neck, which could suggest that he was hanged or strangled,' Bernie added.

'And does anyone have any theories as to *who* could have done it?' Peter asked, making a conscious effort to sound casual, but convinced in his own mind that his apprehension must be obvious to anyone. It seemed clear to him that the most likely explanation – and the explanation that the tabloid press would be sure to leap upon with glee – of a young man having been killed and hidden in a Catholic church, was some sort of misdemeanour on the part of the clergy, probably involving sexual deviancy and a cover-up by those in authority.

'Not yet,' Jonah told him. 'The young man in question used to do odd-jobs around the church, so he would presumably have come into contact with the clergy and any caretaker or verger or whatever they had then.'

'But, apparently the church was left permanently open in those days,' Bernie added quickly. 'So literally *anyone* could have come in and hidden the body.'

'Except – how would they know that there was

anywhere *to* hide it?' Lucy objected. 'It looks to me as if it *must* have been someone who knew about the work on the organ and the layout of the church *and* when there was likely to be nobody else around.'

'Which does rather point towards the clergy, or else some lay person who was around the church a lot,' Bernie agreed, gloomily. She shared Peter's uneasiness regarding the reaction of the popular press.

'And the body being wrapped in that ... altar frontal was it, you said?' Jonah added, 'would fit with it being a priest that did it, wouldn't it?'

'A priest or anyone who knew where they were kept,' Bernie pointed out. 'Henry Chandler could easily have found one in the vestry. He was there in the church for weeks, building the organ, wasn't he? I bet he knew his way round pretty well. How about this? Henry confronts Julian in his workshop and, like a good old Victorian-style father, demands to know what his intentions are towards his daughter.'

'Julian gives an unsatisfactory answer of some sort,' Peter joined in with a will, 'and Henry blows his top.'

'And whacks him with a heavy organ pipe,' Bernie continued gleefully, 'cracking his ribs and breaking his arm.'

'Julian fights back,' Peter continued, 'and Henry grabs him by the neck and squeezes; and, before he knows what's happened, it dawns on him that he's dead. So he stuffs the body into the corner of the workshop, right on top of the heating pipes ...'

'Heating pipes? In a workshop?' Jonah queried sceptically.

'Why not? We don't know what sort of place it was, do we?'

'OK. Go on.'

'He knows that it isn't safe to keep it there forever,' Bernie resumed, 'so a few days later, he takes it out and puts it in the van that he uses for transporting the organ parts and takes it to St Cyprian's. He wraps it up in an altar frontal from the vestry – an old one that isn't currently in use – and pushes it in under the organ platform and nails the panels on the sides and breathes a sigh of relief, thinking that nobody will ever know what happened.'

'Well, that does seem to cover all the facts as we know them so far,' Jonah admitted. 'And, to be honest, I wasn't looking forward to digging up a whole lot of dirt on your Father Damien's predecessors; but for all we know, Julian Stamp is still alive and well.'

'Come to that, so could Patrick Doughty be,' Bernie commented. 'We'll only know that he's definitely dead, if his dental records match our mystery corpse.'

'But his disappearance was reported to the police at the time,' Jonah insisted, 'whereas nobody seems to have been at all concerned about Julian Stamp. And the timing is just right: he vanishes in April 1982, the same month that the organ is being built, and-'

'April?' Lucy queried, with a puzzled frown on her face.

'Yes,' Jonah answered. 'They were hoping to do it earlier in the year, but had to delay until after Easter in the end. The work wasn't actually finished until mid-May. Why?'

'I was thinking about this idea that the body dried out on top of central heating pipes. Would they still be on by then?'

'Maybe it was a particularly cold year,' Peter suggested.

'Even so,' Bernie argued, 'Lucy has a point. It does seem quite unlikely that anyone would have the heating on enough to mummify a body, even if it was lying on top of the pipes. And especially not in a church. The treasurer would do his nut!'

'In fact,' Jonah agreed, remembering his conversation with Father Damien, 'that was the whole point of waiting until after Easter to fit the organ. They were waiting until the heating was turned off to re-route the pipes.'

They all sat looking at one another for a minute or two.

'So, whoever the corpse is and whoever killed him,' Jonah summarised at last, 'the place that he was kept after death must have been somewhere quite special.'

'What exactly is involved in building an organ?' Peter asked. 'Might an organ builder need to heat things up? To bend metal to shape or something?'

'You mean, like a blacksmith?' suggested Lucy. 'We visited one once, on a school trip, and the place where he was working was incredibly hot.'

'But would it *stay* hot?' Jonah asked sceptically. 'Aren't we really looking for something more like a blast furnace, where it's a continuous process that carries on day and night?'

'I'm not so sure,' Bernie said slowly. 'When we had a coal fire in the living room, if you let it go out overnight, the bricks around it were often still quite warm in the morning. Or think about storage radiators: they're basically just a lump of concrete with a heating element inside them. If you had some sort of furnace surrounded by stone walls, with some sort of niche where the body was put, mightn't it stay warm enough for this mummification process to take place?'

'I suppose we'd better ask Penny just exactly *how* hot and dry it has to be,' Jonah sighed. 'Maybe she'll have some suggestions as to what sort of place we're looking for.'

They finished their meal and then Lucy and Jonah went into the living room, while Peter and Bernie tackled the washing up.

'I got a very strange letter the day before yesterday,' Peter began hesitantly, once they were alone together.

'Oh?' Bernie waited for him to go on.

'Do you remember Jane Carrington?'

'The name sounds familiar, but … you don't mean …?' Bernie faltered to a stop. She did not know how to refer to the woman who, biologically, was Peter's half-sister, but whom he steadfastly refused to acknowledge as any sort of relation.

'Yes. That's right: my "sister" Jane.' The inverted commas were clearly discernible in his voice.

'Funny her writing after so long,' Bernie said cautiously. 'Was there a particular reason?'

'She's getting married again.'

Bernie said nothing, sensing that there was more to come. After a long pause, Peter continued.

'She wants me to give her away.'

'What?' Bernie exploded into laughter. 'Surely she can't be serious! In this day and age? And she must be well into her forties. How can she possibly want to be handed over from one man to another like some sort of parcel? It beggar's belief!'

'I think she probably just wants someone to walk down the aisle with her,' Peter said, smiling in spite of himself at his wife's outrage. 'I don't suppose she sees it as an affront to womanhood the way you do. She just wants her wedding to look like anyone else's.'

'Yes, well she did always seem like a bit of a weed,' Bernie snorted in derision. 'But even so, why pick on you? Surely she must have a friend she could ask.'

'She says that her new bloke has got a big family and she doesn't want there to be no blood relatives at all on her side. You're invited to go – and the kids and grandkids.'

'But she must know that you haven't even told Hannah and Eddie that she exists. How are you supposed to explain to them that they've suddenly acquired a new aunt?'

'Of course there's no way I'm going to tell them anything – not after the way her mother ...,' Peter's voice died away into an angry silence.

'So, presumably you're going to write back to her to say you're not doing it?'

'Yes ... at least, that's what I'd *like* to do. I just ... I don't know ...,' Peter sighed. 'Oh! I wish she'd just leave me alone!'

'I thought she'd agreed that she would,' Bernie said in a very decided voice. 'And I think that you shouldn't feel under any obligation to her. She's broken her side of the bargain and it's not fair of her trying to make you feel bad about it. Just write back saying thanks, but no thanks.'

'Yes. I was hoping you'd say that. It's just …,' Peter sighed again. 'I suppose I can't help feeling a bit sorry for the poor woman, and it's not as if she actually did me any harm. If only it wasn't for that dreadful mother of hers!'

'But if you were to go,' Bernie argued, 'you'd only be thinking about that awful meeting and what she said. Think about it? What on earth would you say in your speech? People will be expecting you to reminisce about Jane's childhood and the rest of her family and …'

'But I don't know the first thing about any of that!'

'Exactly! She just hasn't thought things through at all. If she's introducing you to her in-laws as her brother, they're going to expect you to have some sort of idea of what she's like and what she's been doing with her life up to now.'

'Surely she'll have to explain …'

'To her fiancé maybe, but there'll be uncles and aunts and cousins popping up from all over, who won't have been properly briefed. I say, don't touch it with a barge pole. Just send a polite refusal. She can't *make* you do it.'

'Yes,' Peter suddenly felt better. 'You're right. I shouldn't feel guilty about it. I've told her any number of times that, as far as I'm concerned, she and her mother are nothing to do with me. If she can't accept that, then that's not *my* fault. I'll write tomorrow.'

9 PRELIMINARY DIAGNOSIS

'Come through! Come through!' Father Carey greeted them warmly, leading the way down a rather dark hallway to a room at the back of the presbytery. He was a small, rotund man with white hair around a bald crown. This tonsure-like hairstyle, together with his faded black cassock, put Jonah in mind of mediaeval monks.

The priest threw the door open and they found themselves in a spacious room furnished with worn, but serviceable, leather-bound armchairs and a few low tables. The morning sun was slanting in through a window in the wall ahead of them, making it very bright compared with the dingy hall. One wall was lined with bookcases, while another was adorned with a crucifix and numerous religious paintings.

'I know,' Father Carey said, seeing Jonah looking at a particularly gory representation of the sacred heart. 'I sometimes wonder what the attraction is of that sort of thing. That one was given to me by the sweetest little old lady you could imagine. I could hardly refuse it, but I told her that, rather than having it over my desk as inspiration while I write my sermons, I thought it should go here, where we have all our church committee meetings, so that more people would get the opportunity to see it.'

'I'm sorry,' Jonah was taken aback at the priest's apparent ability to read his mind. 'I hope I didn't look disapproving; I'm just not very familiar with … er …'

'Why should you be? Now, can I get you something to drink? Or would you rather get straight down to business?'

'Down to business, if that's OK with you. It shouldn't take long, and then we can get out of your hair.'

Bernie sat down and took out the laptop from the storage space at the back of Jonah's wheelchair, ready to take notes. Father Carey settled himself in a chair opposite them both.

'I'm sorry I couldn't see you yesterday. I had three funerals and then a wedding rehearsal in the evening.'

'That's quite alright,' Jonah assured him. 'Now, I think you are aware that this is about your time at St Cyprian's in Headington?'

'Yes, of course. I suppose I ought to have got over there to see you the moment I saw the report on the TV. But, I knew that Thursday was going to be so very busy and I suppose I hoped that … well, it had all gone unnoticed for so long that …'

Father Carey suddenly appeared strangely flustered and incoherent. Jonah watched him in silence, wondering what this was all about and judging that the best way to find out was to wait without speaking so that the priest was forced to explain his words. Father Carey closed his eyes for a few moments as if in deep thought – or could it be in prayer? Then he took a deep breath and started again.

'I'm sorry. I'm not making a lot of sense, am I? Perhaps we could start by you confirming that you are wanting to question me about a body that you've found under the organ in St Cyprian's – a man's body wrapped in a green altar frontal – is that correct?'

'Yes – but how did you know about the green cloth? We didn't release those details to the public.'

'That's simple: I know what he was wrapped in, because I put him there.'

Jonah and Bernie sat staring in amazement at these words, trying to think of a fitting response.

'I didn't kill him, I hasten to add,' Father Carey went on, speaking more easily now that he had unburdened himself of the thrust of the secret that he had been keeping for more than thirty years. 'I found him, hidden away in the bottom of an old trunk in the vestry, when I was clearing out all Father O'Leary's old things, after he died. I know I ought to have reported it then, but I was young and Father O'Leary was not even buried yet and I was afraid of a scandal.'

'Are you saying that you thought Father O'Leary had killed him?' Jonah asked.

'I don't know what I thought!' Father Carey sighed. He thought for a moment and then continued. 'You've got to remember that things were different in those days – especially in the Catholic Church. I'd been brought up to revere the priesthood. Father O'Leary was my Parish Priest, and my mentor. I was convinced – or I managed to convince myself – that whatever he'd done must have been for the best. And I thought that, if he'd kept this thing secret for two years, what was the point of bringing it all to light now and causing a scandal?'

'Two years?' Jonah asked sharply. 'Why do you say *two years*?'

'Because that's how long it was since the lad had gone missing.'

'You mean you recognised who it was?'

'Not exactly recognised,' Father Carey admitted, 'but it never occurred to me that it could've been anyone else.'

'Anyone else but who?' Jonah was feeling more and more bewildered by these cryptic remarks.

'Leonard O'Connell.'

'And Leonard O'Connell is?'

'I'm sorry!' Father Carey sighed. 'I'm telling this all

back-to-front, aren't I? Let me start again. We need to go back to March 1979, when I first came to be Father O'Leary's assistant.'

'OK,' Jonah agreed. 'Tell me all about it.'

'When I arrived, Father O'Leary had already been there for over twenty years. As far as I could tell, everyone liked him. He was hardworking and never refused an appeal for help. I was a bit surprised to find this young man living in the presbytery guest room; but it was typical of Father O'Leary's way. Apparently, Leonard O'Connell had been drifting around for a few years when he washed up at St Cyprian's. He had no job and nowhere to stay. Father O'Leary felt sorry for him and took him in. He gave him a "temporary" bed in the presbytery guest room and found odd-jobs for him to do around the church.'

'You say you came to St Cyprian's in March 1979. How long before that had O'Connell been living there?' Bernie asked when Father Carey paused. 'Just so we've got the chronology right.'

'I'm not sure. A month or two maybe, possibly longer. It was supposed to be a temporary arrangement until Leonard found somewhere else to live, but the months went on and he was still there. Father O'Leary trained him up to be an altar server, and he started helping out at the Boys' Club that Father O'Leary ran. These days, maybe the alarm bells would have started ringing in my head, but it just never occurred to me to question it. I just thought how great it was that he'd found somewhere that he belonged at last. You see, a bit at a time, he told us about himself. He'd been abused by his father from an early age and ran away from home as soon as he'd left school. He'd never had any proper job and he'd spent a lot of time sleeping rough and scavenging from bins. The only thing that had kept him from sliding into a life of crime had been his mother's Catholic faith, which she'd impressed on him from birth. He told us he'd once been so hungry that he'd been tempted to steal food from a supermarket, but he put it back when he thought about what his mum would have said. So, I admired Father O'Leary for giving him a purpose in life and a roof over his head. Do you see what I'm getting at?'

'Perfectly,' Jonah assured him. 'But I take it something happened to change your opinion?'

'Not really – or not as much as perhaps it should have, in the light of the sorts of things we know now. My mother died in January 1980. I went to her funeral, which was in Plymouth. I was away for about three days. When I got back, Father O'Leary told me that Leonard had decided to move on. He was gone and the guest room had been cleared, but a few weeks later, I came across some of Leonard's possessions in a cupboard in the vestry – personal things that I wouldn't have thought he'd have wanted to leave behind. It seemed strange to me, but I assumed that he must have just forgotten about them. I took them to Father O'Leary, thinking that he'd have a forwarding address for him, but he said that he didn't know where he'd gone and just to put them somewhere safe in case he came back.'

'And you now think that what actually happened was that Leonard died and Father O'Leary hid his body in the vestry?'

'That was what I thought must have happened, when I found the body two years later.'

'But you say you didn't actually recognise him, you just assumed it must be him?'

'I don't think anyone would have been able to recognise him,' Father Carey shuddered at the memory. 'It was all brown and shrivelled up, like a bag of bones, only more rigid. I've seen lots of dead bodies in my time – it goes with the territory – but never anything like that!'

'Something like this?' Jonah asked, swivelling the computer screen attached to his chair so that Father Carey could see a photograph of the body that had been retrieved from under the organ.'

'Yes. That's it alright.'

'OK. Now, this Leonard O'Connell: can you describe him to me?'

'I'm not sure. Taller than me, but that's not saying a lot. Brown hair, blue eyes, I think. I'm sorry, I can't remember any more than that.'

'What about his age?'

'He told us he was nineteen.'

'And that was in 1979?' Bernie asked.

'Yes.'

'I don't suppose you have a photograph with him in it?' Jonah suggested, without much hope.

'No. I'm afraid not. There might be some pictures of the Boys' Club, back at St Cyprian's, but I didn't bring anything of that sort away with me.' Father Carey hesitated before going on. 'Actually, there *was* a photograph of Leonard. I found it in Father O'Leary's desk, when I was clearing out his things. I thought it might be taken the wrong way, so I destroyed it. I – I – that was one of the things that made me so sure it was Leonard's body, when I came across it a day or two later.'

'Can you describe this photograph?' Jonah asked cautiously, wondering what sort of debauchery might be about to be revealed.

'Not really. It was just a photograph.' Father Carey frowned in puzzlement.

'Full length? Any particular pose?'

'No, no. It was a portrait – just head and shoulders.'

'And your concern? The reason that you decided to destroy it?'

'It just seemed strange, that's all: a Catholic priest keeping a photograph of a young man in his desk drawer. I was afraid that people would think ... OK. This is what crossed my mind, after I found the photo and before I found the body. I remembered how close Father O'Leary had been to Leonard and I did just wonder if there was any possibility that he could have been his father. It's not unknown for priests to father children and keep it secret. If Leonard's mother hadn't wanted to cause a scandal, she might have married the first man who came along afterwards, or I suppose she could even have been already married when they … Anyway, that was what I thought. Make of it what you will. It may be all moonshine. I hope it is, but that's why I destroyed the photograph.'

'Alright,' Jonah leaned his head back and pursed his lips in thought. 'I'll need a formal signed statement from you about all this. I'll arrange for someone to sort that out. Meanwhile, we'd better ask all the questions that we came here to ask you, just in case you're wrong about the identity of the man that you found in the vestry. Let's start with this man.'

A flick of Jonah's index finger produced a new picture on the screen in front of them.

'This man went missing in April 1982, shortly before the organ was installed. Do you recognise him?'

Father Carey peered at the screen for a few seconds and then looked back towards Jonah, shaking his head.

'No. Does he have a name?'

'Patrick Doughty. He was an unemployed labourer. He used to go to St Cyprian's occasionally and sometimes did odd jobs there, according to one of the congregation who remembers him.'

'I can't honestly say it rings any bells, but my memory isn't what it used to be, I have to admit. I could well imagine Father O'Leary giving him work to do, if he was unemployed. Leonard was by no means his only protégé. As I said at the beginning, he never refused a cry for help.' Father Carey sat staring at the photograph in silence for several seconds. 'But, surely you can't be suggesting that this man was the body that I found? I would have known if it was only a few weeks old. It *couldn't* have been someone who disappeared that April. It was already all shrunk to skin and bones – just like your photograph.'

'According to our forensic anthropologist, the

mummification process could have taken only a matter of days, in the right conditions.'

'You mean I could have been completely wrong about it having been in the vestry for two years?'

'Yes.' Jonah waited for a few moments, watching the priest's face as this information sank in. 'Now, I need to ask you about someone else. You presumably met the organ builder, Henry Chandler?'

'Yes. With Father O'Leary dying suddenly in the middle of the work, I was responsible for signing it off and paying the bill.'

'And do you remember his assistant?'

'Julian? Yes. He seemed a nice boy.'

'Were you aware of any sort of quarrel between the two men?'

'I did hear rumours that they'd fallen out, yes.'

'Do you know what it was about?'

'No. I don't even know how true the rumours were. I did notice that Julian wasn't there anymore, but then the heavy lifting part was all finished, so I assumed that he just wasn't needed. You're not suggesting that *he* was the victim?'

'He's just another young man who seems to have vanished at much the same time as you discovered a body and hid it under the organ. We have to look into all the possibilities.'

'I don't know!' Father Carey sighed and shook his head in bewilderment. 'I thought that I was going to tell you what happened and then it would all be over. Now ...' he sighed again, 'what happens next?'

'As I said, I'll arrange an appointment for you to go down to your local police station and make a formal statement. You may want to take a lawyer with you, because you do need to realise that what you did was at very least perverting the course of justice.'

'And, for all you know, *I* may have been the one who killed whoever it turns out to be and I've invented all the stuff about a man going missing while I was away to throw you off the scent.'

'Precisely. I'm glad you understand the situation.' Jonah turned to Bernie. 'I think we'll call it a day now. Let's get back and see what more we can find out about this Leonard O'Connell.'

They returned to the car. While Bernie was still strapping him in, Jonah spoke on his mobile phone to Andy Lepage.

'I want you to get over to St Cyprian's and have another look through all those documents in the office there. See if you can find any mention of a Leonard O'Connell. Apparently, he lived at the presbytery from sometime in 1979 until January 1980, doing odd jobs and helping around the place. And find out as much as you can about the Boys' Club that Father O'Leary used to run. In particular, see if there are any photographs taken between 1979 and 1982.'

Satisfied that Jonah's chair was secure in the back, Bernie got out and climbed into the driving seat.

'I'd say that puts the kybosh on the theory that the organ builder killed his assistant and hid the body under the organ,' she said, as they headed back to Oxford. 'It looks as if the murderer must either be Father O'Leary – if Father Carey is telling the truth – or Father Carey himself, if he isn't. Do you believe his story?'

'I think I probably do. After all, he didn't have to tell us anything. He could have simply said that he was as surprised as anyone to hear about the body being found, and that he didn't remember anything strange going on back in 1980. If he killed O'Connell – or whoever it really is – why admit to having moved the body?'

'And, if it *was* O'Connell, and he'd killed him two years earlier, why bother moving it? If it hadn't been found after two years, it must have already been in a pretty safe place. Why risk being seen moving it?'

'I suppose he might have been afraid that any new

Parish Priest coming in after Father O'Leary died might instigate changes that would bring it to light. Or it might not be O'Connell. Father Carey could have killed Patrick Doughty – or even Julian Stamp – and then told us about O'Connell to put us off the scent.'

'He seemed genuinely surprised to hear that the body could have been relatively fresh in 1982,' Bernie pointed out.

'Yes. I'm only playing devil's advocate. I think the chances are that Father Carey is telling the truth and he really did find the body, already mummified, and hide it to avoid a scandal. Whether he's telling us the whole truth about his suspicions of Father O'Leary, I'm not so sure.'

'Yes,' Bernie sighed. 'I must say I'm starting to feel very uneasy about Father O'Leary and his Boys' Club. I hope this isn't going to open up a whole new clergy abuse scandal with St Cyprian's at the centre of it.'

When they arrived back at base, they found Monica Philipson waiting, eager to speak to Jonah.

'Penny Black has sent us her report on the dental records,' she told him eagerly. 'The body definitely *isn't* Patrick Doughty. And Belinda Chandler arrived five minutes ago, saying she's got more information on Julian Stamp. I knew you were on your way, so I've put her in Interview Room 3 with a cup of tea. I thought you'd like to meet her yourself.'

'Thanks. Let's do that right away – although what we've just learnt from Father Carey does rather suggest that the fight between Henry Chandler and his assistant is a red herring.'

Belinda Chandler was a small, dumpy woman with auburn-dyed hair and a plump, much-lined face. She looked up anxiously as Jonah and Monica entered.

'Miss Chandler: this is DCI Jonah Porter,' Monica said. 'He's in charge of the case. He'd like to hear what you have to say about Julian Stamp.'

'I'm sorry I didn't tell you everything when you came,'

Belinda smiled up apologetically at Monica, who smiled back reassuringly.

'That's quite alright,' Jonah said kindly, positioning his wheelchair so that they could converse conveniently. 'Witnesses often think of things later that they wish they'd remembered during the initial interview.'

'But, it isn't that I've only just remembered,' Belinda explained, still looking anxious. 'It's that I didn't like to say anything in front of Mum. She never approved of Julian, you see, and even after all these years ...,' she sighed. 'I never told her that I carried on seeing him after he left. As far as she and Dad were concerned it was all over.'

'So, is Julian Stamp still alive?' Monica asked eagerly.

'No,' Belinda shook her head sadly. 'He joined the army. The Falklands war had just started and he thought it would be exciting to go off down there and fight. He was rather impetuous like that, and rather romantic. It was all over, of course, by the time he was actually recruited, but he went through with it and I think he rather enjoyed army life. Anyway,' she sighed again. 'All you need to know is that he was blown up by a nationalist bomb in Northern Ireland a couple of years later. I'm sure you'd have found all this out eventually, but I thought I ought to tell you, so you didn't waste a lot of time thinking he might have been that body in the church.'

10 VISITING TIME

'Peter!' Father Damien smiled broadly at the sight of his visitor standing on the doorstep of the presbytery. 'What brings you here?' He threw open the door and gestured to Peter to go inside.

'I wanted to warn you that you can expect a surge of interest in St Cyprian's and some of the publicity could be rather unpleasant,' Peter explained as he followed the priest into his study.

'Is this to do with the stuff that young police officer took away with him this afternoon? About Father O'Leary's Boys' Club?'

'Yes. The club and a young man who used to help with it – Leonard O'Connell. Father Carey thinks that's who the body under the organ is.'

'Oh?'

'And that's another thing that you need to be prepared for. Father Carey has admitted to being the person who put the body under the organ, where we found it. He says that he came across it amongst Father O'Leary's things when he was sorting out after O'Leary died suddenly. Now you can imagine what the press are likely to make of that when it comes out!'

'Another attempt by the clergy to cover up ... what

exactly? Is the idea that Father O'Leary was abusing this Leonard O'Connell and ended up killing him?'

'I don't know. According to Jonah, Father Carey claims not to have thought beyond preserving the good name of a well-liked Parish Priest who had only just passed away. I don't think there's any evidence of abuse – only that O'Connell somehow ended up dead and Father O'Leary hid his body, instead of reporting it to the authorities. The thing is,' Peter continued earnestly, 'in the short term, it's not what actually happened that matters – it's the press speculation that you're going to need to be ready to deal with. The police are putting out a public appeal for information about where O'Connell went after he left St Cyprian's in 1980 and they're also going to be asking for anyone who was in the Boys' Club at that time to come forward. You can expect to be besieged by journalists wanting to see the exact place where the body was found and hanging around waiting to pounce on anyone who looks as if they might be willing to talk to them – especially older people who might have been around long enough to remember Father O'Leary.'

'Oh, we've already had a few people round!' Father Damien sounded unperturbed. 'There was a nice young woman from the Oxford Mail and someone from local radio. They just asked politely to be shown where the body was found and chatted about the organ restoration and left a little donation for the repair work.'

'This will be different,' Peter insisted. 'As soon as the national tabloids get a whiff of another clergy abuse scandal, they'll be all over you like a rash wanting to dig out any dirt they can find. You need to be ready for them. And it may become bigger than just St Cyprian's. Perhaps you'd better tell the bishop. Won't he have a press secretary or someone to deal with this sort of thing? Someone who can help you to work out a damage-limitation strategy?'

'Hold on there!' Father Damien put up his hand to stop

Peter's flow. 'I dare say you're right about informing the bishop. He ought to know what's going on. But I don't like the suggestion of a *damage-limitation strategy*. Isn't that exactly what the Church has been criticised for in the past? If Father O'Leary or Father Carey or anyone else in the church has done wrong, then surely the right thing for us to do is to wait for the police to complete their investigation and then to apologise to the victims and look for ways to put things right!'

'But that's not how these people operate! They won't be sitting around waiting for the police to report their findings. They'll be lying in wait after Mass on Sunday, on the lookout for anyone who looks old enough to have been around back in the seventies, and then following them home and pestering them to tell their story. And they'll be scouring the back issues of the local papers, hoping to find news of that Boys' Club and then tracking down names in the hope of finding someone who'll claim to have been abused. I really don't think you've realised how very nasty this could get. There are a lot of people out there who make money by dragging people through the dirt; and there are a lot of people who are on the lookout for ways of showing up what they see as the hypocrisy of religious people. And if you're not prepared for them, they'll trick you into saying something that they'll be able to hold up as proof that the church is guilty!'

'Peter! Peter!' Father Damien said gently, holding up his hand again. 'You worry too much. *Take no thought for the morrow*, remember? And *Can any man by worrying add so much as an hour to his life?* Just relax and leave it in God's hands.'

'That's all very well, but you don't know these people. They twist what you say. You need to be prepared with answers that they can't turn against you.'

'*When they hand you over, do not worry about how you are to speak or what you are to say; for what you are to say will be given to you at that time*,' Father Damien quoted.

'I still think you need to be on the alert not to let them

trip you up. You don't have any idea how unpleasant this could get. Isn't there something in the Bible about needing to be *as wise as serpents?*'

'*And as innocent as doves*, yes. Believe me: I'm not complacent, but no amount of preparation will alter the fact that all we can really do is to take things as they come.'

'I wish I had your faith. The thing is: I've seen this sort of thing get out of hand so many times.' Peter sighed. 'Anyway, at least you know now. The appeal is already out on Social Media and it'll probably be on the Ten O'clock News tonight and the radio tomorrow morning – just nice time for some of the more unsavoury characters to do a bit of background reading and be waiting for everyone to come out from Mass on Sunday morning.'

'I'll make a point of sending someone out with a collecting box for the repair fund. If that doesn't scare them away, at least we may be able to pay the builder for fixing the roof.'

'I don't know how you can stay so calm,' Peter smiled. 'I just hope I really am worrying unnecessarily. Now, before I go, there was something else I'd like to have a word with you about – if you're not too busy; I've already taken up a lot of your time.'

'No, no. I've got nothing planned for this evening. Go ahead.'

Father Damien waited patiently, while Peter sat across the table from him looking rather awkward and fumbling with something in his pocket.

'Is it about the confirmation service?' he prompted gently.

'No. It's nothing to do with that' Peter said quickly. 'Or … well, maybe it does sort of relate to my First Confession. I mean, I'm supposed to tell you all my sins, aren't I? And I'm supposed to forgive my enemies and stuff.'

There was another long silence.

'It doesn't have to be all at once,' Father Damien said

at last. 'You could do it bit by bit, if that would make it any easier. You can even start now, if you like.'

'Well, can I tell you the whole story and then maybe you can decide what I ought to do?'

'Yes. I think the whole story would be a good idea. Let me get us some coffee. It sounds as if this could be a long session.'

'You remember I said that I was brought up in the National Children's Home,' Peter began, once they were settled comfortably with their elbows on the table and their hands around comforting mugs of coffee. 'I never knew who my parents were, and I never wanted to. I was quite content with what I had and I never regretted not having a normal family. When I was small, I suppose I thought that my parents were dead, and then, when I started to know more about the world, I assumed that I was probably illegitimate and my mother hadn't been in a position to care for me. I left school and went into the Police Service and then I met Angie and we got married and we had the kids and I still didn't give a thought for my birth mother. Everything was fine and dandy until just a few years ago. It was round about when Bernie and I got married. I was on the television news appealing for witnesses to a particularly nasty run of arson attacks against ethnic minority families.' He broke off and grinned across at Father Damien. 'You see the trouble these appeals to the public can cause!'

'Not yet, I don't. Go on. What happened?'

'This woman rang in. Her name was Valerie.' Peter stopped short. 'OK. I'd better be honest about this. My mother rang in. She'd seen me on the TV and heard my name and she claimed that she recognised me. According to her, I look very like my father – who thankfully was already dead by then, so at least I didn't have to face him too.'

'And how did you feel about that?'

'Angry. I told her to stop wasting police time and to get

off the line so that real witnesses could get through.'

'I take it that wasn't the end of the matter.'

'No. She wouldn't take *no* for an answer. She pestered and pleaded and in the end this other woman – Jane – turned up, saying she was my half-sister and begging me to meet her mother.'

'Who is also *your* mother?'

'Yes,' Peter grunted. 'Yes. I said I'd be honest, so yes, she was my mother.'

'And why is that so hard to accept?'

'Because she was the most blatant, most offensive, most bigoted, most insensitive, self-obsessed racist I've ever had the misfortune to meet!' Peter snarled.

There was another long silence. Father Damien sipped his coffee and waited for Peter to resume his story.

'I'm sorry,' he said at last. 'I shouldn't have said that. The woman's dead now, but I still can't forget what she said. I'd better explain what happened.'

He took a long draught from his mug. Then he wiped his mouth with his hand and continued.

'Eventually they wore me down and I agreed to meet them. Bernie and I went up to Manchester – they lived in Stockport – and we met at Piccadilly Station. As far as I was concerned, that was the end of the matter. She'd had a chance to see how her baby had turned out. I'd reassured her that I didn't feel betrayed by her and that I'd had a happy life. I hoped that, after that, she'd accept that we had nothing in common and it was better for everyone if we never saw one another again.'

'And did she see it that way too?'

'No. I foolishly let slip that I had children. She immediately wanted to meet them too. Jane had let her down rather badly by not having any, so I was her last chance to be a grandmother. There was no way I was allowing her to get her claws into Hannah and Eddie. They could do without having a grandmother and aunt appearing out of nowhere expecting to pay them visits and give presents and all the things that grandparents do. And I told myself that it wasn't fair on Jane either. After all, she'd been the dutiful daughter all those years and now she was being pushed out by this older brother who had suddenly become the apple of her mother's eye. So I made it very clear that they were to stay away from me and I was not having any more to do with either of them.'

Peter drained his mug, trying to delay the moment at which he had to put into words the most distressing part of his story. He replaced it on the table and clasped his hands together in front of him.

'About two years later, Jane turned up again. Her mother – our mother – was dying of cancer. She wanted more than anything to see her grandchildren before she died. I still wasn't prepared to tell Hannah or Eddie about her, still less to allow them to meet – and I'm just so glad that I stood firm on that – but in the end, I agreed to go and see her, just once more and to take some photos with me. I really didn't think I had any other option. The wretched woman was dying, after all.'

He relapsed back into silence. Father Damien sat without speaking, waiting for him to go on.

'I got there and she was pathetically grateful to me for coming. I began to wonder if I'd been rather cruel not agreeing to see her before. And then I got out a photograph of Hannah at her graduation, which I'd brought for her to see. I'd chosen a full-length one, showing her dressed up in her gown and mortarboard, with Angie and me standing on either side of her, all smiling proudly because she was the first in the family to get a degree. Valerie – that's my mother – took one look at it and …'

Peter trailed off as he fought to keep down his emotion. He took two or three deep breaths and tightened the grip of his two hands together.

'I've never seen anything like it. She seemed to be physically repelled. She sort of gasped and dropped back on the pillows. And she said a whole load of nonsense about how it was impossible that this black woman could be her granddaughter. She looked at my beautiful, intelligent daughter and it disgusted her!'

'Perhaps she was just taken aback,' Father Damien suggested, without much hope. 'If she'd never come across a mixed-race family before, it must have been a surprise.'

'No,' Peter said decidedly. 'No. It gets worse. She started asking questions about why I'd married a black woman. Not, why I'd married Angie. To her, Angie wasn't a person; she was just a *black woman*. And she kept bringing it all back to herself and her obsession with the idea that not having a proper family must have ruined my life. That was the other thing that got to me: she didn't *want* me to have had a good life! She wanted me to have been constantly regretting being brought up in a Home. She *said* she wanted me to forgive her for deserting me, but she really just wanted to wallow in her own self-pity that her parents wouldn't let her keep her baby. She kept asking: was it because I came from a Children's Home that nice white women wouldn't have me? As if I'd been scraping the bottom of the barrel when I asked Angie to marry me! She was so – so,' Peter's voice rose in indignation, 'she was so convinced that I was doing *that black woman* a tremendous favour by allowing her to marry me. It never occurred to her that I could feel *privileged* that *Angie* chose *me*. And she couldn't even bear to look at my kids' photos because of the colour of their skin! And it just makes me feel so angry and ... and ... well not exactly ashamed, but that's the nearest I can get ... ashamed that she gave birth to me. I don't want to be descended from that sort of bigoted racist. It makes me feel ... dirty! And, if you're asking me to forgive her for what she said ... well, I don't think I can.'

'Let's take this a bit at a time,' Father Damien said, putting his hands around Peter's fists, which were still clenched together on the table. 'And let's deal with that last bit first. You say that having this Valerie for a mother makes you feel dirty. Well, maybe you need to realise that everyone has things about their families that they feel ashamed of. My dad, for example: he was a great *spare the rod and spoil the child* man. His idea for disciplining me and my brothers would be called assault these days. And going back further, I don't suppose any of us doesn't have a good few racists in their family tree. My mum traced her family back to some wealthy mill owners up north somewhere. They must have been importing cotton from slave plantations – not to mention exploiting their own workers.'

'But you've never met those people,' Peter argued. 'And that was centuries ago. Valerie was still treating black people as beneath contempt less than a decade ago.'

'And that was wrong of her; but it doesn't contaminate you. What I'm trying to say is that we all have things in our family tree that we'd feel ashamed of if we knew about them. That's only worth thinking about insofar as it reminds us that we're all part of fallen humanity and liable to succumb to similar temptations.'

'But that's just it!' Peter protested. 'I can't help thinking that *I* might think the same way as she did if she'd brought me up instead of putting me in the Home.'

'That's just speculation – and if you don't mind me saying it pointless and dangerous speculation. I daresay you would have seen things rather differently if you'd been brought up among different people, but that doesn't absolve you from making your own decisions and value-judgements. We each have responsibility for our own soul. We each have to educate our conscience to pull us up on the things that matter. Your mother gave you her genes – the basic building blocks of your life, the raw material if you like. Those may have determined the way you look – your build, your red hair, your-'

'Actually, according to Valerie, that's all down to my father.'

'But those aren't the things that make you who you are. She just provided you with a blank canvas on which you have painted your life. Yes, you've been influenced by the people around you, but at the end of the day, you are morally responsible for your actions – just as she is. You think her racism is reprehensible – so do I – so would any right-thinking person. Is it understandable, given her background and upbringing? Perhaps it is, but that doesn't make it right. She was wrong to denigrate your wife and children because of their colour. Nobody is asking you to make excuses for her or to explain it away. If you had lived all your life with her and, as a consequence, had entertained similar views and had not modified them in the light of clear moral certainties and Christian teaching, then you would also have been culpable. However, that is only hypothetical. It didn't happen, so it's pointless to consider it – except insofar as it may remind you not to take pride in your racial inclusivity and broadmindedness, which may be largely a product of your actual upbringing and subsequent life experience. Do you see what I'm getting at?'

'I *think* so,' Peter said slowly. 'You're saying that our background and upbringing do affect the way we think, but that we still have a responsibility to work things out for ourselves and change our views if they turn out to be wrong. And I shouldn't congratulate myself on never having been tempted to look down on black people, because that's just good luck on my part.'

'Yes. I think you've hit on what I was trying to say with that idea of temptation. Our upbringing and circumstances affect which sins we are tempted to commit and the moral issue for us is deciding whether or not to give in to the temptation. Now, are we finished with the business of Valerie making you feel bad by association? Can we move on?'

'Yes. I suppose so. I'm going to have to think about it a bit, but I think I get the general gist.'

'Right! Now let's consider forgiveness. What do you have to forgive Valerie for?'

'For being a bigoted racist, of course!' Peter exclaimed in surprise.

'No,' Father Damien said firmly. 'That won't do. That's far too general and not in your power to forgive. You'll have to leave that to God. No. What I'm asking you is: what harm did she do to you personally?'

'She racially abused my wife and kids.'

'Well, strictly, she made racist remarks about them to you. She didn't actually abuse them. They weren't there.'

'That's just splitting hairs.'

'Well, of course, we Catholic priests are famous for that; but I don't think so. I'm trying to get you to analyse exactly what harm she did and to whom. Your wife was already dead and your children presumably still don't know anything about it, and yet I agree those remarks were wrong. She said things to you that were hurtful. Do you agree?'

'Yes. I suppose so.'

'And she pursued you after you'd said you didn't want to have anything to do with her. So you resent that too?'

'Yes! If she could only have accepted that we were nothing to one another, none of the rest of this would have happened. Or if only she'd never seen that stupid TV appearance!'

'That's another issue altogether. Let's stick with forgiveness. You need to forgive her for continuing to try to see you after you'd told her to back off, and for saying racist things about your wife and children, which you found hurtful. Is that it?'

'Well, I suppose so,' Peter sounded reluctant to agree. 'But it's not the number of things that's important! It's what she said – and the way she said it and – and the fact that she just wouldn't even try to understand!'

'OK. That's fine. I didn't say it was a small thing, or that it was going to be easy to forgive. I just wanted you to be clear what it is that you need to forgive. Your mother was racist. That's bad, but it isn't your responsibility to deal with it. Your mother hurt you by saying racist things about your wife and kids – *that's* what you need to learn to forgive. Now, I'm going into the church and I'm going to take my rosary and meditate on the Sorrowful Mysteries, praying for the right words to say when your horde of journalists descends on me like a pack of wolves. And I think you ought to join me. Your intention can be the salvation of your mother's soul. If you can't forgive her, you can at least pray for her.'

'I don't have a rosary.'

Father Damien opened a drawer and took out a string of black beads. 'Take this one. You can keep it. People keep giving them to me. I can't think why.'

He led the way down the corridor, through the vestry and into the church. It was dark and silent. In the sanctuary, the light burning in front of the tabernacle containing the blessed sacrament shone eerily bright. Father Damien felt for the switch and light flooded the church from fittings in the ceiling. He gazed across at the entrails of the organ and the rows of pipes still lying on the floor waiting to be set in their places.

'Keith keeps assuring me that it will all be finished before Easter,' he sighed, 'but I can't see any difference from when they started back to work on Wednesday afternoon.'

'Take no thought for the morrow,' Peter reminded him. 'Doesn't your faith in Providence extend to organ refurbishments?'

'Mea culpa!' Father Damien beat his clenched right hand against his breast and bowed his head. 'I admit it: I am a great hypocrite!' He looked up again and grinned. 'And past experience tells me that, however hard I pray, Our Lord has a habit of ignoring my pleas not to be left embarrassed by something going wrong during important services! Did I tell you about the bird that got in and left a deposit on the Bishop's head? Or the time I dropped a baby in the font? I keep telling myself that it's good for the people to know that their Parish Priest has as many human faults as they do themselves – I just hope *they* realise it's good for them too!'

Peter grinned back. 'I remember Angie saying to the kids once, "Life is unfair, and I'm unfair; so I'm preparing you for Life!" I wished I'd thought of that one myself.'

'I'll save it up for the next time I have to give the casting vote in an impossible dispute between the factions on the school governing body. Now, we agreed on these prayers, so we'd better get on with it or we'll be here all night.'

They knelt down together in a pew, close to the statue of the Virgin and Child.

'Tell you what,' Peter whispered mischievously. 'Could we do a swap? I'll pray for you not to make a fool of yourself when the journalists come prying; and you pray for eternal rest for Valerie's soul.'

Father Damien looked at him for a second or two, trying to decide whether he ought to reprimand this levity. He struggled to keep a straight face, finally giving up and breaking into a grin.

'I'm not sure you're treating all this with appropriate seriousness,' he gasped, suppressing, with a supreme effort, the laughter that threatened.

'I was only following your example.'

'But I'm a priest. I'm allowed to be irreverent. Why do you want to swap anyway?'

'I just thought that that way probably both lots of prayers will be more sincere. If you like, I'll add in an extra decade of Hail Marys for the safe restoration of health to the organ.'

Father Damien's shoulders shook with laughter. He reached out his arm and clapped Peter on the shoulder.

'OK, you're on! It's a deal!'

11 REVISED PROGNOSIS

'I'm putting on another piece of toast for myself,' Peter called across the kitchen, 'Does anyone else want one?'

'No thanks.' The others shook their heads.

Peter put a single slice into the toaster and pushed it down. Lucy resumed her task of feeding Jonah with breakfast cereal, while simultaneously eating her own slice of toast and marmalade. Bernie put down her spoon and pushed her empty bowl away. Saturday breakfast was a more relaxed affair than the weekday rush to get Jonah ready for work and Lucy off to school on time. She could afford to sit for a few minutes of conversation before starting the tasks of the day.

The mobile phone attachment on Jonah's wheelchair rang out. Seeing that it was from the police station, he swiftly answered the call.

'I thought you'd want to know right away,' came the eager voice of DC Joshua Pitchfork. 'A man's just walked into the station in Brighton claiming to be Leonard O'Connell.'

'Really?' Jonah asked excitedly. 'Is he still there? I'd like to speak to him.'

'Yes. They've got him writing a statement for them, but they wanted to know what to do with him after that.'

'Get a video link set up. I'll be down directly. I want to interview him.'

Leaving the rest of his cereal uneaten, Jonah turned his chair and headed for his bathroom to complete his morning routine. Bernie was already on her feet, anticipating the move and ready to help. Realising the futility of arguing that he was not on duty over the weekend, she contented herself with ensuring that he would not rush out without cleaning his teeth.

It was not long before they were both sitting in front of a large computer screen, upon which was displayed an empty interview room. Then a uniformed police officer walked across, blocking the view for a moment before taking a seat behind the table. She was followed by a middle-aged man with grey hair, brushed back from a high forehead, and a prominent bulbous nose. He sat down next to her. There was a murmur of voices as she explained the video system to him and pointed out the screen and camera.

'Can you hear us?' Jonah asked.

'Yes,' replied the uniformed officer, looking directly into the camera. 'I'm PC Janet Strange and this is Leonard O'Connell.'

'And I'm DCI Jonah Porter and I have with me DC Joshua Pitchfork, DS Andrew Lepage and Dr Bernie Fazakerley. Now Mr O'Connell, please can you just confirm that you are the same Leonard O'Connell who stayed at St Cyprian's presbytery for several months back in 1979?'

'That's right. I was right down in the gutter back then and Father O'Leary got me back on my feet and gave me a home for a while.'

'I see. But in January 1980 you went off again. Why was that?'

'I just decided it was time to move on.'

'Leaving some of your possessions behind in the vestry. Why was that? Were you in a hurry to leave?'

'I just forgot about them until it was too late to go back.'

'How was it too late? Why didn't you contact Father O'Leary and ask him to send them on to you?'

'I never thought.'

'You say he picked you up out of the gutter. Didn't you feel you owed it to him at least to leave a forwarding address so that he'd know you were alright?'

'I suppose I should've, but I never thought.'

'Father Carey was worried that something might have happened to you.'

'I told you: I never thought about that. I just thought it was time I moved on, so I did.'

'Why was it time to move on?' Jonah persisted. 'What prompted you to think that?'

'Nothing. I just thought I'd been there long enough.'

'So you went, without saying anything to either of the two priests who had befriended you? Father Carey came back from his mother's funeral and found you'd gone. He hadn't had any idea that you were thinking of leaving. That strikes me as rather strange.'

'I was young. I didn't think things through. I just got an idea into my head and then I did it, just like that.'

'People are going to say that you ran away because of something that Father O'Leary did to you. Was that what really happened?'

'No. Not at all. I just decided it was time for me to move on.'

'Without saying where you were going?'

'I didn't *know* where I was going. I was just drifting.'

'OK. Let's talk about the Boys' Club. You used to help with that, I gather?'

'I did, yes. What of it'

'Did the boys seem happy? Were you aware of any complaints?'

'Yes, they seemed happy enough; and no, none of them complained that I know of. Why?'

'No bullying?'

Silence.

'None of them ever came to you with any stories of inappropriate touching?'

No reply.

'None of them seemed uncomfortable around Father O'Leary – or Father Carey?'

'No! Nothing like that. Father O'Leary was really good with the boys. They all loved coming to the club. Stop trying to make it sound like he was some sort of pervert.'

'And yet, round about that time, some young man died in or around St Cyprian's and his body was hidden inside the church. Father Carey thought it must be you, because you disappeared and never got in touch. Do you have any idea who it might have been?'

'No. But I do know it wasn't any of them boys. The same boys used to come to the club all the time I was there. None of them went missing.'

'So you have no idea at all who the body that we found there a few days ago could be?'

'No. And I don't believe Father O'Leary had anything to do with it either. I don't know what people've been telling you, but take it from me he's not a killer – or a child-molester. Have you asked him what *he* thinks? What does *he* say?'

'We haven't asked him for the very good reason that he died only a couple of years after you left Headington.'

'No! You're joking! He wasn't old. I suppose he would be old by now, but he couldn't have been more than – what? – fifties?'

'He was fifty-two. He suffered a heart attack, quite unexpectedly. And that's why we're relying on people like you to tell us what went on in the last few years of his life.'

'I see.' O'Connell thought for a few moments. 'OK. Maybe I'd better tell you the real reason why I left in such a hurry. It wasn't what you think, mind!' he added hastily. 'Father O'Leary never laid a finger on me or any of the boys in the club and I don't believe he ever would.'

'OK. So what *did* happen?'

'He was just getting a bit too ... It felt like he thought he was my Dad. He kept on at me to go to college and get some qualifications. He even started talking about me going into the priesthood. I just suddenly thought, "I can't take any more of this!" I wasn't ready to settle down to studying and then a regular job and all that. I wanted my freedom; and I wanted to make my own choices, not have someone else deciding things for me. I went to Father O'Leary, while Father Carey was away, and I explained it all to him. He tried to persuade me to stay, but when he saw I wasn't going to, he gave me money so's I'd be able to pay for a bed in a hostel for a few nights and an old rucksack to carry my things in; and he gave me a list of parishes where he knew the priests would be sympathetic. I know I should've rung him to say I was OK, but, like I said, I was only young and I never thought.'

'I see. OK. I believe what you say about Father O'Leary, but I still need to work out who it was who was killed and hidden in the church. What can you tell me about Father Carey? Did he get involved in the Boys' Club at all?'

'I didn't know him as well as Father O'Leary,' O'Connell began slowly. 'He seemed very young for a priest. I don't remember him coming to the Boys' Club. I don't remember much about him at all to be honest. It was a long time ago now.'

'You were an altar server. Didn't that mean you got to know both priests?'

'Well, yes, but Father Carey was more stand-offish. He was only interested in seeing that the Mass was done right. He didn't keep on at me to make something of my life the way Father O'Leary did. Mind you,' O'Connell went on, suddenly becoming expansive in an effort to exonerate his benefactor from all suspicion, 'he was right about the studying. I only realised when I met my wife and found that she could get a better wage than me because she'd got qualifications. She's in the catering and hospitality business. That's why we moved down to Brighton. She got a job managing one of the big hotels here, while the best I could do was waiting on and washing dishes. I should've listened to Father O'Leary and gone to college.'

'Yes. Well, thank you for speaking to me. The Brighton police will type up a statement for you to sign, for the record, and then you can go. If you think of anything else that could throw any light on who the body in St Cyprian's could be, please let us know.'

The screen went blank. Jonah turned to his colleagues.

'Well!' He pursed his lips in thought. 'We've now excluded Patrick Doughty, Julian Stamp and Leonard O'Connell. It looks as if we're back to the drawing board with finding the identity of our corpse.'

'I'll do another trawl of the Missing Persons' files,' Andy offered. 'Assuming Father Carey is telling the truth about finding the body in the vestry, we could be looking at someone who went missing several years before the organ was built.'

12 ALTERNATIVE DIAGNOSIS

The family was sitting round the kitchen table enjoying an after lunch cup of coffee and arguing over whose turn it was to do the washing up, when Jonah's phone rang again. It was Andy Lepage.

'I didn't know whether you'd want to be disturbed, seeing as you're off-duty,' he began tentatively, 'but I've found a rather promising Missing Person that you might like to know about.'

'Sounds interesting. Tell me more.'

'It's a Kevin Molyneux. He disappeared from his home, which is only a stone's throw from St Cyprian's, in January 1978. He was twenty, but with a mental age of six, whatever that means, according to the notes.'

'That's how we used to talk about people with learning difficulties,' Jonah told him. 'You don't hear it so much now, probably because it's bound to be misleading to suggest that an adult thinks the way a small child does. But go on. What makes you think this could be our man?'

'He's the right age and height and there's something in the notes that suggests that he may have been at St Cyprian's on the day he disappeared or shortly before.

They had dogs out looking for him, in case he was just hiding somewhere in the neighbourhood. It says that they got excited when they got to St Cyprian's. Officers searched the grounds at the back of the church, but didn't find anything. It all seemed to fit. I thought maybe he was killed there and then hidden away inside the church where the dogs couldn't get to.'

'Yes. That does sound interesting. I'll be right o-,' Jonah said excitedly, breaking off as Bernie caught his eye. 'Or, could you bring the file round here?' he amended. 'So I can have a quick look at it?'

'No problem. See you in a bit.'

'1978,' Bernie mused. 'That was the year you got your sergeant's stripes wasn't it, Peter?'

'Yes – and the year I married Angie.'

'Do you remember this case?'

'I think I do – vaguely. For some reason I only came in after everyone had more or less given up hope of finding the fellow alive, but I do remember Richard taking me round the back of St Cyprian's and showing me a sort of "den" that some kids had made in amongst the bushes there. And I remember his mother crying and saying she couldn't believe he would have gone off with a stranger.'

'You mean Richard was in charge?' Jonah asked eagerly.

'Yes. He must've been. I just can't work out where *I* was when the lad went missing.'

'Why don't we have a look in his diary?' Lucy suggested, her eyes lighting up at the thought of re-opening one of her father's old cases. He wrote about everything he did. He's bound to have said what he thought might have happened.'

'Yes. You're right,' Bernie agreed. I'll see if I can find the right one.

She got up and headed upstairs to her study where she kept the huge quantity of A4 books that made up her late husband's diary. Richard Paige had been meticulous in writing an entry for every day of his life, from his early teens up until the day before his death, shortly before his sixtieth birthday. Lucy followed her. Together they sat on the floor pulling out volumes from the shelf, trying to find the relevant one.

'Here it is!' Bernie said triumphantly at last. '1977 to '78. That *must* include January 78, surely.'

She opened the book and studied the untidy scrawl. Lucy peered over her shoulder, trying to make out the strange sloping handwriting.

'Yes! Look!' she squealed, reaching out her hand to point at an entry that started near the bottom of the page, '*no progress with finding K. M.* That must be talking about this Kevin Molyneux, mustn't it?'

'The twelfth of January. Yes. I think you're right,' Bernie agreed. OK. Let's take this downstairs and show the others.'

The doorbell rang as they were descending the stairs, and they almost collided with Peter, who was on his way into the hall to answer it. He opened the door to reveal Andy Lepage, who was standing on the doorstep clutching a thick file of papers. They all made their way into the living room and sat down. Andy put down his papers on the coffee table and started shuffling through them.

'The officer in charge of the investigation was DI Richard Paige,' he began.

'Yes. We know,' Jonah interrupted. 'And old Peter here was on the team as well.'

'I didn't do much,' Peter added hastily. 'I only came in when it was almost over, as far as I remember.'

'Yes. Richard complains about that in his diary,' Bernie said, grinning up from where she had been engrossed in speed-reading her husband's thoughts about the case. 'Apparently you were off on some training course and, in your absence, he had to rely on some foot-in-mouth DC called Broadbent, who managed to upset the lad's parents.'

'Of course! I remember now. It was a residential course

for DCs who were being promoted to sergeant. The beds were hard and the rooms were freezing.'

'OK Andy,' Jonah said briskly, cutting across Peter's reminiscences. 'Can you summarise the case and why you think this might be our man.'

'Kevin Molyneux, aged twenty, was reported missing by his parents on the tenth of January 1978,' Andy began, reading from his notes. 'He lived with his parents in their house in Headington and, because of his mental disability, he was very much dependent on them. He had been clearing snow from the garden path. His mother went out to call him in for a mid-morning drink of cocoa and found that he'd gone. It was completely out of character for him to leave the house without telling his parents, so they were immediately worried. They knocked up some of the neighbours to see if he could have gone in to visit any of them, and a few of them made a search of the area. When he wasn't back by lunch time, they reported it to the police.'

Andy turned over a page in his notes, scanning it with his eyes to pick out the salient facts.

'They didn't take it very seriously at first, because he was an adult. Nothing much was done until the next day, when DI Paige was assigned to investigate. I've got the detailed description that he took down and the photos that his parents provided.'

Andy spread out three photographs on the table in front of them. Everyone leaned forward to look. The first was a head-and-shoulders portrait of a young man smiling towards the camera, a mop of brown hair falling untidily over his blue eyes. Then there was a family group, sitting around a table with paper hats on their heads, all smiling as an older man carved a Christmas turkey. The last picture showed the young man at work, sticking tape on to a cardboard box to seal it.

'I wonder whether Penny's student has done that artist's impression yet,' Jonah mused. 'I'll get on to her and find out. It would be good to compare it with these photos.'

'He was five foot eleven tall – which exactly matches Penny Black's estimate – with dark brown hair and blue eyes. When he went missing, he was wearing blue trousers, a blue sweatshirt and a duffle coat – and brown suede shoes!'

'That fits,' Jonah agreed. 'Apart from the duffle coat. But he could have taken that off.'

'The shoes were size ten,' Andy went on, 'which is the same as the ones on our corpse.'

'This is certainly looking promising,' Jonah murmured. 'I don't suppose they kept any DNA that we could use to check if it *is* the same man?'

'No. I suppose there wasn't much point until they had a body to compare it with.'

'In any case,' Peter intervened, 'in those days it wasn't so easy to get DNA from someone who'd gone missing. Picking up traces from his hairbrush or whatever probably wasn't an option. I suppose we might be able to get DNA from a relative – except, no! I'd forgotten: he was adopted, so his family aren't actually related to him.'

'OK. I suppose there will be dental records we can use, so it probably doesn't matter.' Jonah turned back to Andy. 'Now, you said that they found signs that he might have visited St Cyprian's the day he disappeared. Tell us about that.'

'They had dogs out, trying to follow where he went after he left the garden. They seemed to pick up a scent at the entrance to the church grounds and led the handlers round the back. Apparently, there was a sort of garden back there, with bushes in it. The dogs found a place in amongst them that looked like kids had been playing there.'

'I remember it now,' Peter chipped in. 'Richard took me to see it – after I got back from the course. It was a sort of hidey-hole under a big rhododendron bush. There were a couple of orange boxes that we thought they must've used for sitting on, and a tea chest for a table. It was all hidden away behind other bushes, so you wouldn't know it was there.'

'It says here,' Bernie added, 'looking up from the diary, 'that Kevin's parents were Catholics and went to St Cyprian's. So, on the one hand, the dogs could've picked up a scent from the Sunday before, if he went with them, but on the other, it would be natural that he might have been in the habit of playing in that den round the back.'

'Yes, I remember now,' Peter added. 'There was a priest with Mrs Molyneux one time when we went to see her. He seemed quite old, but then I was younger then. He was very tall with a great hooked beak of a nose. I suppose that must've been Father O'Leary. There was a young one too. We met them both one time when we went to the church. They held some sort of service there to pray for Kevin's safe return. I can't remember his name. He may never have told us. He was smaller and didn't say much.'

'Could that have been Father Carey?' Bernie asked.

'No.' Jonah immediately had the facts at his fingertips. 'He didn't come until '79. It must've been Father O'Leary's previous assistant. Andy! Make a note to have a look in the records at St Cyprian's and find out what his name was. Now that we're looking at Kevin Molyneux as a possible candidate for our corpse, he could be a crucial witness.'

'According to Richard's diary,' Bernie continued, 'Kevin's parents thought he must have been abducted. Richard sort of agreed with them, but he was convinced it must've been by someone known to him.'

'Such as Father O'Leary,' Andy suggested. 'He could've walked past and asked Kevin to come with him – maybe he wanted him to clear the snow from outside the church. With him being an authority-figure, Kevin might have gone without telling his parents. Father O'Leary could even have said that they already knew.'

'Yes,' agreed Jonah. 'This Father O'Leary does seem to

be shaping up as a very plausible villain. As the senior priest, who would be better placed to conceal the body in the church? I have to say that I'm becoming very suspicious of this Boys' Club of his!'

They talked on for some time, studying Richard's notes about the case in his diary and comparing them with the official records. Eventually Andy looked at his watch and got up to go.

'I'd better get these back to the station,' he said, shuffling the papers back into their folder and picking it up. 'My shift ends soon.'

'Stay for tea,' Bernie urged. 'It's ages since you did.'

'And Mike's coming over,' Jonah added. 'He may be able to tell us where Penny's student is up to with that artist's impression.'

Andy hesitated. He knew that Saturday High Tea was something of an event in Bernie's household. If he agreed to stay, he would be unlikely to get away until late in the evening.

'OK,' he said, after a moment's thought. 'I'll ring Mum and let her know I won't be in until later.'

While Bernie supervised Jonah's physiotherapy and Lucy, very proud to have passed her driving test a few weeks earlier, went to the station to meet Dominic, Peter and Andy chatted in the living room. Peter had been Andy's mentor during his time as a trainee detective constable and he still felt a proprietorial interest in his career. After a while, the conversation stalled. Peter sat, looking a little uncomfortable and twisting his hands together in his lap. Andy watched him, puzzled at his change in mood.

'Andy?' Peter looked up abruptly. 'There's something I'd like to ask you, but it's a bit personal, so don't answer if you don't want to.'

'Sir?' Andy reverted to formality in his surprise at this remark.

'I'd better explain first why I'm asking. Did I ever tell you that I grew up in a children's home?'

'*You* didn't, but I sort of knew.'

'Sort of knew?' Peter echoed.

'When I was assigned to you for my training, some of the guys at the station decided to fill me in on what you were like. It was part of the gossip that you'd come from an orphanage and tended to be a bit soft on kids who'd been in Care.'

'I see. Well, anyway, I never knew who my real parents were, and I was never interested in knowing. I assumed they'd had their reasons why they couldn't look after me, and that was fine by me. But then, a few years back, this woman, Valerie, suddenly turned up out of the blue claiming to be my mother. And then there was this other woman, Jane, who was her daughter.'

He paused. Andy waited patiently for him to go on, wondering where this could be leading.

'To cut to the chase,' Peter continued, 'although I thought it was a bad idea, I eventually agreed to meet them both. They twisted my arm rather after it turned out that Valerie was dying of cancer. Anyway, I went up to Stockport to see them. Bernie came too for moral support. I didn't tell Hannah or Eddie anything, and I still haven't. As far as they're concerned, they don't have any family on my side. But I took some photographs with me – at Valerie's request – so that she could see what her grandchildren looked like.'

He got up, walked across to the wall opposite and took down a photograph of a young black woman wearing gown and mortarboard and holding a scroll of paper tied in red ribbon. He held it out for Andy to see.

'I showed her this. That's Hannah in the middle with Angie and me on either side. I thought she'd be pleased to know that her grandchildren had both got degrees, but …'

'But?'

'All she could see was the colour of their skin! I've

never seen anything like it before or since. She actually recoiled in disgust! It was as if the idea of having black grandchildren made her feel sick!' Peter shuddered and fell silent.

Andy sat staring down at the photograph, not knowing what to say. Peter took the picture back and returned it to its place on the wall.

'I'm sorry, sir,' Andy ventured at last. 'I can see how distressing that must have been, but I'm not sure what you want me to say.'

'No. I'm sorry. I … I was hoping you might be able to advise me about what to do about this.' Peter pulled out Jane's letter – now very crumpled – from his pocket. 'Jane – that's Valerie's daughter – wrote this. She's getting married in the summer and she wants me to give her away. She says I'm her only living relative. I don't want to have anything to do with her, and I can't think why she wants me to be there, but …'

'I'd say, if you don't want to do it then just say *no*, but I still don't see why you're asking me.'

'It's because I thought you might be able to see it from Hannah and Eddie's point of view. It's them that I'm worrying about. I didn't tell them about Valerie turning up, because I didn't want them getting excited about having a new grandmother and then having it turn out to be a disappointment. And then, after I met her and she turned out to be … well a raving racist, I was jolly glad I hadn't said anything to them. But now, I do just wonder whether I'm doing the right thing, concealing it all from them. And I was wondering … what do you think? Would you want to know if you were in their place?'

'I don't honestly know. I've never had any interest in finding my dad. I always took the line that, if he ran off and left my mum to bring me up on her own, I wasn't interested in knowing him. I don't know what I'd do if he, or any of his family, turned up and wanted to see me.' Andy paused in thought, before going on more vehemently. 'But I do know that I wouldn't hold it against my mum if he approached her and she didn't tell me about it. I'd know that she was only trying to shield me from getting hurt.'

'I see. That's interesting. I hadn't seen it quite like that. Now there was something else – and don't answer if you don't want to. It's about Valerie's reaction to seeing Hannah's photo. I was wondering … I just thought … well, you're the only black member of your family, aren't you? I mean, your Mum's relatives are all white. Did any of them find it hard to accept you as part of the family, do you think?'

'Not that I'm aware of, but then it was different with me. They all saw me when I was a baby. By the time I was old enough to take notice, they'd had plenty of time to come to terms with it. There were a couple of my cousins who teased me a bit – just some silly name-calling – but Mum soon put them in their place! I'm sure she wouldn't have …,' Andy's voice tailed off as a thought struck him. 'You know, I hadn't thought of it until now, but I suppose that could've been the reason she won't have anything to do with my Aunt Clare.'

Peter looked at him enquiringly. Andy gathered his thoughts and then continued.

'Mum's the third of four girls. The oldest and youngest – my Aunt Pauline and Aunt Jennifer – come visiting quite often, and I used to play with their kids. But Mum won't have anything to do with Clare or her kids. I remember, in particular, when we went round to my grandparents' house on their golden wedding; the moment Mum realised that Clare was there, she took me straight back out again and we went home. She's never said anything about what was wrong between them, but now you mention it, I can see that it could be to do with something she said about me when I was a baby, and Mum's never forgiven her. That would sort of fit with one or two things Aunt Jennifer let slip over the years.'

'I'm sorry,' Peter said anxiously. 'I didn't mean to open up a can of worms for you. I really shouldn't have put you on the spot like that.'

'No. That's OK. I'm not going to lose any sleep over what Aunty Clare thinks about me or why Mum and she don't get on. I suppose maybe now I *can* answer your question. I think that, in your kids' place, I wouldn't hold it against you if I found out you'd deliberately prevented them from knowing about their grandmother and aunt. I'd know you were trying to do the best for them.'

'So I wouldn't be selling them short if I just tell Jane to get lost and find someone else to walk her down the aisle?'

'Not in my book, but that's just my opinion; you know your kids best.'

13 CASE NOTES

On Sunday morning, Peter declared his intention of attending the first Mass of the day at St Cyprian's. He wanted to be there if any journalists attempted to speak to members of the congregation. After checking that Lucy was happy to finish Jonah's morning routine with him, Bernie opted to go as well. She would be back in plenty of time to take Jonah and Lucy to the service at their Methodist church afterwards.

'What about you, Dominic?' she asked, as she put on her coat in the hall. 'You're welcome to come with Peter and me now or there's another Mass at eleven or you can come with us to Cowley Road at half ten.'

Dominic considered the matter. He knew that his mother would like him to go to Mass. On the other hand, perhaps he could be useful helping Lucy and Jonah. He would only be missing one Sunday Mass, and he was going to be spending upwards of two hours at the Easter Vigil on Saturday night, which must surely make up for it. Now that he had discovered that Lucy would be at school for much of his stay in Oxford, every minute in her company felt precious.

'I think I'll just go with you all to Cowley Road,' he answered at last. 'I'd like to see what a Methodist service is like. I've never been to one before.'

Jonah scowled as he watched them go. Was this going to be a new Sunday morning routine? Was Bernie thinking of reverting to the Catholic faith in which she had been brought up by her father? She and Lucy had always attended St Cyprian's occasionally, but it had never seemed to be more than a token acknowledgement of Bernie's religious heritage. Once Peter had become a Catholic, would that increasingly be Bernie's church too? Of course, they would always see to it that he was able to attend somewhere more suited to his staunchly Protestant taste, but it would not be the same if the rest of the family was only going along for his benefit.

He became aware that Lucy was speaking to him.

'OK. If you don't want any more toast, let's go and get your teeth brushed.'

Father Damien stood at the door shaking hands with his flock as they left the church. The eight o'clock mass was never as well-attended as the more popular family-friendly one at eleven, but he knew that it was valued by the, mostly elderly, stalwarts who preferred the dignified solemnity and prayerful silences of the more traditional service.

'Good morning, Grace! It's nice to see you back on your feet. How's Bill doing? ... I'll be over to see your mother on Tuesday, if that's alright with you, Jean. ... Are you still OK to do a reading at the Vigil, Siobhan? ... Godfrey! I was hoping you'd be here ...'

Peter held back until last. He wanted to bring Father Damien up to date with the latest developments in the case.

'Hello there!' Father Damien greeted them heartily. 'All set for the Big Day? Not too nervous, I hope?'

'Absolutely terrified,' Peter grinned back at him, 'but I thought we were supposed to be *taking no thought for the morrow*!'

'And you'll be there to support him, I trust,' Father Damien turned to Bernie.

'You bet! And we've got reinforcements down from Liverpool too. My first-cousin-once-removed has descended on us, wanting to see the show. But I must dash,' Bernie added, looking at her watch. 'I'm on stewarding duty today, so I must be there in good time.'

She hurried off, leaving Peter and Father Damien standing alone in the porch.

'Don't you want to be off too?' Father Damien asked.

'No. I'd like to fill you in on some developments in the police investigation, if you've got a few minutes.'

'They're making progress then? Did you get a response to the TV appeal?'

'Yes. But not quite what everyone was expecting.'

'It sounds intriguing. Tell you what – you go on into the presbytery and make us some coffee, while I disrobe. Then I'll join you in my study in a few minutes. You know where everything is, don't you?'

Ten minutes later, they were sitting comfortably in the familiar surroundings of Father Damien's study, with elbows resting on the circular table and hands around steaming mugs of coffee.

'I thought you were supposed to fast before celebrating the Eucharist,' Peter commented. 'Doesn't coffee count?'

'Fasting is only for an hour these days. You're well out of date if you think we all have to abstain from food and drink from midnight, the way it used to be.'

'Of course! I remember you going through the rules with me now. It's just the way Bernie wouldn't have breakfast before we came that threw me.'

'And, in any case, priests who celebrate several Masses in one day are allowed to eat between them, even if they are less than an hour apart. So I'm doubly safe. But that's enough of canon law – tell me about those *developments* that you were talking about.'

'Well, the good news is that Leonard O'Connell has turned up alive and well. He reported to the police in Brighton yesterday morning, after he'd heard the appeal on the radio.'

'And the bad news?'

'Father O'Leary is still shaping up as the most likely person to have hidden that body – whoever it is – in the vestry, where Father Carey found it. That is, unless Father Carey has been lying to us, and he was the murderer himself.'

'But that's just supposition? You can't be sure, can you?'

'No, but it does look very much as if that Boys' Club of his could be involved. We've got another theory as to who the victim might be, and he used to be a member of the club.'

'Oh?'

'We're going even further back in time now – to January 1978. A young man went missing from his home, just round the corner from here. His name was Kevin Molyneux. His parents used to go to St Cyprian's and he used to be a member of Father O'Leary's Boys' Club.'

'Molyneux?' Father Damien queried. 'Would that be Mary and Norman Molyneux?'

'I'm not sure. I always addressed them as Mr and Mrs. Do they still live here then? Do they go to St Cyprian's?'

'Mary Molyneux does. Norman passed away before my time, but we always say a Mass for the repose of his soul on the anniversary of his death.'

'She must be very old by now. I remember thinking that she was old to be Kevin's mother, when we interviewed her back then. But then she wasn't actually his mother. He was adopted, and I think they waited until they were sure they couldn't have their own kids before …'

'She's in her nineties,' Father Damien agreed, 'but

amazingly active still. She'll most likely be at the eleven o'clock Mass.'

'You mustn't say anything to her about Kevin,' Peter said quickly. 'It's only guesswork that the body could be him. That theory could turn out to be as wrong as the other three that we've had. I think Jonah's got it in mind to check the dental records tomorrow. Then we'll know.'

'She's never mentioned a son to me,' Father Damien murmured, half to himself. 'I always thought she had no family.'

'I suppose, after forty years, it's not an easy thing to talk about,' Peter suggested. 'Although, to be honest, I'd have thought there was more point in asking you to say masses for the safe return of Kevin, who might still be alive, than for the soul of her husband, who … well, he's in God's hands now, isn't he? But I suppose that's just my Protestant upbringing coming out.'

'Yes. No. I think you have a point there. I don't know. Maybe, after all these years, she's resigned to the idea that Kevin will never be found. Or maybe she just didn't want to have to explain what happened to a newcomer like me. Or … hang on! Did you say you interviewed her? *You* were involved in investigating her son's disappearance?'

'Yes' Peter admitted. 'I'm afraid I don't remember much about it; but I do remember Mr Molyneux being angry and Mrs Molyneux crying a lot, and there was a priest who seemed to spend a lot of time with them. That must've been Father O'Leary. And I'd forgotten but we found it in Richard's diary: Kevin had been a member of the Boys' Club, but he'd recently been told he had to leave because he was too old. He had Learning Difficulties – only we called it being mentally handicapped in those days – and liked being with the younger boys. That's what I meant by everything still seeming to centre around that Boys' Club and Father O'Leary.'

'Are you suggesting that there might have been more than just Kevin's age that made it expedient to ban him from the club?'

'You mean *he* could've been ... let's say, exhibiting inappropriate behaviour towards the boys, and Father O'Leary was trying to protect him from accusations? I hadn't thought of that, but ... I suppose it would fit. It doesn't explain how he ended up dead, though.'

'No, but it might explain Father O'Leary hiding the body – if he was trying to cover up something that went on between this Kevin and one or more of the boys. It doesn't excuse him,' Father Damien added hastily, 'but I could sort of understand it happening – if he thought he was protecting them from ... I don't know: public censure or prosecution even.'

'I suppose it might even not have been Father O'Leary who hid the body. Could that have been some of the boys? If any of them were altar servers, they might have known that there was a trunk with old altar cloths that were never used.'

'I don't know which is worse! At least Father O'Leary is dead and nothing that comes out now can do him any personal damage, but it'll be another blow to the reputation of the church if he was responsible for covering up murder and who knows what else. On the other hand, if it's boys from the club, the repercussions on them and their families don't bear thinking about.'

The doorbell sounded. Father Damien hurried to answer it, wondering who could be calling so early on a Sunday morning. It was a young woman in a pinstriped trouser suit. She looked up at him through large, round glasses and held out a business card, which informed him that she was representing a well-known national newspaper.

'My name's Jocelyn Crabtree,' she said in a business-like tone. 'You must be Father Rowland. I was hoping that you might answer a few questions about the body that was found in your church and about the recent police appeal for information.'

'I'm sorry. I really can't help you there. I'm not privy to the police investigation.'

'But you must know something about this latest line of enquiry,' the journalist persisted. 'What can you tell me about your predecessor, Father O'Leary? Is the Boys' Club still running?'

'I never met Father O'Leary. He died twenty-five years before I came here. And no: there isn't a Boys' Club here any longer. We have a flourishing Youth Group and an after school club for younger girls and boys. Let me give you a copy of our weekly newsletter, which has all the details.'

'Could I see the place where the body was found?'

'I'm afraid not. It's all sealed in again now. And besides, we've got Mass starting in under half an hour. There will be people arriving and wanting to spend time in prayer. I couldn't allow you to disturb them by taking photographs or whatever.'

'Who do *you* think the body is? Is it Leonard O'Connell, the man that the police are looking for?'

'As I said, it isn't for me to say. It's the job of the police to find out.'

'But you must have thought about it,' the woman's tone became just a little more aggressive. 'Are you afraid that this is going to be another clergy abuse scandal?'

'At the moment, nobody knows what happened, and there is nothing to be gained by speculating ahead of the evidence.' Peter stepped out from the study, where he had been listening from behind the open door. 'The police are exploring a number of lines of enquiry, many of which are concerned with eliminating potential victims and witnesses. If you are interested in Leonard O'Connell's whereabouts, I suggest that you contact Sussex Police, who will be able to confirm that he made a statement at their Brighton station yesterday.'

'And you are?'

'DI Peter Johns.'

'Peter was here when we found the body,' Father Damien explained. 'He's retired now, but he's been keeping in touch with his colleagues and seeing that I'm kept informed about how the investigation is going.'

'And how *is* the investigation getting on?' Crabtree asked.

'Slowly,' Peter replied. 'As is normal when a case concerns an incident that took place many years ago, it is taking some time to discover who and what was involved. There have been a number of lines of enquiry, of which Leonard O'Connell was just one. The police will make an announcement to the press as soon as there is anything concrete to report.'

'But the very fact that the body was found actually *inside* the church must surely indicate that someone from the church was involved,' Crabtree persisted. She turned back to Father Damien. 'What is the Church doing to hold its clergy to account?'

'When we know what they have to be held to account for, we will, of course, take appropriate action,' Father Damien replied stiffly. 'But until the police have completed their enquiries, it would be premature for the Church to act.'

Crabtree looked dissatisfied with this answer and opened her mouth to ask another question, but Peter cut in before she could speak.

'And now, I'm afraid we must ask you to leave,' he said firmly. 'Father Damien has to prepare for Mass. As I told you, the police will issue a statement as soon as they have anything to say about the matter.'

He closed the door and then hurried into the study so that he could check, through the window, that the journalist had left the premises. He watched her walk down the path and round the end of the church towards the car park, where the first of the eleven o'clock congregation were arriving.

'I'm going outside,' he told Father Damien, who had

come up behind him. 'I can't see properly from here. I want to make sure nobody tries to question your parishioners as they come to Mass.'

'She seemed harmless enough,' Father Damien observed placidly. 'I really think you are worrying unnecessarily.'

'Well you fended her off very well, but other people may be less savvy. And whatever else, we don't want journalists questioning Mrs Molyneux about the Boys' Club and suggesting that there could be any connection with the body under the organ.'

'I hadn't thought of that,' Father Damien's voice took on a note of alarm. 'You're right. You'd better get out there and head them off at the pass. And I'll make a point of telling people during Mass not to speak to journalists, in case they try to catch them as they're coming out.'

Peter, as it turned out, had been right in his expectation that there would be considerable interest from the press in St Cyprian's Church and its congregation. By the time the Mass was over, there was a substantial cluster of journalists and photographers waiting outside the gate. Peter watched anxiously from the porch, while Father Damien stood at the inner door, gently enjoining the congregation to remain inside the church and partake of the excellent coffee and biscuits being served by Margaret Kenny and her helpers.

A police car drew up and two uniformed officers got out. Peter's telephone call a few minutes earlier had borne fruit. Soon the group at the gate started to disperse in response to Sergeant Burton's polite injunction to "move along, there's nothing to see here." Peter smiled. It would not be long before the congregation could go home without having to run the gauntlet of prying newspaper correspondents hoping for some juicy revelations of clerical misconduct.

Going back inside, he was greeted in the Welcome Area by Father Damien, who took him by the arm and conducted him from table to table, introducing him to members of the congregation. An elderly woman in a blue hat and coat looked vaguely familiar.

'Mary,' Father Damien addressed her. 'Let me introduce you to Peter Johns, who is going to be confirmed at the Easter Vigil. He's a retired policeman, which has been very handy this last week.'

The woman fixed deep-set brown eyes on Peter's face and smiled a welcome.

'I don't suppose you remember me,' she said, unexpectedly. 'I remember you. You were a lot younger then, but your face isn't so different.'

'You're Mary Molyneux?' Peter stammered, uncertainly. 'Kevin's mother?'

'That's right. So you *do* remember!'

'I wouldn't have if you hadn't reminded me – and if I hadn't been thinking about Kevin, because that was the first time I came across St Cyprian's. I never thought for a moment that it would become *my* church one day! It's strange how things pan out.'

'What made you decide to become a Catholic?'

'I – I – it was last summer. Did you see on the news, a baby was snatched from her pram in the playground on the corner of Margaret Road?'

'Oh yes! It brought back all the memories from when Kevin went missing – not that I don't think about him every day in any case. I felt for the poor parents, not knowing if they were ever going to see their little girl again.'

'She was my granddaughter.'

'Yes. I think I saw you on the news, asking people to come forward if they'd seen anything.'

'That's right. Anyway, I wandered in here one day, when it was looking as if nobody was ever going to find her and thinking that it couldn't do any harm to ask God to help, and …,' Peter stopped speaking and looked across the church towards the Madonna and Child statue. 'Our Lady told me that she understood what it was like to lose a child. And I promised her that I'd become a Catholic if Abigail came home safe.'

Mary Molyneux reached out a wrinkled, blue-veined hand and took hold of Peter's arm.

'Thank you,' she said earnestly. 'I pray to Our Lady every day that Kevin is at peace. I've given up expecting him home, but I just hope that he isn't suffering. You hear about people being kept hidden away for years and forced to do terrible things.' She shuddered. 'I almost hope that he was killed all those years ago, rather than that. And most of all, I'd just like to *know*.'

'The case isn't closed,' Peter tried to think of something reassuring to say. 'If anything new comes to light, the police will look at it again. I don't suppose it helps, but I do know that the officer in charge was very disappointed not to have found him.'

'He was very kind. I know he did his best.' Mary Molyneux sighed. 'I don't blame them for giving up, but …'

14 DIAGNOSTIC TESTS

'OK. Settle down now!' Jonah called the room to order. 'There have been a few developments over the weekend, so let's start with a recap of what we know so far.'

A movement of his finger on the keypad beneath his left hand brought up a sequence of photographs on the screen attached to his chair and, simultaneously, on the larger screen at the front of the room.

'We have now eliminated three potential candidates for our mystery corpse,' he continued. 'Patrick Doughty's dental records prove that it is not him. Julian Stamp, we now know, died in Northern Ireland some years after the organ platform was sealed. Leonard O'Connell is alive and well, and living in Brighton. However, Andy has come up with a new possibility.'

Everyone looked intently at the screen as an unfamiliar face appeared.

'This is Kevin Molyneux, a young man with learning disabilities, who lived only a matter of yards from St Cyprian's church. He was reported missing in January 1978. That is, more than three years before Father Carey discovered a body in a chest of old altar cloths and vestments in the vestry at St Cyprian's church. His description and the clothes that he was wearing when he disappeared are consistent with the appearance and clothing of the body that the organ builders found last week. His family had connections with the church and, indeed, his mother still attends there.'

'What's the idea, sir?' Monica Philipson asked from the back of the room. 'Did someone kill him and hide him in the vestry? Or could that Father Carey be lying, and he killed him himself?'

'No. If it *is* Kevin Molyneux, then Father Carey must be in the clear, and hence is presumably telling the truth. He didn't arrive in the parish until more than a year *after* Kevin went missing.'

'So then, who killed Kevin?' Monica asked.

'That's not at all clear, at present. Father Carey seemed to think that it must have been Father O'Leary who hid the body in the vestry. But that's not the same as saying that he killed him.'

'Except, why would he hide the body if he *hadn't* killed him?' Alice Ray asked, with a puzzled frown.

'That I don't know. Father Carey seemed to think that he must have had his reasons, but whether he has any basis for saying that, I have no idea. He may just have been trying to justify his own actions in not reporting the body when he found it, or he may have some idea of what was going on and not want to say. It's just a hunch, but I can't help feeling that it could have something to do with the Boys' Club that Father O'Leary used to run, and which Kevin Molyneux used to go to.'

A black and white photograph appeared on the screen. It showed a group of boys wearing shorts and football jerseys.

'This is the class of seventy-seven,' Jonah told them. 'The tall lad on the right is Kevin Molyneux. This was shortly before he was asked to leave the club because he was too old. We originally started looking into the club because Leonard O'Connell used to help with it. He insists that there was nothing untoward going on there, and yet he ran away without telling anyone where he was going.'

Jonah turned his chair and scanned the faces of his team.

'The first thing we need to do is to establish whether or not it really *is* Kevin's body lying in the mortuary. Alice! I want you to locate his dental records. They weren't in the Missing Person's file that Andy found, but surely they must have been preserved.'

'Right you are, sir. I'll get on to it right away.'

'And I'd like to find out more about the Boys' Club. Andy!'

'Yes sir.' Andy looked up hastily from the photographs of the corpse, which he had on his own computer screen, and had been comparing with the picture of Kevin. They did not look all that similar to him, but it was difficult to tell, with the corpse being so shrunken and discoloured.

'You must be pretty familiar with the filing system at St Cyprian's by now. I'd like you to go back there and find out as much as you can about the club. In particular, try to put some names to the faces in that picture. And, better still, see if you can find out where they are now.'

'Yes sir.'

'We've asked for anyone who belonged to the club in the late seventies to come forward,' Jonah continued. 'I'm putting Monica in charge of co-ordinating our response to any calls that we get. Two or three came in over the weekend. They don't look particularly promising, but they'd better be followed up. Pitchfork: you liaise with Monica about that.' He paused, as he looked round the room again. 'I think that's all. Get to it, all of you.'

The screen went dark, as Jonah prepared to leave the room. Bernie walked ahead of him to open the door. He passed through and then headed down the corridor towards his private office.

'Close the door,' Jonah instructed her as soon as they

were both inside. 'I need to think.'

Bernie did as she was told, and then crossed the room to switch on the kettle that stood on top of one of the filing cabinets.

'I'll make a brew to stimulate the little grey cells.'

While she busied herself with cups and teabags, Jonah sat behind his desk, staring blankly at pictures of Kevin on his computer screen.

'I'm wondering what to do about Kevin's mother,' he said at last, as Bernie set his cup on the tray attachment on his chair and directed the straw to within his reach. 'I'd like to talk to her about his disappearance, but I'm not sure that we ought to bring her into this until we know for certain that it really is him. What do you think?'

'Peter seemed to think she was a resilient old girl,' Bernie ventured slowly, 'but he only spoke to her for about five minutes, so he may be wrong.'

'Mmmm! And he also said that there were a load of journalists sniffing around the church. That's another thing to consider. How long will it be before one of them gets hold of reports about Kevin's disappearance and starts putting two and two together?'

'If I was Kevin's mum,' Bernie said forthrightly, 'I would definitely prefer to hear it from the police than from some journalist with an eye for an exclusive. And don't you think she may well have worked it out for herself by now, in any case?'

'You're right!' Jonah snapped into action. 'She's bound to have made the connection, now that we've appealed for people from the Boys' Club to come forward. Let's get over there right away.'

15 FAMILY HISTORY

'Good morning,' Jonah said politely to the middle-aged man who opened the door of Mary Molyneux's house. 'I'm Detective Chief Inspector Porter, and this is my personal assistant, Bernadette Fazakerley. I'd like to speak to Mrs Mary Molyneux. Is she at home?'

The man peered closely at the warrant card and identification that Bernie was holding up. Then he looked across the road at the shadowy figure of one of their neighbours behind the net curtains.

'I suppose you'd better come in,' he grunted, opening the door a little wider.

Bernie set up the portable ramp, which she had brought from the car, so that Jonah could drive his wheelchair over the doorstep and into the house. She followed him inside. The man led the way to a room at the back of the house, overlooking a small, well-kept garden, bright with daffodils and crocuses.

'Someone to see you Aunt Mary,' he said as he entered. 'From the police.'

Mary Molyneux looked up from the book that she was reading, taking off her glasses and putting them down on the broad windowsill of the low bow window.

'Is it about Kevin?' she asked.

'Yes, but it's important that you realise that we don't know anything for certain yet. I just thought you ought to know that ... that one of the possibilities that we're exploring is that the body that was hidden under the organ at St Cyprian's could be Kevin's.'

'Do you want me to look at him? To identify him?'

'No. We have other ways of doing that. And ... after all this time ...,' Jonah trailed off, hoping that Mrs Molyneux would be able to fill in for herself the unspoken story of the transformation of a human body over a period of thirty or more years.

'So what is it you want, then?' the man asked bluntly.

'And you are?' Jonah turned to him, smiling politely.

'Aidan O'Brien.'

'Aidan is my nephew,' Mrs Molyneux explained. 'He lives with me, now that I'm not as young as I was.'

'First of all, I wanted to warn you that it's quite possible that you may be bothered by journalists wanting to talk to you about Kevin's disappearance. We are being careful not to let them know about the possible link to the body in St Cyprian's, but it won't take much for them to work out for themselves that it's a possibility. Unfortunately, we'd already put out a call for information about the St Cyprian's Boys' Club, before we realised about Kevin. We thought ... well, a witness had told us that it was most likely another man associated with the club.'

'I see. Is that why Father Damien told us all not to speak to journalists if they approached us?'

'Yes. And also because he didn't want to encourage speculation about anyone else who'd belonged to the club.' Jonah paused for a moment, before continuing. 'The other thing that I'd like to talk to you about is Kevin's relationship with the Boys' Club and with Father O'Leary in particular. It's important to emphasise that we really don't know whether or not we've found Kevin's body. It's still quite possible that he may be alive.'

Mary Molyneux smiled indulgently at this suggestion.

'As I told your friend yesterday, I've got to the stage where I feel that it would be preferable for him to have died all those years ago, rather than to have been held somewhere against his will in whatever ghastly conditions it may have been.'

'Well, rest assured, we're doing our best to establish whether or not that is his body. You may be able to help with that. We need to find his dental records. Can you tell us the name of his dentist?'

'We always took him to the hospital. They understood him better there.'

'And there's something else,' Jonah recollected the description that Penny Black had given of the injuries sustained by the deceased prior to death. 'Had Kevin had any accidents? Any broken bones at any time?'

'Yes. He fell off his bike when he was sixteen and broke his elbow.'

'Which arm?' Jonah asked eagerly.

'His right. It made it very awkward for him because he was right-handed.' Mary Molyneux looked searchingly at Jonah. 'Does that tell you anything?'

'It's important that you don't read too much into this,' Jonah said slowly and emphatically, 'but, the body under the organ also had a healed fracture to the right elbow.'

Everyone fell silent for a few moments, digesting this information.

'Surely that proves it?' Aidan said at last. 'There can't have been two people with broken elbows abducted at the same time!'

'It certainly does increase the chances that we've found Kevin,' Jonah agreed cautiously, 'but that particular injury is quite a common one – especially in Oxford where so many people ride bicycles, and fall off them.'

'Do you actually have anyone else in mind?' Aidan

demanded.

'Not at the moment, but we have considered three other possible victims, whom we have now been able to eliminate.' Jonah turned back to his aunt. 'Mrs Molyneux, if you don't mind, please could you tell me more about Kevin? If it is his body that we've found, then I need to know as much about him as possible in order to find who killed him; and if not, it looks as if we may have at least two members of the Boys' Club who have mysteriously disappeared.'

'Get out the album, will you, Aidan?' Mary said briskly. 'That'll be the easiest way to show you what Kevin was like.'

Aidan got up and went over to a bureau in the corner of the room. He opened a drawer and took out a large old-fashioned album, with tissue interleaving to protect the pictures, which were attached to the pages by photograph corners. He brought it over to his aunt and placed it into her hands without speaking. She reached for her reading glasses and put them on before opening the album.

'Here's Kevin when he first came to live with us,' she said, opening the album at the first page. 'You do know that he was adopted, don't you?'

Jonah manoeuvred his chair alongside hers, so that he could see the photograph. It was a black-and-white picture of a small child sitting in a high chair and looking rather startled.

'He was eight months old, but he looks a lot younger, because he was born premature. His heart stopped during the birth, which is why ... and I think his mother had a hard time and that made it difficult for her ... and then, with his brain damage, she couldn't face ...'

She turned the pages.

'This is his first birthday ... and this is our first seaside holiday ... and here he is being introduced to my brother's Old English Sheepdog.'

'Do you have any pictures of him with his friends from

the Boys' Club?' Jonah asked gently.

'This is his first communion.' Mary turned several more pages to reach a colour photograph of a row of children. The girls were dressed in long white dresses, while the boys were in smart suits. She pointed at a boy of eight or nine, standing near the centre of the group smiling broadly. He had on a grey suit, with a white carnation in the buttonhole. His shirt was a dazzling white with a blue bow tie. 'Father Gould – he was Father O'Leary's assistant at that time – tried to say that he couldn't take communion because he didn't understand properly, but Father O'Leary insisted that it was alright. He said that, if the only people we allowed to take communion were the ones who completely understood, then our churches would all be empty. He always used to stick up for Kevin. He knew that there are things that are more important than book learning.'

'It looks as if there were quite a few other children his age at St Cyprian's in those days,' Jonah commented. 'How did Kevin get on with them?'

'Not too badly,' Mary sighed. 'Some of them used to tease him and call him names, but he never seemed to mind about it as much as I did. I don't think he always realised that they were making fun of him. And he always used to see the best in everyone. He was very trusting. It would never have occurred to him to want to hurt anyone, and so it never crossed his mind that anyone else might want to hurt him.'

She continued to turn the pages.

'Here he is in his altar server's vestments. He loved St Cyprian's, and he loved being trusted to help at the Mass.'

'We've got a picture here of the Boy's Club,' Jonah said, when she reached the end of the album. 'Could you have a look at it with me?'

Bernie took out a rather yellowing copy of the photograph that Jonah had displayed to his colleagues earlier that morning and held it where Mary and Jonah could both see it.

'Can you remember the names of any of the boys?' Jonah asked. 'Were any of them Kevin's special friends?'

Mary Molyneux peered closely at the photograph.

'That's Gerard Cooke,' she murmured, pointing at a curly-haired boy standing in the centre of the picture holding a football. 'He was captain of their football team. They didn't play regularly, but they got up a team for a tournament that someone organised for church youth clubs. He's an accountant now, I think. Aidan probably knows better than I do.'

Her nephew obligingly came over and stood behind them to look at the photograph.

'Yes. That's Gerry alright,' he agreed. 'And that's me, next to Kevin. Gerry didn't rate me as a footballer so he put me in goal.'

'Do you recognise any of the others?' Jonah pressed them gently.

'Those two there are Brendan Connolly and Timothy Norcott,' Aidan said, pointing at two boys standing next to one another towards the right of the picture. 'They always went round together. At least …,' he paused as if in thought. 'At least they did until Kevin disappeared. I never thought about it before, but it must've been round about then that they fell out.'

'Tim Norcott was very good to us,' Mary said warmly. 'He seemed very cut-up about Kevin. He used to bring flowers round for us every year on his birthday – until the family moved away, that is. And when Norman was ill, he did all sorts of odd-jobs around the house for me.'

'So, was he a special friend of Kevin's?' Jonah asked.

'I suppose he must have been, although I hadn't realised before.'

'No,' Aidan disagreed. 'He and Brendan were some of the worst. They used to bully Kevin and call him names. I reckon it was guilt that made him start coming round to help.'

'Whatever it was, he was a big help when Norman was in hospital. We missed him when they moved away.'

'And when was that? Can you remember?'

'It must have been a couple of years after Kevin disappeared. Norman's heart attack was the October of that year and Tim was still around for a while after that.'

'It was 1982,' Aidan said confidently. 'We'd both just finished our O' Levels[7].'

'Do you have any idea where he went?'

'Somewhere on the south coast, I think,' Mary answered. 'He did promise to write, but ... Well, you can't expect a young man to remember a couple of old fogeys like us, once he's got all his new friends.'

'OK. Have another look at the picture. Do you recognise any of the others?'

'There's my brother George,' Aidan volunteered, pointing at a plump youth with socks around his ankles. 'He's in Australia now.'

'That boy standing next to Kevin was called Robert,' Mary said. 'I can't remember his surname – can you, Aidan?'

Aidan peered down and appeared to be thinking.

'Lewis,' he said at last. 'Robert Lewis. He wasn't too bad with Kevin. Nobody seemed to like *him* much either, so I suppose he had a bit of sympathy for him.'

'Any others?'

---

[7] The General Certificate of Education (GCE), Ordinary Level (commonly known as O' Level) was an examination-based qualification taken by school students in England, Wales and Northern Ireland at the age of 16. It replaced the School Certificate in 1951 and was itself replaced by the General Certificate of Secondary Education in 1988. GCE Advanced Level qualifications still exist and are the main qualification for entry into English and Welsh universities.

Mary and Aidan continued to scan the photograph for a minute or more before looking up and shaking their heads.

'No,' Mary said. 'One or two of them look familiar, but I couldn't put a name to them.'

'Not to worry. You've given us a few leads for us to follow up. You don't happen to know how we might get in touch with any of them, do you?'

'I can give you George's email address if you like,' Aidan offered, 'but I don't suppose he'll be able to help you much.'

'Thank you. Could you write it down for us? He may remember something that would help us piece together what happened.'

'There was Colin Kennedy,' Mary said suddenly. 'I don't think he's in that picture, but he went to the club, and he came back here a few times to play with Kevin. That was when they were much younger. I used to know his mother quite well, but they moved away after Colin killed himself.'

'Really? When was that?'

'It must have been …,' Mary frowned in thought. 'I think it was about ten years after Kevin went missing.'

'I see. And do you know where his parents moved to?'

'No. I'm sorry.'

'Never mind. Someone else may know. Can you just tell me their names, perhaps?'

'Agnes … and … I *think* he was Gordon. I didn't really know him.'

'Good. Now, perhaps we could just go through the list again. I've got Gerard Cooke, Brendan Connolly and Tim Norcott … and then there's Colin Kennedy and …'

While Jonah and Bernie were engrossed in their conversation with Mrs Molyneux and her nephew, Peter was at home, doing his best to entertain their guest.

Dominic had watched, downcast, as Lucy set off for school on her bicycle. He had not realised until after he arrived that she did not break up for four more days. It had not occurred to him that Oxford schools might have different holidays from those in Liverpool.

Now he was sitting in the living room, pretending to read a book while Peter got them both a mid-morning drink of coffee and tried to remember the schedule of housework that he had planned for himself before Bernie's young cousin had insisted on helping with the chores. It was very good of him to offer, but it upset Peter's routine.

He poured the coffee and carried it through to the large room with its French windows facing on to the extensive back garden.

'Why don't we get the bus into town this afternoon?' he suggested. 'You can't go home without seeing the dreaming spires of Oxford.'

'I suppose not,' Dominic replied languidly. 'But maybe I could go with Lucy on Saturday.'

'I think she's got a match on Saturday afternoon,' Peter warned him. 'And she said she was going out in Martin's boat in the morning. I'm sure you'd be welcome to go too,' he added hurriedly, seeing Dominic's face fall.

'If I'd realised she was going to be at school this week, I'd have come later and stayed longer,' Dominic lamented. 'Why d'you think she didn't tell me?'

'I rather think she didn't want to suggest that she thought that you were coming here primarily to see her.'

Dominic sat in silence, trying to work out the implications of this statement.

'Do you mean she's trying to avoid me?' he asked at last.

'No. It's just ... if she'd said, "don't come this week because I'll be at school", it would have implied that she thought you were coming *in order* to spend time with her.'

'Or that she wanted to spend time with me.'

'Well, yes, I suppose so.'

'So that means she doesn't want to.'

'Not necessarily – only that she doesn't want to make it obvious to *you* that she does.'

'So do you think she does want me here?'

'I'm quite sure she doesn't mind you being here,' Peter hedged. Then, seeing the disconsolate look on Dominic's face, he felt compelled to go on. 'Look Dom: Lucy's very busy at the moment, swotting for her A' Levels. She doesn't want any distractions. And then she's got five years of medical training ahead of her. I'm sure she's happy to have you for a friend, but if you're after something more than that, you've either got to be patient and wait or look elsewhere.'

'Yeah, I know all that. I just wish … well, I think she might have told me, that's all.'

They relapsed back into silence. Dominic gazed morosely down into his mug while Peter racked his brains to think of some new topic of conversation.

'You studied religion at university, didn't you?' he asked at last.

'Yes. English Literature and Religious Studies, why?'

'I've got an ethical dilemma. Maybe you could help me think it through.'

'I dunno. Wouldn't a priest be better? I mean … I'm not qualified to …'

'It's this letter.' Peter pulled out a screwed-up ball of paper from his pocket. 'I can't decide what to do about it.'

Dominic flattened out Jane's letter and began to read. His brow puckered as he struggled to work out what it was all about.

'Who is this Jane woman?' he asked eventually.

'She's my half-sister,' Peter explained. 'Our mother was only a teenager when I was born and her parents made her leave me in the hands of the National Children's Home. I only discovered that she existed a few years ago. She's dead now and, according to Jane, so are all the rest of her family, which is why she's on at me to give her away.'

'So, where's the moral dilemma?'

'I don't want to do it. I don't want to have anything to do with any of them, but … well, I keep wondering if I'm being unfair to this Jane woman. It's not her fault that …'

'That what?' Dominic was still at a loss to understand.

'That her mother was a disgusting racist bastard, who insulted my wife and my kids,' Peter growled with more vehemence than he intended. 'She insisted on seeing photos of them and then she … well, what she said was unrepeatable.'

'Does this Jane know about that?' Dominic gasped, completely taken aback at this outburst from the normally placid Peter.

'She was there.'

'Then surely she can't really expect you to … don't you think she may just have asked you out of politeness – to show that she doesn't bear a grudge?'

'I never thought of that. I suppose you could be right.' This suggestion made Peter feel suddenly more cheerful. 'Yes. Maybe she's *hoping* I'll refuse.'

'What do your kids think?'

'They don't know anything about it. I never let on to them that Jane and her mother had turned up – and I don't want them to know. That's another reason why I don't want to go to this wedding. If I do, I'll have to explain why I've got to go off up to Stockport all of a sudden. And then they'll wonder why I didn't tell them before – and why I didn't let them see their grandmother when she was dying. And I don't want them to know what she said about them.'

'It all seems simple enough to me then,' Dominic said, relieved to have reached a conclusion and hoping to move away from this awkward subject. 'Just write to her and say *no thank you.*'

They sat for several minutes in uncomfortable silence. Peter felt relieved to hear his young companion advising him to do what he would most like to do, and at the same time, uneasy that he would not be treating Jane fairly. Dominic also had mixed feelings. He was honoured by Peter's confidence in him and yet embarrassed by it as well.

'Does Lucy know?' He asked suddenly. 'I mean, if you haven't told your own kids ...?'

'Oh Lucy knows. It's not the same at all. I wouldn't be having to tell her that her own grandmother considers her and her mother to be something less than human. That's why I can't tell Hannah and Eddie. They can do without knowing that.'

'Do you really think that's what she meant? Couldn't it just have been surprise at seeing the photos? Don't you think that maybe she'd have come round in the end?'

'No. I saw her face. And she didn't need to go on and on about what a pity it was that I couldn't find a nice white girl to marry instead of *that black woman*. She'd never have been able to accept them. I'm sure of it.'

16 CASE RECORDS

'Morning sir!' Since the press invasion the previous day, a uniformed police officer had been stationed at the door of St Cyprian's to scrutinise visitors and prevent parishioners being harassed. PC Appleton was on duty.

'Morning Malcolm!' Jonah responded cheerfully. 'Is the Father around, do you know?'

'Yes. He's in the church having a word with the organ builders. And Andy Lepage is in there too, rummaging in the parish records.'

'Good.' Jonah steered his wheelchair up the long slope that led to the porch, and in through the open door. Then he had to wait for Bernie to open the inner door to allow him inside the church. At the sound of Bernie's footsteps on the tiles, Father Damien hurried over to greet them.

'DCI Porter! And Bernie! What can I do for you?'

'I've been speaking with Mary Molyneux.' Jonah came straight to the point. 'I expect Peter told you that it's a fair bet the body in your church is her son Kevin. She and her nephew gave us a lot of interesting information about the Boys' Club, including some names. I was hoping that you might be able to help me find where they are now.'

'It's a long time ago,' Father Damien replied dubiously, 'but I suppose some of the families may still be around. Come through into the office where we can talk.'

He led the way down the aisle, past the organ platform, where the two Boswells were engaged in lifting the large pipes and fitting them into place behind the console, and then across the front of the church to the door that led to the vestries and office. He gestured to his left as they passed through the choir vestry.

'As if things weren't bad enough already,' he sighed, 'the boiler's started playing up. What with that and the organ, I can see Saturday's vigil being a complete disaster!'

'That's the boiler that powers the central heating?' Jonah asked, remembering that they still needed to locate a place where the corpse could have been stored in conditions suited to mummification. 'What sort is it? I mean – how is it powered?'

'It's gas now. Originally it was solid fuel. There was a boiler house and coke store with a door through from the vestry. That's been blocked up now and you can only get in from the courtyard. I can't think why they did that. It's tremendously inconvenient having to go outside to get to it.'

'And when was the change to gas made?' Jonah asked with interest.

'Well before my time. We replaced the old gas boiler not long after I came, which was in 2009. So it must've been a good few years before that.'

'But in 1978, would the old solid fuel boiler still have been there? And the door from the boiler room to the vestry?'

'I suppose it probably would. I'm not sure. Does it matter?'

'It might. I was just thinking about ways of a body getting into a chest in the vestry, ready for Father Carey to find it.'

Andy Lepage looked up when the door opened and

Jonah came in.

'Hello sir! I'm glad you've come. I think I may have what you wanted.' He held up a dog-eared exercise book. 'This is the 1977 attendance register for the Boys' Club. It's got a list of names and addresses and a record of their attendance each week.'

'Good man!' Jonah said warmly. 'And I've got some names of boys who may have been particularly close to Kevin Molyneux, our potential victim. Pull up a chair,' he added, turning to Father Damien, 'and let's put our heads together and see what we can come up with.'

Father Damien sat down on the dilapidated computer chair that stood next to the table bearing the printer. Andy sat back down in his own chair and then leapt to his feet again as he realised that Bernie had nowhere to sit. She motioned him to sit down and hurried out of the room in search of another chair. Jonah, ignoring this pantomime, pressed buttons on his computer keypad to bring up his list of Kevin's friends on the screen attached to his chair.

'Here we are! Let's start with Timothy Norcott. According to Mrs Molyneux, he was very upset by Kevin's disappearance. Is he on your list?'

'Yes,' Andy answered. 'And there's an address in Cranley Road.'

'Unfortunately the family moved away not long after Kevin went missing, but that address gives us a starting point. One of the neighbours may know where they went.'

'Or Father O'Leary may have noted down their address,' Father Damien suggested. 'So that he could keep in touch or let their new Parish Priest know about them.'

'If he did write to the priest in the place where they went, the letter may be in the correspondence file,' Andy added. 'Shall I have a look?'

'Later. Let's check the other names first. How about Gerard Cooke? I think he stayed in the Oxford area.'

Bernie slipped quietly back into the room, carrying a chair that she had found in the Choir Vestry. She set it down next to one of the tables and began setting up her laptop ready to take notes.

'Yes,' Andy confirmed, after consulting his list. 'There's a Gerard Cooke and a younger brother Martin, living in Ringwood Road.'

'I think I may have known their mother,' Father Damien told them. 'Mabel Cooke passed away about five years ago. She was already a widow when I came here. She lived in Ringwood Road.'

'Presumably her sons will have come to the funeral. Did you get to speak to them?' Jonah asked eagerly.

'I don't really remember, I'm afraid. There were a good few relatives there, and I didn't know any of them.'

'Never mind. We may be able to trace Gerard through his work. According to Aidan O'Brien – that's Mrs Molyneux's nephew, Andy – he became an accountant. If he's a partner in an accountancy firm, he's bound to have some sort of internet profile. Now, how about Robert Lewis?'

'Yes. He's here, with an address in Edgecombe Road.'

Before long they had addresses for all of the boys that Mary Molyneux had mentioned and an additional list of nearly twenty more members of the Boys' Club. Three families still attended St Cyprian's, although all the boys had long since left home and were unknown to Father Damien. It looked like a good morning's work, which had yielded plenty of new leads for Jonah's team to follow up.

'Good,' he said with satisfaction, 'now there's something else I'd like to ask you about. We're trying to trace the priests who assisted Father O'Leary before Father Carey. There was a Michael Bannister, who was at St Cyprian's until November 1978 and then in a parish in Coventry for a year or two after that, at which point he left the priesthood and nobody seems to be able to say where he went. Do you have any idea where a priest might go under such circumstances, or how we might find him?'

'Hmm,' Father Damien pondered. 'It's difficult to say.

There aren't very many obvious career options for an ex-priest. Catholics tend to be less than welcoming towards them and non-religious people tend to be suspicious of anyone trying to take on a secular role after having been ordained. If he was a scholar, then he might be able to make his way in academia or maybe he could become a teacher – unless there was some sort of cloud hanging over him that would make him unsuitable to be working with children. Often it's to do with a woman and she may help to support him until he gets back on his feet. I could ask around. There could well be people who remember him – that's not the sort of thing that people forget in a hurry.'

'What else might make a priest resign? Jonah asked, 'apart from the celibacy issue?'

'I suppose losing one's faith must be high on the list,' Father Damien shrugged. 'Or maybe loneliness – as distinct from wanting to marry. It can be quite isolating being the person that everyone looks up to and expects to have all the answers; and maybe feeling inadequate, when you realise that you don't. I'm sorry. I can't really help. For understandable reasons, that isn't something that we are encouraged to give a great deal of thought to.'

'Yes. I can see that. Thanks for the suggestions, anyway. It's given us a few ideas to work on.' Jonah smiled up at Father Damien. 'And now, we'll leave you in peace and get started chasing up these names and addresses.'

Meanwhile, Peter was showing Dominic around Oxford.

'That's the Martyrs' Memorial,' he told him, stopping in front of the ornate gothic-style monument on the intersection of three roads outside Balliol College. 'It commemorates the death of some Protestants who were burnt at the stake under Queen Mary. I don't remember their names, but you probably know all about it, with your Religious Studies degree.'

Dominic walked forward and bent down to read the

inscription.

'Cranmer, Ridley and Latimer,' he murmured. 'Yes, I've heard of them. Of course, at home there was always more said about St Thomas More and St John Fisher and the Forty English Martyrs![8] I can't understand it myself,' he added as they left the memorial and walked on past St Mary Magdalen's Church towards Cornmarket Street. 'I can't see why anyone would either go to the stake or send someone else to it for the sake of a dispute about how the national religion should be organised – and all in the name of a man who spent most of his time campaigning against organised religion!'

'How do you make that out?' Peter asked, surprised at this outburst. Up until this week, he had only met Dominic in his home, under the watchful eye of his mother, who seemed intent on ensuring that all her children kept to strict orthodox Catholic doctrine and practice.

'It's there all through the gospels: "woe to you, scribes and Pharisees", "the first shall be last", "Is it not written: 'My house will be called a house of prayer for all the nations'? But you have made it a den of robbers". Jesus had no time for the organised religion of his time and I'm sure he never intended to set up anything like the Vatican or the Church of England or any of our big church bureaucracies.'

'That's more the sort of thing I'd expect to hear from my Methodist friends,' Peter observed with a smile. 'How come you're still a Catholic?'

'How come you're all set to become one?' Dominic countered. 'I'm just going with the flow and not upsetting Mum, but you've got no reason to switch.'

'That's what Jonah thinks. And I sometimes wish …,' he hesitated. 'I don't like the way it's coming between us, but I promised … and it's the only church where people

---

[8] Catholics, who were put to death during the English Reformation.

understand about Mary. Bernie says she's just a way of anthropomorphising the feminine side of God; and Jonah says I'm just using her as a substitute for Angie. What about you? Do you pray to Mary?'

'Well I do say Hail Marys often enough,' Dominic admitted. 'It's a sort of habit. But I guess I always think of it as praying to God and those are just the words of a sort of mantra, I suppose.'

'A mantra? Isn't that a Buddhist idea or something?'

'It's to do with meditation,' Dominic agreed, 'but you can have Christian meditation too. I suppose, what I'm saying is that you don't need words to tell God things, because he's omniscient. The words are just to help us to focus and stop our minds wandering. So, I don't have a problem with saying a few Hail Marys for … for someone who's having a hard time, say. They're just words that come easily to me because I've said them so often, and God knows what it is I'm concerned about without me telling Him. Does that make sense?' he added anxiously, going red in the face as he remembered that Peter was a new convert to Catholicism and might not relish having his new faith called into question by a lad more than forty years his junior.

'I think I see what you mean, but she is real, you know.' Peter paused, unsure whether to go on. Then, deciding that he had come too far to stop now, he took a deep breath and continued. 'She speaks to me. She understands. Do you believe that?'

'I – I – when you say she speaks to you, do you mean audibly? A voice from the sky or something?' Dominic stammered, unsure how to take this statement, which seemed so out of character for the staid and down-to-Earth ex-policeman whom he had thought he was starting to get to know.

'The first time, it did seem like that; but Lucy was there – and some cleaning lady from the church – and they didn't hear anything, so I think it must really have been in my head.' Peter came to a halt at the end of the road and pointed to their right towards a tall, square-based tower with a clock on the side of it. 'That's Carfax Tower,' he said. 'Students all have to live within a set distance from here during term time. I suppose I ought to be worried about hearing voices in my head, shouldn't I?' he added with a little laugh. 'Do you think it's a sign of incipient madness?'

'I've never met anyone who seemed saner than you,' Dominic assured him, smiling at the suggestion.

'Now, down there,' Peter went on, conscious of his role as a tour guide for his young guest, 'you can see Tom Tower. It's a bell tower over the main entrance to Christ Church College. We ought to have a look inside there. It's got some very fine architecture, I'm told – not that I know anything about that sort of thing.'

They started down St Aldates, heading towards the octagonal tower, with its distinctive dome.

'In my experience, God usually speaks to me through other people or even just through circumstances,' Dominic said, trying to think of a way of conveying that he did not question Peter's sincerity, while not sharing his experience. 'Like, sometimes I get the feeling that some words in church are sort of directed at me or ... or, well, when I told Lucy I was thinking of becoming a teacher, she said she thought that was a bit of a cop out. I only said it because she asked me what I was going to do with my degree and I didn't like to say that I hadn't thought about it. But then afterwards, I thought I'd better find out more about it, because she'd made me feel a bit stupid. And I found that I needed to get some experience in school or I wouldn't get on the course. And then, when I was helping out at a school run by nuns, one of them said something to me that convinced me that I ought to be a teacher.'

'Oh?' Peter said encouragingly, as Dominic stopped abruptly.

'I was just thinking,' he laughed. 'Lucy said, why didn't

I become a priest, seeing as I'd studied religion, and I told her that I didn't have a vocation, but I suppose I do now – just not the one I was thinking of.'

'And the nun?'

'She must have been in her seventies, maybe older, and she'd gone into the order when she was sixteen. So, you wouldn't think she'd have much idea about ... well anything really.'

'But?'

'It turned out she was very knowledgeable and very concerned about the way kids these days pick up so many of their ideas from social media and how that makes it easy for them to be ... radicalised, for want of a better expression. And she said something along the lines of: we always used to be so keen to teach children the catechism and to make them repeat what we believe, but I'm convinced that we ought to be encouraging them to learn about what everyone else believes and to understand that there isn't only one right way of doing things. And I thought about all the stuff I'd learnt about other religions and I somehow felt that this was God giving me a nudge to say that teaching Religious Studies was the right thing for me.'

'Ah well! Perhaps I'm such a reprobate that I needed a bit more than just a nudge to get me back on track,' Peter smiled, as they crossed the road to stand at the entrance to Christ Church.

'Oh no! I don't believe in right and wrong tracks,' Dominic protested. 'I think everyone has to find their own way to God. I suppose that's something else your friend would take issue with, if he's an evangelical?'

'Jonah? No. He'd be with you all the way there. He had some very choice words to say about the evangelicals who tried to convince a friend of ours that he couldn't be a Christian and have a gay relationship. It's not my soul that he thinks I'm putting at risk – it's my reason! And he says Catholics are closet polytheists, with all their saints and

147

statues and stuff.'

'I used to worry about that myself,' Dominic admitted, 'but then I met some real polytheists – Hindus – who said that, the way they saw it, the different Hindu gods were all aspects, or incarnations if you like, of the one God. That's what really convinced me that what you believe isn't as important as what your beliefs lead you to do. And the more I read what Jesus said, the more I think that he must've thought that too. But you won't tell Mum I said all that,' he added hastily. 'She'll start worrying that I might be a heretic.'

'Of course not,' Peter smiled. 'I don't want to spoil her pleasure at my conversion by letting on that I'm one too. Now let's go in.'

'Are you sure it's OK?' Dominic asked doubtfully, pointing at a notice board standing in the middle of the wide archway. 'It says it's *closed to visitors*.'

'Just walk in confidently and everyone will think you're one of the students.'

Dominic still looked dubious, so Peter led the way further down St Aldates and in through the wrought iron gates that led to Broad Walk, the path that runs along between the college and Christchurch Meadow. There was no notice here to warn off tourists.

'This was where Angie – that's my first wife – and I had our first proper talk together,' Peter said, wondering why he felt the urge to confide in this young cousin of Bernie's. 'We'd been at a "do" in the Town Hall and we came out here for a breather.'

They sauntered along the wide path in the bright spring sunshine. Dominic gazed around at the lush pastureland and the pale golden Cotswold stone mediaeval colleges, thinking how different this was from the modern buildings of Lancaster University, where he had studied. He plucked up courage to tackle Peter on a subject that he had been wondering about since before he arrived.

'Can you tell me any more about that body that they

found in the church? Or is it all a police secret?'

'Well, what do you know so far?' Peter asked cautiously.

'I heard the news reports about them looking for some down-and-out called O'Connell, but I wasn't sure whether he was supposed to be the victim or the murderer. And then there was something about a Boys' Club. And there was something on the radio this morning about O'Connell having come forward, so I guess that means he can't be the corpse.'

'Well, yes,' Peter admitted. 'He walked into a police station in Brighton and told them that he just moved on without telling anyone. The theory had been that he was the victim. In fact – and don't tell anyone about this because it isn't being made public yet – the Assistant Priest at St Cyprian's at the time, admitted to having put the body under the organ so that it wouldn't be found, thinking that it was Leonard O'Connell.'

'But why? I don't understand?'

'Neither do I. What he told Jonah was that he thought that Father O'Leary, the Parish Priest, must have hidden the body in the vestry some time earlier. He *said* that he was sure that Father O'Leary must have had a good reason for doing it and he didn't want to risk tarnishing his memory by reporting it to the police and instigating an investigation. It doesn't make any sense to me, but I was forty-odd years in the Police Service, so my instinct would always be to report anything that might be a crime. Maybe a priest would see things differently, but I can't understand why.'

'I suppose he was protecting his friend and fellow-priest,' Dominic suggested, 'but what reason could the other one – Father O'Leary, I mean – have had for hiding the body in the first place? Could he have been protecting someone else? Or was he somehow bound by the seal of the confessional?'

'I could see why he might not feel able to tell the police

who killed him, but why conceal the body? How could he justify all the anguish that the victim's family would go through, not knowing what had happened to him?'

'Maybe he didn't have any family?' Dominic suggested. 'Or – or maybe he thought that they would be more upset if they knew the truth; if he died because he was engaged in doing something disreputable, say.'

'Such as?'

'I don't know,' Dominic thought quickly, 'a heart attack while he was in the act of committing adultery, maybe. And then, there would be the other person to consider as well.'

'I suppose so,' Peter agreed reluctantly. 'I still think it would be better for everyone to be told the truth, but I suppose, if you're used to keeping secrets to preserve other people's reputations, you might see things differently. At least that's a lot better than some of the things that I've been imagining.'

'Why? What are they?'

'I have a nasty feeling that Father O'Leary's Boys' Club is at the bottom of it all, and I can't help thinking that, despite what everyone says, Father O'Leary's conduct may turn out to be … well, questionable, let's say. And the bottom line is: wouldn't the most likely reason for him concealing the body be that he was the murderer?'

'But does it have to be him? Does it even have to be him who hid the body? Just because that's what that other priest *thought* doesn't make it true.'

'Except that Father Carey found it hidden in a trunk of old altar cloths and vestments in Father O'Leary's vestry. Who else would be confident of hiding it there? … Except … hang about … I think Jonah said that O'Connell used to be an altar server. Maybe you were right when you said you didn't know whether he was the victim or the perpetrator. Maybe O'Connell killed whoever it was and hid the body and nobody looked in the trunk until after Father O'Leary was dead. I wonder if Jonah has thought of that. I got the impression that he's decided that O'Connell's out of the picture now that he's turned up alive.'

17 DENTAL WORK

'Quiet everyone!' Jonah called the morning team meeting to order. 'Yesterday afternoon I left you with a number of leads to follow up. Let's start with Alice: I think you have something to report regarding Kevin Molyneux's dental records?'

'Yes, sir.' Alice got to her feet and addressed the room. 'We've been able to confirm that the body that was found in St Cyprian's church *is* that of Kevin Molyneux. Both the dental records and the X-rays of his elbow injury match perfectly.'

'So now we know who our victim is,' Jonah concluded, 'and now we need to get to work on discovering who killed him and why.'

'Isn't it obvious that the killer must be that old priest? Father O'Leary wasn't he called?' Monica Philipson asked confidently. 'Who else could have hidden the body like that? And that other priest – Father Carey – who hid it again; he was obviously just covering up for his friend – if he didn't do it himself!'

'I don't think we can be as sure as that,' Jonah said patiently. 'And you can forget about Father Carey killing

Kevin Molyneux. Kevin was dead more than a year before he came on the scene. I've had it suggested to me that the killer could have been Leonard O'Connell. He was an altar server while he was at St Cyprian's, which means that he might have known where he could safely hide the body where nobody would look; and he did run away in rather a hurry, without telling anyone where he was going. Could that have been because something happened to make him think he might be going to be rumbled? Basically, we just don't know, which is why we need to find as many of the boys from the club as we can and try to persuade them to tell us what was really going on there.'

'I can help with that, sir,' Monica called out eagerly. 'One of them rang in yesterday afternoon. He's agreed to be interviewed later this morning. He's a GP in Abingdon and he said we can go over there and he'll speak to us after his morning surgery.'

'Good. I'll leave that to you and Alice. What's his name? Was he one of the ones we were looking for?'

'No. He's a Dr Philip Dodds. I think he was a year or two older than Connolly, Norcott and the others.'

'OK.' Jonah looked round the room. 'Has anyone managed to track down any of the other boys?'

The officers all shook their heads.

'I got some addresses for the Norcotts when they moved away,' Joshua Pitchfork contributed nervously. 'They went to Hastings and then to Colchester, but I haven't managed to trace them after that.'

'OK. Keep working on it. And that goes for the rest of you too,' Jonah added, looking round the room again. 'Now I'm going to break the news to Mrs Molyneux. I'll be back at lunch time and I hope you'll have something more for me by then.'

Jonah did not go straight to Mary Molyneux's house. Instead, he called at St Cyprian's and explained the situation to Father Damien.

'She told me yesterday that she almost hoped that Kevin was dead, because it was better than the alternative,' Jonah told the priest, 'but I'm sure it will come as a massive shock to her all the same. I'd like you to be there to provide her some support.'

'Of course; I'll be glad to.' Father Damien followed Jonah and Bernie down the path and out on to the pavement.

'We might as well walk,' Jonah said, leading the way. 'It's not far.'

'And there is absolutely no doubt that it *is* Kevin?' Father Damien asked, hurrying to keep up.

'Yes. Both the dental records and the medical records confirm it – not to mention the clothes and shoes.'

They turned a corner and found themselves face-to-face with Peter and Dominic. Peter was pushing a double buggy, in which were sitting his two youngest grandchildren: two-year-old Ricky and not-quite-one Abigail. Their parents both had full-time jobs, so Peter was often called upon to care for the youngsters. They all stopped.

'We're on our way to the C. S. Lewis Nature Reserve[9],' Peter explained.

'Got my net!' Ricky crowed excitedly, waving a long-handled shrimping net and hitting Father Damien on his legs.

'Careful Ricky!' Peter admonished, catching hold of the child's hand. 'I'll have to give the net to Dominic to carry if you wave it around like that. We're going pond-dipping

[9] The C. S. Lewis Nature Reserve (http://www.bbowt.org.uk/reserves/cs-lewis-nature-reserve) is an area of land in the site of the garden of "The Kilns" which is the house where the academic, author and Christian apologist, C. S. Lewis lived. It is managed by the Berks, Bucks and Oxon Wildlife Trust.

and mini-beast hunting,' he added, turning back to address the adults.

'And I'm keen to see the place where C. S. Lewis wrote the Narnia books,' Dominic added. 'What about you? Are you on the trail of the body in the church?'

'We've identified the body,' Jonah told him gravely. 'We're on our way to tell his mother.'

'So it *is* Kevin, is it?' Peter asked.

'Yes. I wasn't in much doubt, to be honest,' Jonah replied, 'but we had to wait for confirmation.'

'Fwog! Toad!' Ricky was becoming impatient with the delay. Ignoring Peter's injunction, he waved the net wildly again.

Dominic reached down and plucked it from his hand. 'Tell you what,' he said, 'I'll carry this and you look after my special key ring.' He reached into his pocket and brought out a key ring bearing the Everton Football Club logo. He held it out to Ricky, who happily made the exchange.

'I hope it hasn't got any keys on it that you mind losing,' Peter warned. 'I can't guarantee it won't end up in the pond!'

'Don't worry! I don't use it for keys. I only have it with me because it's got a torch built into it, which is sometimes useful.' Dominic addressed Ricky solemnly: 'Now you take good care of that for me, won't you? I'm trusting you.'

Ricky nodded vigorously, holding the keyring tightly in his small fist.

'We'd better go,' Peter said, starting forward again. 'These two don't like having to wait for their amusements.'

'Who's the young man?' asked Father Damien, after they were out of earshot.

'Oh! I'm sorry,' Bernie apologised. 'I should have introduced you. That was my cousin Joey's youngest. His name's Dominic. He invited himself to stay, ostensibly to see Peter confirmed.'

'And his real reason?'

'It's not for me to say, but he did seem a bit annoyed that Lucy hasn't broken up for Easter yet.'

They turned in at the gate of Mrs Molyneux's trim front garden, bright with daffodils and early tulips. Bernie went ahead to set up the portable ramp. She had hardly finished when the door opened. Aidan O'Brien had seen them from the window and hastened to let them in before they were observed by the neighbours.

'Is your aunt in?' Jonah asked him as soon as they were all inside with the front door closed behind them.

'Yes. Come through to the back room.'

Soon they were once more in the cosy back room. Father Damien went straight over to Mrs Molyneux, who was sitting in her accustomed chair by the window, and took her hands between his.

'The inspector has some news for you, Mary,' he said gently.

'I was expecting it.' She looked towards Jonah. 'It *was* Kevin there under the organ all these years, wasn't it?'

'Yes, Mrs Molyneux, it was. We now have definitive evidence that the body that Father Damien and the organ builders found is that of your son. I'm sorry.'

'Can I see him now?'

'That may not be a good idea,' Jonah began.

'I'm his mother. I need to see him.' Mary Molyneux spoke softly but with determination.

'If that's what you want, we'll arrange for you to do that,' Jonah conceded cautiously. 'However, I do need to warn you that you may find it distressing. His body has gone through a mummification process, which means that in some ways it has been preserved, but in others, it is very different from how you remember him. You might find it easier to see some pictures first.'

'I realise all that,' Mary Molyneux still spoke with quiet determination, 'but I know what I have to do, and I would like to do it as soon as possible. When can you take me to him?'

'I can ring the mortuary now, if you like,' Jonah answered, seeing that there was no point in trying to dissuade her and deciding that she was probably right in thinking that the sooner it was done the better. 'They'll want to do some preparation I expect, but I don't think it need take long.'

'Thank you. I'd like that.'

Jonah made his telephone call and arranged to take Mrs Molyneux to see her son's body that afternoon. He explained this to her and then, after a brief pause, began the hardest part of the interview.

'I know that this is a difficult time for you, Mrs Molyneux, but I'm afraid that I do need to ask you some more questions about Kevin. If you would prefer, it can wait until another time – after you've been to see him, for example?'

'No. It's alright. Go ahead. I don't want to hold things up. I want you to find out what happened to him.'

'Thank you. I don't think this need take long. You've already told us a lot. The first thing I'd like to ask about is Leonard O'Connell. Do you remember him?'

'I remember you were looking for him. The reports said that he was a homeless man that Father O'Leary took in, but I don't remember ever meeting him.'

'He helped with the Boys' Club for a while,' Jonah told her, 'and he was an altar server. Does that ring any bells?'

'No,' Mary shook her head. 'I'm sorry.'

'Never mind,' Jonah said reassuringly. 'That may be an indication that he has nothing to do with all this. If he and Kevin had been mates, Kevin would have talked about him, don't you think?'

'Yes. I think he would.'

'I've been looking into the other priest who was at St Cyprian's when Kevin went missing – Father Michael Bannister. Do you remember him?'

'Oh yes! He was very quiet and studious, and he gave rather long, complicated sermons. Not much of a talker. I think he was rather shy – especially around the ladies.'

'Did he help with the Boys' Club at all?'

'I don't think so,' Mary paused in thought. 'Although … I think maybe he did go with them when they went camping. That was the summer before Kevin …'

'That's interesting. You're saying that the boys went camping in summer 1977. Was that before or after Kevin was asked to leave?'

'About a month before, maybe a bit less.'

'And did Kevin go with them?'

'Oh yes! He loved it – didn't he, Aidan?'

'He certainly did!' her nephew agreed. 'He came back absolutely full of it.'

'Did you go?'

'No. My parents had already booked a holiday flat in Eastbourne, so my brother and I couldn't go on the camp.'

'So you don't know anything about what went on there? – apart from what the other boys, including Kevin, told you?'

'That's right,' Aidan nodded, then rather defensively, 'but that doesn't mean that anything went on that shouldn't have. Father O'Leary was very strict about good behaviour. And if you're thinking that *he* might have been up to something, you've got him all wrong.'

'And what about Father Bannister?'

'Father Mike?' Aidan sounded incredulous. 'Like Aunt Mary said, he was very quiet and shy – always had his nose in a book. We kids used to make fun of him behind his back, but I don't think he ever took enough notice of us to realise.'

'He left the priesthood a few years after he moved on from St Cyprian's. Do either of you have any idea why that might have been?'

'No.' both Aidan and Mary shook their heads.

'I thought he had the makings of a good priest,' Mary said, looking puzzled and a little anxious, 'once he got over his shyness and realised that ordinary people just want simple sermons, not lots of stuff from all the difficult books he'd been reading. What happened to him? Where did he go?'

'That's what we don't know,' Jonah told them. 'We haven't been able to track him down after he left the Church. Presumably you don't know anything about any family he may have had?'

'No,' they shook their heads again.

'We didn't really know Father Bannister,' Mary added. 'It was Father O'Leary who did most of the parish visiting – especially he was the one who looked after us when Kevin was missing.'

'Alright, we'll leave you for the present.' Jonah brought the interview to an end, judging that Mrs Molyneux and her nephew had nothing more to tell him. 'Would you like me to arrange for one of our family liaison officers to come and stay with you until it's time to go to see Kevin?'

Mary looked towards Father Damien, who answered for her: 'no, no. I'll stay.'

'Until this afternoon then,' Jonah said, looking towards Mary and then Aidan, while Bernie got up and shook hands with them both by way of farewell. 'We'll come for you at about two.'

18 MEDICAL OPINION

Dr Philip Dodds was a small, plump man with a red face and black hair combed back from a "widow's peak" hairline. He looked at Monica and Alice over half-moon glasses, which he took off his nose and allowed to drop around his neck on a chain as he got up to greet them.

'Come in and take a seat,' he said, indicating two plastic chairs in the centre of the room. 'I'm sorry to have kept you waiting.'

'I'm Detective Sergeant Philipson and this is Detective Constable Ray,' Monica said, holding up her warrant card briefly before sitting down.

'And what can I do for you?'

'You were a member of the Boys' Club at St Cyprian's Roman Catholic Church from 1975 to 1979. Is that correct?'

'Yes. At least, it must have been round about then.'

'Over four years, you must have got to know some of the other boys quite well,' Monica suggested. 'Do you still see any of them?'

'No. We all went our separate ways, and I haven't been to church since I went to university – apart from my parents funerals, that is.'

'Do you remember Kevin Molyneux?'

'The guy with Learning Difficulties who went off into the snow and never came back?'

'Is that how you and your friends perceived it?' Monica asked sharply. 'Did you think he'd gone of his own accord?'

'I don't really know. I was speaking rather flippantly just then, I'm afraid. We boys didn't take it all that seriously. We always thought he was a bit odd, and this seemed like just another manifestation of that oddness, I suppose. I'm sorry – that must sound very callous, but teenage boys aren't noted for their ability to empathise.'

'You say that none of you had much empathy with Kevin,' Alice said, picking up on the suggestion that the other boys had seen him as an outsider, 'was that as far as it went? Or was there any bullying or name-calling or anything of that sort?'

'Mostly we just ignored him, but there were one or two of the boys who seemed to enjoy teasing him.'

'Can you give us any names?' Monica asked quickly.

'I wouldn't want to point the finger at anyone,' he hedged, 'after all this time …'

'We are talking about murder, Dr Dodds,' Monica said firmly. 'And a murder that took place in January 1978 – exactly the time that you are talking about. We need to know about anyone who might have been on bad terms with Kevin Molyneux in the months leading up to that.'

'But they were all only young boys,' Dodds protested, still reluctant to reveal their identities.

'OK,' Alice said, opening her notebook. 'Let's try another way. We've been told that Brendan Connolly used to bully Kevin. Did you see anything to confirm that?'

'Yes,' Dodds mumbled. Then louder, 'yes, I did. He and Timothy Norcott used to always be on at him, talking nonsense, which he didn't know any better but to believe, and then laughing at him when he repeated it to other people.'

'Thank you,' Monica took over again. 'That fits in with what other people have told us. I don't suppose you know how we might find either Connolly or Norcott, by any chance?'

'No. Norcott's family moved away and Brendan dropped out of school and disappeared off my radar. I rather fancy he got mixed up with some rather wild lads from the Blackbird Leys estate and ended up in trouble with the police – but that's just rumours that I heard,' he added hurriedly. 'I don't know for sure.'

'Thank you. That's helpful.' Monica looked towards Alice, who once more consulted her notes.

'I've got some more names for you,' she said, looking up again, 'Robert Lewis and Colin Kennedy. Kevin's mother seems to think they were particular friends of his. Is that how you saw it?'

'Robert was a loner. Or rather – I think he wanted to belong but no one seemed to want him to be in their gang. Colin? Now he was very thick with Tim Norcott. I don't think either of them were particularly friendly towards Kevin, but as I said before, they did used to talk to him and tell him tall stories, and then laugh at him when he believed them. Maybe he thought they were his friends. He was like a very placid, trusting infant in many ways. He didn't seem to notice when people were making fun of him.'

'I see,' Monica resumed her questioning. 'And I don't suppose you can tell us where we might find either of them?'

'Rob joined a firm of accountants – a big one with offices in Reading and Swindon as well as Oxford. I can't remember the name, I'm afraid. Colin? He's dead now – killed himself by shutting himself in his mother's car and running a hose from the exhaust in through the window. He could only have been twenty or thereabouts: I remember my mum writing to me when I was still in medical school.'

'And do you – or your Mum – know how we might get in touch with his family?' Monica asked.

'Not off-hand. I remember Mum telling me they'd moved away after Colin died, but I don't know if she kept in touch with them at all. I doubt it. I think they moved in order to get away from all the people they knew in Oxford.' Dodds looked at his watch. 'Are we done yet? I'm sorry to have to rush you, but I've got some home visits I need to fit in this afternoon and I haven't had any lunch yet.'

'Alright, I think that's all,' Monica said, getting to her feet and holding out a business card towards him. 'If you think of anything else – or if you remember the names or contact details of any of the other boys from the club – ring me on this number.'

Alice, following Monica's lead, also got up to go. Then she hesitated.

'Just one more thing,' she said, looking directly into Dr Dodds' eyes. 'Do you remember Leonard O'Connell? How did he get on with the boys?'

'Leonard O'Connell?' The doctor looked puzzled.

'He was a friend of Father O'Leary's,' Monica prompted. 'He used to help with the Boys' Club.'

'Oh yes! I think I know who you mean: tall, thin guy with long brown hair? I don't remember much about him. I don't think he was there all that long.'

'OK. Never mind.' Monica opened the door and led Alice outside to their car. 'What do you think?' She asked, as soon as the door was closed.

'It looks to me as if there was something going on back then, but they're all closing ranks to protect whoever it was that was responsible.'

'I agree,' Monica concurred, putting the car into gear and preparing to reverse out of the parking bay. 'My guess is that one out of Father O'Leary and his assistant – or else Leonard O'Connell – or maybe all three of them together

– were paedophiles, and they were afraid that Kevin would say something that would give them away. Everyone seems to agree that he didn't always understand what was going on and trusted everyone too much. He might have seen something and they were afraid he'd tell his parents, say, without realising what it meant.'

19 SURGICAL PROCEDURE

The team was in buoyant mood when they assembled to compare notes towards the end of the afternoon. Now that the body had been positively identified, work on tracking down anyone who might be able to throw light on who had killed Kevin Molyneux had been proceeding apace. Jonah called for silence and then asked Andy Lepage to deliver the first update.

'Josh and I have managed to trace four of the boys that Mrs Molyneux told us used to associate with Kevin,' he began, looking towards DC Pitchfork, who nodded in acknowledgement. 'Two of them are dead: Colin Kennedy committed suicide in 1987 and Robert Lewis died of liver failure in 2010. According to the coroner's report on Kennedy's death, he'd been suffering from depression for some time before he killed himself. Lewis had had an alcohol problem for several years. He'd been in rehab twice, but still couldn't kick the habit.'

'It might be an idea to talk to the therapists at the rehab centres to see if they can throw any light on *why* he drank,' Jonah suggested. 'There seems to be a pattern emerging of boys from the club suffering from mental health problems in later life.'

'I'll look into that,' Andy promised. 'The other person who may be able to tell us more about Lewis is his wife. I've got her address. She's still living in the family home in Littlemore. Then, moving on, we have Brendan Connolly. As soon as Monica and Alice found out that he'd been in trouble with the police, we managed to track him down. He's served time for possession of a variety of illegal drugs. Currently he's back in Oxford, begging and sleeping on the streets. Gav Hughes thinks he can locate him and bring him in.'

PC Gavin Hughes was well known among the Oxford police officers as having established a rapport with the homeless people in the city. Now approaching middle age, he had no ambition to progress beyond the rank of constable, being content to continue in his role of "Bobby on the beat" and proud to be a familiar and trusted figure in his community.

'Good – and the fourth boy?'

'Gerard Cooke and his brother both suffer from Huntington's disease, which also killed their father. They're both in nursing homes and unable to talk.'

'That rules them out as potential witnesses,' Jonah agreed, 'and with Kennedy and Lewis both dead – not to mention Father O'Leary, who probably holds the key to the whole mystery if only he were still with us – we're not as much further forward as I'd like. However, Monica and Alice seem to have had a productive time with Dr Dodds. Perhaps you could tell us what you found out next.'

Andy sat down again and Monica rose to her feet.

'As Andy said, Dr Dodds, who was a member of the Boys' Club at the same time as Kevin Molyneux, told us about Connolly's criminal record. He also confirmed that Kevin was the subject of bullying by some of the other boys, notably Timothy Norcott, Brendan Connolly and Colin Kennedy. He said that Kennedy and Norcott were great mates and Brendan used to hang around with them too. He thought that Robert Lewis would have liked to have been mates with them too, but he wasn't welcome.'

There was a knock at the door, which opened to admit the bulky figure of PC Gavin Hughes. He looked round the room until he caught Jonah's eye.

'I'm sorry to interrupt, sir, but I've got Brendan Connolly in Interview Room two. I thought you'd like to know.'

'Thank you. I'll come and speak to him right away.'

'And sir,' Gavin said hesitantly, looking at the board at the side of the room, where photographs of key people relating to the case were displayed. He was slightly in awe of the CID and was always nervous of putting forward his own ideas to them. 'Were you wanting to speak to Mr Bannister too?'

Jonah looked towards the board. They had obtained the photograph of Father Bannister from a back issue of the church newsletter in the Parish that he had moved to when he left St Cyprian's. It was a small black-and-white picture, which he had not held out much hope of being useful, but it was the best that they had been able to find.

'You know him?' he asked in surprise.

'Oh yes! He's the manager of the homeless shelter in Rose Hill. Didn't you know? I thought maybe that was why you had his picture up there.'

'No. We're interested in him because he used to be a priest and he was at St Cyprian's at the time when our murder took place. I had no idea he was back in Oxford.' Jonah turned back to address the team. 'OK. I'm going to interview Connolly now. I'd like you all to carry on trying to locate more of the boys – especially Norcott. His name keeps cropping up.'

Brendan Connolly looked older than his fifty-two years. His grey hair was sparse, wispy and unkempt; his skin was blotchy red and white; his eyes were sunken and moist. He looked up briefly when Jonah, Bernie and Gavin entered the room, and then fixed his gaze on the paper cup of tea on the table in front of him, carefully avoiding Jonah's attempts to make eye contact.

'This is Detective Inspector Porter,' Gavin told him, speaking slowly and carefully. 'You aren't in trouble. He just wants to ask you a few questions about something that happened a long time ago.'

'Do you remember St Cyprian's church?' Jonah asked gently, conscious that Connolly might well be suspicious of the police and reluctant to get involved in a murder enquiry.

Connolly did not respond. He continued to gaze down into his tea.

'There used to be a club there, for boys. We've been talking to some of the members. They remember you.' Connolly remained silent. 'They also remember a lad called Kevin Molyneux. Do you remember him? He went missing forty years ago. Do you remember that?'

'Yeah. I remember,' Connolly mumbled.

'We've found his body, and now we need to find out what happened to him. You may be able to help us. We need you to tell us anything you can remember about Kevin and the other boys in the club.'

'What sort of things?' Connolly asked suspiciously.

'Let's start with Kevin. Did he have any particular friends, would you say?'

'I wouldn't know about that.' Connolly shook his head.

'We've heard that some of the boys used to make fun of him. Were you aware of that?'

'Maybe.' Connolly shrugged.

'Any boys in particular?'

'I never did anything to him,' Connolly spat out defensively.

'Nobody's saying you did,' Gavin intervened gently.

'That's right,' Jonah agreed. 'We're not accusing you of anything. We just need you to try to remember. There was another boy, called Timothy Norcott. Do you remember him?'

'I remember Tim, yeah. What about it?'

'We're a bit confused about him. Someone told us that he was one of Kevin's best friends, but someone else said that Timothy used to bully Kevin. Which of them was right?'

'I dunno. Why're you asking me?'

'Because you were there – and we haven't managed to find Timothy Norcott yet. You don't happen to know where he is, by any chance?'

'Nah!' Connolly shook his head vigorously, still keeping his eyes down. 'He went off years ago. The whole family up and left.'

'OK. Let's leave Norcott for now. A couple of other names have come up. Did you know Robert Lewis or Colin Kennedy?'

'What if I did?'

'We're trying to find out more about them. Unfortunately, they're both dead, so we can't ask them themselves. We think they, and maybe Kevin as well, may have been subjected to some sort of abuse, while they were in the club. Did you hear about anything of that sort? Or did you see anything?'

'No.' Connolly continued to stare down into his cup.

'It's alright, Brendan,' Gavin intervened. 'Nobody's saying it's your fault. We just need to know what happened. Was there anything – anything at all – that went on in the club that you were uncomfortable with?'

Connolly sat in silence, biting his lip. Jonah waited patiently. After several minutes, Connolly took a deep breath as if about to speak. Then he let it out again. Jonah continued to wait.

'Rob and Colin bunked off school 'cos of the snow,' Connolly mumbled, speaking rapidly as if wanting to get an unpleasant job done as soon as he could. 'They wanted me to go with them, but I didn't. They said they were going to build an igloo and have a snowball fight. I heard afterwards Kev went with them. They went round the back of St Cyprian's where no one could see them.'

He stopped suddenly and sat staring down at the table, crumpling the empty paper cup between his hands. Jonah waited for him to continue. Bernie and Gavin watched expectantly, willing Brendan to go on. After two or three minutes, Jonah tried again.

'I can see it's difficult for you,' he said kindly, 'but we really do need to know what happened. Tell me – was that the day Kevin disappeared?'

Brendan nodded.

'And do you have any idea what else went on – apart from messing about in the snow?'

'No.' Brendan shook his head, still staring down at the table.

'OK.' Jonah looked round at the others. 'I think we'll leave it there.' Then, turning to address the witness again, 'Thank you, Brendan. You've been a great help. PC Hughes will take you for a meal in the canteen and then he'll drive you back to the hostel. I'd be grateful if you can stick around Oxford for the next few weeks, just in case we need to speak to you again, but that's all for now.'

20 STRESS FRACTURE

'Anyone at home?' Peter called out, as he opened the front door when he and Dominic arrived home.

'Only me!' came Lucy's voice from above, responding to this familiar ritual.

'Come in the kitchen,' Peter said in a lower voice, putting his hand on Dominic's shoulder and steering him across the hall. 'I'll put the kettle on. I could do with a cuppa after so much culture and architecture!'

Dominic gazed up the stairs as he passed them, hoping that Lucy would appear.

'It must be weird, living in one of those old college rooms,' he said, making conversation while listening out for Lucy's footsteps on the stairs. 'That place that you said used to be Bernie's room, for instance, with those narrow, pointy windows and that spiral staircase up to it! And fancy eating in that dining hall with those long wooden benches to sit on – it was like something out of Harry Potter!'

'Well, the Great Hall in the film was based on the hall in Christ Church and they did some of the filming inside the Bodleian Library and in the cloisters at New College;

so that's not surprising,' Peter told him, as he busied himself with filling the kettle and measuring loose tea into a large pot. 'If you ask me, the university is about as plausible as Hogwarts – and about as relevant to most ordinary people!'

Dominic was pleased to see that Peter put out three bone china mugs on the table. It looked as if he was expecting Lucy to join them. He was about to sit down at the table, when a buzzing in his pocket signalled an incoming call on his mobile phone. He took it out and looked at the screen.

'It's Mum,' he said, not sounding as pleased as perhaps a dutiful son should have done, 'checking up on me.'

'You go on into the lounge,' Peter suggested, sensing that the young man felt embarrassed at his mother's solicitude. 'I'll bring in the tea when it's ready.'

In a matter of minutes, Peter had a tray loaded with three mugs of steaming tea and a plate of biscuits. He carried it out into the hall. The door into the living room was closed. He put down the tray on the hall-stand and stood listening. He could hear the murmur of Dominic's voice interspersed with lengthy pauses. It sounded as if this could be a long session!

Peter left the tray in the hall and set off upstairs carrying Lucy's mug. She turned and smiled as he entered her room, pushing her Chemistry textbook to one side to make room for the mug on her desk.

'Thanks Peter.'

'A lot of homework tonight?'

'Quite a bit, but I think I'll be able to get it done before tea, and then I'll help entertain Dom for you.'

'You make it sound like a chore.'

'No. Not really,' Lucy smiled. 'I just thought you seemed a bit fed up these last few days, and I wondered if it was having him foisted on you. When he said he wanted to come for Easter, I never thought he meant to be here for so long.'

'Don't worry about me. He's quite good company when you get to know him.'

'So what is it that's bothering you then?' Lucy asked, with her usual directness. 'You're not getting cold feet about Saturday, are you?'

'No. Not at all.' Peter hesitated. He had not realised that his anxiety had been so obvious – or was it that Lucy was exceptionally perceptive? He sighed and reached into his pocket for *The Letter*. 'It's this,' he said, handing over the crumpled paper.

Lucy took it, scanning rapidly over the lines until she reached the signature.

'*With love from your sister Jane!*' she read aloud, looking up at Peter with an expression that combined puzzlement with something close to anger. 'What does she want with you now?'

'She's getting married again. She's asking me to give her away.'

'But why?'

'Apparently I'm her only living relative.'

'So what?'

'I think her intended has a big family and she doesn't want there to be no one from the bride's side.'

'She must be mad!' Lucy's voice was scornful. 'You could say anything! You could claim to have a *just cause or impediment* or you could tell her fiancé's family all about what her mother said about Hannah and Eddie or–'

'Don't be silly. You know I'd never do anything like that.'

'But *she* doesn't. She's hardly even met you. For all she knows, you could have been brooding on it all these years, just waiting for an opportunity to get your revenge. She's taking a tremendous risk. It doesn't make sense. And, what about her fiancé? What can she possibly have told him about you?'

'How do you mean?'

'She must have told him she was writing to you – if

they're making wedding plans together. How's she explained why she never sees you – why she hasn't already introduced you to him? And how is she going to explain if you refuse to go?'

'I don't know. Perhaps she believes in openness and honesty and she's told him everything.'

'Told him that her mother was a white supremacist?'

'Well, maybe not in quite those words.'

'I suppose he could be one too – except that then it would be completely stupid of her to let you meet him.'

'No,' Peter said, surprising himself by hurrying to Jane's defence. 'He can't be – and neither can Jane, for that matter – because she's invited the whole family. She says she'd like to meet her niece and nephew and their kids.'

'Do you think she's trying to make up for – for what her mother did? Or maybe she just wants to show you that *she* isn't like that.'

'I don't know,' Peter sighed. 'That's why I can't make up my mind what to do about it. It would all be so much simpler just to write back telling her to get lost, but … I suppose, like you said, she's taken the risk of asking me and maybe it's not fair to throw it back in her face just because of what her mother said. And then there's Hannah and Eddie – I want to protect them from knowing what Valerie was like, but do they have a right to know who their grandmother was and to meet their aunt?'

Lucy sat in silence, frowning in thought. Peter picked up Jane's letter and stuffed it back into his pocket.

'I'd better let you get on with your homework.'

Peter pondered on Lucy's words as he went back downstairs to join Dominic in the living room. She was right: Jane was taking a big risk asking him to take on a role in her wedding ceremony. She had put him in a position where he could humiliate her in the eyes of her fiancé and his family simply by declining the invitation – never mind the damage that he could do if he were to make a scene in front of all the guests.

There must surely be more to it than simply a desire not to appear completely alone in the world. And inviting Hannah and Eddie was even more hazardous for her. She was not to know that he had concealed her existence from them. For all she knew, he could have been feeding them with poisonous ideas about both her mother and herself for years!

Could it be that she was ashamed of Valerie's behaviour and wanted to make amends? But, in that case, why not say so in the letter? On the other hand, perhaps it was too much to expect that she would put down in writing criticism of her own mother. Never having had any parents, Peter struggled to imagine how it would feel to find oneself totally at odds with one's own mother on a matter as important as that. It was only natural he decided, that Jane would feel loyalty towards Valerie, even if she found her attitude towards people of colour as repugnant as he did himself. Was it reasonable to expect her to express that repugnance in a letter to a comparative stranger? A stranger, moreover, who had already made it abundantly clear that he despised her mother and everything that she stood for?

Perhaps he ought to give Jane the benefit of the doubt and accede to her request – or at least agree to meet her to discuss it? But then it might be difficult to avoid telling Hannah and Eddie about their aunt, and their grandmother, and the reason that he had concealed their existence for so long. It would be so much simpler to decline, but the simple option was not necessarily the right one, was it? And, whatever he was going to do, he must make a decision soon. The worst possible thing for Jane would be to receive no reply and not to know whether or not she needed to make alternative arrangements – and whether or not he might appear unannounced to disrupt her big day!

Over the family meal, with everyone seated around the large kitchen table, the conversation turned to the death of Kevin Molyneux and possible links with the Boys' Club.

'I can't help thinking there must have been something wrong with that club,' Bernie said, pouring custard over her portion of Peter's home-made rhubarb tart, the first of the season. 'The way that so many of them seem to have had mental health problems afterwards. Out of the boys that Mary Molyneux mentioned, we've got one that committed suicide, one alcoholic and one homeless drug addict. It's not exactly a good advertisement for a youth organisation, is it?'

'And yet, without exception, everyone who knew him says that Father O'Leary was an exemplary priest and well-liked by all the boys,' Jonah pointed out. 'I agree that it all looks very suspicious, but I can't make up my mind what sort of thing it was that was going on or who is most likely to be to blame. If Father O'Leary was abusing the boys and killed Kevin – either as part of the abuse or to stop him telling people about what he'd seen – surely someone would have come forward and told us by now, especially seeing as he's dead and can't pose a threat anymore?'

'If not him, then who else is there?' Bernie asked. 'Don't forget: it has to be someone who had access to the vestry and knew how to hide the body where nobody would look.'

'There's Leonard O'Connell,' Peter suggested. 'He was an altar server and close to Father O'Leary, so he might have been able to hide the body – and he did do his own disappearing act only a year after Kevin.'

'If he was around then,' Jonah cautioned. 'We don't have a definite date for when he arrived at St Cyprian's, but the sort of thing that people have said is *a few months before Father Carey arrived*, which was in March 1979. I'm more inclined to suspect Father Bannister, who looked to have a promising career ahead of him in the church, and then chucked it all in. Nobody seems to know why, which could suggest he had a cloud hanging over him when he left.'

'Or that he was suffering from a crisis of conscience,' Bernie nodded. 'Would it be worth trying to find out if there was ever any concern raised about his conduct in the parish he went to after he left St Cyprian's?'

'It's none of my business,' Dominic said tentatively, 'but I've been thinking about those boys. I mean the ones that you said just now went off with Kevin the day he died. I was thinking about the way boys behave when they're in a group together. Sometimes they do things that they'd never think of when they're on their own.'

'Are you suggesting that they killed Kevin?' Jonah asked.

'Maybe not as strong as that. It could've been a game that went wrong – an accident. I remember when I was a teenager, there was this old derelict house where we used to go – me and my mates. The front windows were all boarded up, but they hadn't bothered with the ones round the back, and there was a place where you could get through the fence into the back garden, and then you could get inside easy enough. One day someone started a game of daring each other to do things – stupid things like smashing the glass in the conservatory and climbing on the roof of the outhouse. The dares got more and more dangerous until someone dared us to jump down from one of the upstairs windows.'

'Go on,' Peter urged gently, seeing Dominic hesitate.

'There was this kid, Jeffrey. He was younger than the rest of us, but he kept hanging around us hoping we'd let him join in. He said he'd do it. He went upstairs and climbed out of one of the bedroom windows and ... I remember seeing him hanging there from his arms, with his hands gripping the window frame, and then he dropped and there was this horrible thump as he hit the ground and sort of crumpled up.'

'Was he badly hurt?' Lucy asked.

'Just a broken ankle, but we thought he was dead. He was all white and not moving. We didn't know what to do. Some of the lads ran away, leaving me and my mate John to face the music.'

'What did you do?'

'John wanted to try to carry him home, but I thought he shouldn't be moved. Then he came round and started crying with the pain. In the end, I called 999 and an ambulance came. I was just thinking it could've been something a bit like that that happened to Kevin.'

'But then, why didn't *they* call an ambulance?' Lucy demanded. 'Like you did. Even if they didn't mean to hurt him, it was their fault he died because they didn't do anything. And why didn't they own up afterwards, instead of letting his parents carry on wondering where he was?'

'Too frightened probably,' Peter told her.

'Or maybe they didn't even know there was anything wrong until it was too late,' Dominic suggested, emboldened by Peter's support. 'They were playing in the snow. Couldn't they just have left him there and he froze to death?'

'I read a poem in English lessons at school,' Bernie put in, 'about a child playing hide-and-seek. They hid so well that the other kids got fed up with looking and went off, and the child came out hours later to find themselves all alone.'

'Except,' Jonah objected, 'that the medical evidence suggests that Kevin was strangled and that his body was kept in particularly hot and dry conditions immediately after death.'

'But the cold would preserve the body, wouldn't it?' Lucy argued. 'So couldn't it have been moved into the hot dry place later, without there being evidence of a delay?'

'I think Dom may have an idea here,' Peter insisted. 'It could have been guilt over what happened to Kevin that drove those boys to drink and suicide, rather than trauma from being abused.'

'OK. Let's run with that for the moment,' Jonah said, moving his chair back from the table a little to signify that he had finished eating. 'According to Brendan Connolly – who, we need to remember, may not be the most reliable of witnesses – Robert Lewis and Colin Kennedy passed Kevin's house on the way to St Cyprian's and saw him there in the front garden clearing the snow. They persuaded him to go with them to play in the garden round the back of the church. While they are there, some sort of accident befalls Kevin. Lewis and Kennedy are too scared to tell anyone, so they just run off and leave him there, freezing to death in the snow. So far, so good, but there are still lots of unanswered questions: who moved the body? Where did they put it that provided the conditions for it to mummify like that? Why did they move it again? Or was it even the same person who did the two moves?'

'It's a pity that they're neither of them around to tell us,' Peter observed.

'Yes, isn't it?' Jonah said drily. 'Or, from Connolly's point of view, it's very convenient that the two people that he's put in the frame for Kevin's murder are both dead and unable to contradict what he's said about them.'

'Are you saying he's lying?' Bernie asked.

'I think that it's likely he's not been telling us the whole truth. My guess is that he was there too, but won't admit it. Peter's argument that Kennedy killed himself and Lewis took to drink out of remorse could be applied equally well to Connolly's drug habit. And I keep coming back to the fact that whoever hid the body in the vestry must have been someone who knew their way around the church very well – if not Father O'Leary, one of his close associates. I'm sorry,' he looked round the room at all the expectant faces, 'I know you all want it to be nothing to do with the church – I don't want to stir up another clergy abuse scandal either – but you've got to remember it's the seventies we're talking about. Corporal punishment was still widespread in schools. There was a lot more deference towards authority figures in those days and children were expected to accept anything they said and not to criticise them. How about this as an alternative scenario? The boys – Kevin Molyneux, together with Lewis, Kennedy and most likely Connolly as well-'

'And Tim Norcott,' Bernie interjected. 'Don't forget him. I'd say, if anyone was suffering from a crisis of conscience over Kevin's death, it was him. Don't you remember how Kevin's Mum said how kind he was to her, while everyone else seemed to think he was a bully and used to torment Kevin? I bet he was the ringleader and Connolly didn't mention him either because he's still afraid of him or because he didn't want to get him into trouble.'

'OK,' Jonah conceded. 'Let's say it was all five of them messing about round the back of St Cyprian's. Suppose Father O'Leary sees them there and comes out to find out what they're up to and whatever it is, he doesn't approve. Maybe they've damaged some church property or he thinks they're behaving irreverently or … well, anyway, whatever it is, he decides they need to be punished.'

'Hang on a minute!' Bernie objected. 'I can see how that could explain the broken arm and broken ribs – although it would have to be a very extreme form of physical punishment even for those days – but how could anyone justify strangulation as *reasonable chastisement*?'

'Clearly something went badly wrong,' Jonah admitted. 'Perhaps he got carried away and did things that he didn't intend; or … or perhaps the strangulation came about because he tried to constrain Kevin in some way. Look – I don't want it to be Father O'Leary any more than any of you do, but you can't get away from the fact that, even if he didn't cause Kevin's death, he almost certainly was involved in covering it up afterwards and concealing his body.'

'Father O'Leary or Father Bannister or someone else who knew which places in the church weren't likely to be looked in,' Peter cut in. 'You agreed that O'Connell might have known that the chest in the vestry was never disturbed; what about the other altar servers? They might have been in the know too. Were any of those other boys servers? There would have been a few, wouldn't there?'

'Not that it reflects all that much better on the church if it was one of them,' Bernie sighed. 'However you look at it, someone with a trusted position at St Cyprian's must, at very least, have hidden the body, presumably in order to protect the perpetrators.'

21 MENTAL DISORDER

Catherine Lewis stared blankly at Bernie across Jonah's head when she opened the door of her semi-detached house in the Oxford suburb of Littlemore. In response, Bernie held up Jonah's warrant card and her own identification badge, leaving the talking to Jonah.

'I'm DCI Jonah Porter,' he said briskly, 'and this is my assistant, Bernie Fazakerley. We spoke on the phone earlier. I'm hoping you may be able to help us with our investigation into the death of a young man whom your late husband knew when he was a teenager. May we come in?'

'Er ... yes – yes, of course.' Still looking confused, Mrs Lewis opened the door wider and then looked across at Bernie again. 'Does he need any help?'

'Thank you,' Jonah answered, pretending that she had been addressing him. 'We've brought our own ramp.'

He backed his chair away from the doorstep so that Bernie could set up the portable ramp. She checked that it was secure before standing back to allow him to steer his chair up and over the threshold.

'Come in the lounge,' Mrs Lewis said, opening a door

on their left and then standing back, waiting for them to go through it.

Bernie went ahead. The room was cluttered with a rather bulky three-piece suite and several occasional tables with worryingly breakable-looking ornaments. A large tabby cat lay dozing on one of the chairs. It watched Bernie through half-closed eyelids as she carefully picked up one of the tables and moved it into a corner of the room to make space for Jonah's wheelchair. It took fright at the sight of Jonah gliding in on silent wheels and bolted behind the sofa.

'Can I get you anything to drink?' Mrs Lewis asked standing rather awkwardly in the doorway, watching as Jonah manoeuvred the chair into a space next to a glass-fronted display cabinet.

'No thank you. We won't keep you long.' Jonah maintained his business-like tone. 'Please sit down.'

Mrs Lewis came fully into the room and collapsed into one of the easy chairs. She sat there fiddling nervously with a string of coloured wooden beads, which she wore round her neck. She looked towards Bernie again, but Bernie, studiously ignoring her, was busy setting up her laptop in readiness to take notes of the interview.

'And try to relax,' Jonah added, noting her anxiety. 'Neither you nor your late husband are under suspicion. We just need you to give us some background – if you can – about your husband's childhood and, in particular, about the Boys' Club that he belonged to.'

'I'm sorry. I really don't know anything. Robert never said anything about it. He didn't like to talk about his childhood.' Mrs Lewis spoke quickly, her eyes darting back and forth between Jonah and Bernie.

'Oh?' Jonah asked with interest. 'Why was that?'

'I don't know. He just said there was nothing very interesting to talk about.'

'I see. Well, never mind. Let's go back a bit to check we've got the basic facts right. You were married in 1998 in the Oxford Registry Office – is that right?'

'Yes. Robert's Mum wanted us to have a church wedding, but Robert said he'd renounced all that and he certainly wasn't going to promise to bring up any kids as Catholics. She was always on at him about not going to church any more, but he said he'd had enough of being forced to go when he was a kid.'

'I see. And is Mrs Lewis Senior still with us?'

'No. She passed away ten – no eleven years ago now. His Dad was already dead when we got married.'

'And before she died, did she talk about your husband's childhood at all? Did she show you any photographs, for example?'

'Not that I remember. She ... she wasn't a very easy woman to get on with.'

'Was that because she disapproved of Robert marrying a non-Catholic – I assume you are a non-Catholic?'

'Well, I don't suppose that helped, but it was more just that she had such set ideas about everything – not just religion – and she always thought she was right and everyone else was wrong. I remember when we swapped the car for a Peugeot and she hardly spoke to us for about a year, because she thought we ought to have bought British. Robert's dad used to work at Cowley[10], so I suppose she was thinking about people's jobs, but it was our decision. And then there was the bathroom! Apparently getting rid of the bath and just having a shower is the end of civilisation as we know it. And ... sorry,' she apologised, going a little red in the face, 'I'm wasting your time – not to mention speaking ill of the dead. It's just that she did drive me so mad sometimes.'

'Getting back to your husband,' Jonah said smoothly,

---

[10] Cowley motor works (now known as Plant Oxford) was opened in 1912 by William Morris. After a long history of company mergers, it is now owned by BMW. It houses the central assembly line for the Mini.

pleased to have got his witness talking. 'He died very young, didn't he?'

'Yes. Yes, he did.'

'The death certificate says that he had liver failure.'

'Yes. That's right.'

'Brought on by excessive alcohol consumption.'

'Yes.'

Jonah waited in silence. Mrs Lewis looked away and appeared to be contemplating the row of watercolour pictures on the wall above the fireplace. The cat emerged from behind the sofa and jumped up on to her lap.

'Yes,' Mrs Lewis said at last, stroking the cat and bending over it to avoid meeting Jonah's eye. 'He always liked a drink, ever since I first knew him, but it was just social drinking back then.'

'And when did that change?'

'I'm not sure,' Mrs Lewis sighed, still with her eyes down and with her hands busy petting the cat. 'It got really bad after his mum died, but I'd noticed something was wrong even before that. It was the nightmares that set him off, I think.'

'Nightmares?'

'He used to wake up all in a sweat and shivering. I asked him what they were about, but he wouldn't say, except …'

'Except?' prompted Jonah gently.

'One time, when he was dead drunk, he muttered something about wishing he'd never been to his High School reunion. He said something about everyone else being dead and he wished he was too. And then, I thought back and it did seem as if the drinking – the really bad drinking I mean – and the nightmares, started just after he'd been to a party they put on for everyone in his year as school.'

'Can you remember when this was?'

'It was twenty years on from getting to the end of High School, so … that would be 2001, I suppose.'

'I see.' Jonah thought for a moment or two. 'Do you think the nightmares could have been to do with something traumatic that happened to your husband when he was a child?'

'Maybe. He wouldn't say anything about them.'

'And when he got back from this school reunion, did he say anything about it? Any names of people he met – or whom he had expected to meet, but who weren't there?'

'I don't think so. He did say it had been a waste of time, because none of his mates were there.'

'Did he ever talk about his mates?'

'No.' Mrs Lewis shook her head, looking up at last. 'To be honest, I don't think he had many. Robert always found it difficult in social situations.'

'He belonged to the Boys' Club at St Cyprian's Church. Did he ever talk about that at all?'

'Not that I remember. He did say once what a relief it was when he moved into his own flat and his mum couldn't nag him to go to church all the time. He was the only boy in his family. He reckoned she'd got him marked down to become a priest. He told me all about how he used to have to dress up in funny clothes and parade up and down carrying candles and things.'

'You mean he was an altar server?'

'If that's what you call them.'

'How did you and your husband meet?'

'It was through work. We were both going through our accountancy training at the same time, but with different firms. I can't quite remember, but I think we met on a course somewhere.'

'Do you come from Oxford too?'

'Yes – well Kennington.' Mrs Lewis named another of the villages on the outskirts of Oxford, which had grown rapidly during the twentieth century as new housing developments made it more and more a suburb of the city.

'Do you remember hearing about a young man going missing from Headington one winter? It would have been when your husband was twelve or thirteen.'

'No,' Mrs Lewis shook her head again, 'but then I'd only have been eleven, so I didn't take much interest in the news.'

'I thought your parents might have warned you not to go off with strangers. The police thought at the time that he might have been abducted.'

'No. I don't remember anything about it. I expect my mum and dad thought I already knew about *stranger danger* and all that.'

'And your husband never mentioned it? He knew the man. He had learning difficulties and used to go to St Cyprians' Boys' Club even though he was really too old for it.'

'No. Not that I remember. Like I said, he didn't talk about his childhood or the church.'

'So, I don't suppose he ever mentioned a priest called Father O'Leary?'

'No. At least ... I *think* his mother did once. That may not have been the name, but she did mention one of them in particular and it may have been him. It was an Irish name I'm sure. It was during one of her diatribes about *why didn't he go to Mass anymore?* She said something about poor Father so-and-so turning in his grave, and Robert said he couldn't care less if he wasn't resting in peace. He'd got a lot to answer for.'

'Really?' Jonah asked with renewed interest. 'You don't have any idea what it was that this priest had done to make him say that?'

'No.'

'Well now!' Jonah said to Bernie in the car a few minutes later, as they made their way to their next appointment. 'At last we have someone who doesn't think that Father O'Leary was a saint. I wonder what it was that he did to give Robert Lewis nightmares and put him off going to church for life.'

'You're jumping to conclusions there,' Bernie objected. 'There may have been other things that contributed to Lewis's feelings about the church. *A lot to answer for* is a bit vague, isn't it? It could just mean that he didn't do anything to stop whatever it was, rather than that he actually did anything himself. Or,' she added, remembering a particularly fierce priest from her own childhood, 'it could be that Father O'Leary frightened him with stores about hellfire when he was small and he resented it when he got older and stopped believing in it. And you don't even know for certain that it was Father O'Leary he was talking about. Mrs Lewis couldn't remember the name.'

'She said it was an Irish name. That rules out Father Carey and Father Bannister. Besides, they were only there for a couple of years each, whereas Father O'Leary was the Parish Priest for the whole of Robert Lewis's childhood.'

'Yes. Father O'Leary does seem to have got through a lot of assistants, doesn't he? I wonder whether that's normal or if there was some reason that they all moved on so soon.'

'Hmm,' Jonah murmured. 'You're right. We ought to find out about that. When we get back, I'll ask Andy to make a list of all the assistant priests that were there at any point during Father O'Leary's time at St Cyprian's. The chances are he's already got the names and dates from his trawl through the church archives. Who would know what the normal length of stay is for an assistant priest?'

'Well, for a start, it won't be the same now as it was then,' Bernie pointed out. 'Like all the other churches, they don't have enough priests to go round now. That's why Father Damien doesn't have an assistant. I think Father Carey was the last one.'

'So the fast turnover may not mean anything after all. Perhaps they just needed to get the new priests out into their own parishes as quickly as possible. Still, it's worth looking into.'

PC Gavin Hughes was waiting for them when they pulled up outside the homeless hostel in one of the back streets of South Oxford. 'Mike's in the office, catching up on the paperwork,' he greeted them, waiting while Bernie set up the ramp so that Jonah could descend. 'I'll show you.'

He led the way down the side of the building and in through a small door at the back, which he opened by pressing buttons on the combination lock.

'They keep the main doors locked during the day,' he explained. 'There's an emergency buzzer on this door, but the residents aren't supposed to use it except ...'

'In emergencies,' Jonah finished for him. 'I get the picture. This shelter is here so that people don't have to sleep on the streets, but it's up to them to find somewhere to go in the daytime.'

Gavin led the way down a narrow, dark corridor and knocked on a door at the end of it. It was ajar and swung open further at his touch.

'Come in!' called a voice.

Gavin went ahead, opening the door wide to make room for Jonah's chair to pass through. Bernie squeezed in after them and closed the door again. The office was very small and very cluttered.

A small man with white hair and metal-framed glasses was sitting behind a desk. He jumped to his feet as they entered and took off his spectacles, holding them in both hands for a few seconds before folding them and putting them down on top of the pile of papers that he had been studying. He came out from behind the desk, holding out both hands towards them in greeting.

'Come in!' he repeated, grasping Bernie's outstretched hand between his. 'Make yourselves at home.'

He looked round the room. There were only two chairs.

'I'm sorry it's so cramped in here,' he apologised. 'Perhaps you could go round there and take my chair,' he said to Bernie, gesturing with one arm, 'and Gavin – you can have the other one. I don't mind standing. It'll do me good after being at my desk all morning.'

'That's alright, Mike,' Gavin smiled. 'I'm just going. I only came to introduce you to DI Porter.'

'That's right,' Bernie backed him up. 'You sit back down and make yourself comfortable.'

Gavin left, closing the door behind him. Bernie moved her chair to the side of the room so that Jonah could position himself opposite Michael Bannister, who squeezed back behind the desk and sat down again.

'As PC Hughes will have told you,' Jonah began, 'I'm DCI Jonah Porter and this is my Personal Assistant, Bernie Fazakerley. We want to talk to you about your time as Assistant Priest at St Cyprian's church in Headington.'

'In connection with the disappearance of Kevin Molyneux?'

'That's right. His disappearance in 1978 and his unexpected reappearance last week.'

'What do you want to know?'

'Let's start with what you remember about Kevin's disappearance.'

'Not a lot, I'm afraid. I didn't know the family all that well – not the way Father O'Leary did. I'm afraid I wasn't really that good at the pastoral side of things. I didn't find it easy getting to know people. And it was difficult having them all ... In those days, Catholics all tended to be rather deferential towards priests. They assumed we knew all the answers, which was difficult when you were starting to wonder if you knew anything at all really!'

'How did you get to hear that Kevin was missing?'

'His mother rang the presbytery. That would be the evening of the day he disappeared. She thought he might have gone to see Father O'Leary. I don't think she really thought it was likely that he'd have done it without telling her, but she was just trying all the places she could think of.'

'Did you speak to her yourself or did Father O'Leary take the call?'

'Mrs Wimbourne answered the phone and she handed it over to Father O'Leary.'

'Mrs Wimbourne?'

'Our housekeeper.'

'I see. And what did Father O'Leary do when he heard that Kevin was gone?'

'He went straight round to see Mr and Mrs Molyneux.'

'And you? What did you do?'

'I went into the church to pray for Kevin's safe return. Father O'Leary joined me later – it must have been close to midnight by then – and we stayed praying until it was time to get ready for the morning Mass.'

'Alright. Now, I know it's a long time ago, but I'd like you to think back to earlier that day. It was snowy. We think that some of the boys from the Boys' Club bunked off school to play in it, and we think that they came to St Cyprian's and built an igloo round the back there. Did you see anything of them?'

'No – not that I remember.' Bannister paused in thought. 'I cleared the snow from the path at the front in the morning, so I don't think they can have come until after I finished that. But then I stayed indoors with my books for the rest of the day.'

'What about Father O'Leary? Can you remember what he was doing that day?'

'No.' Bannister shook his head. 'He was out in the morning, I think. Let's see … what day of the week was it?'

'A Wednesday,' Bernie told him, after consulting the case notes on her computer.

'Ah! Then he'd have been at the hospital in the morning. I don't know about after lunch.'

'And he didn't say anything to you about seeing the

boys – or their igloo – in the courtyard or the gardens?'

'No. Not that I remember, but it *is* a long time ago, and Kevin's disappearance rather overshadowed everything else.'

'Of course. Now, tell me – how did Father O'Leary seem when he heard about Kevin?'

'What do you mean? He was worried for the boy's safety, naturally, and upset for his parents.'

'But nothing more? He didn't seem agitated – or guilty?'

'No!' Bannister leapt to his feet, pushing back his chair so that it banged against the cupboard behind it. He glared at Jonah who smiled blandly back. 'What are you suggesting?' he demanded angrily.

'I'm not suggesting anything. I'm merely exploring the possibilities.'

'Well I can tell you for certain that you're barking up the wrong tree if you think Father O'Leary had anything to do with what happened to Kevin. He'd known Kevin all his life, and Kevin absolutely adored him. He'd never have done anything to harm him.'

'Alright,' Jonah said equably. 'We'll leave that.' He waited for Bannister to sit down again before continuing. 'I'd like you to tell us about the Boys' Club. Were you involved with that at all?'

'I went along sometimes. Father O'Leary thought that they might find a younger priest easier to talk to, but I never seemed to be on their wavelength somehow, whereas he … well, he was a born Parish Priest. He managed to empathise with everyone, whether it was a homeless drunk or a young mother or a grandmother worried that her grandchildren wouldn't go to Mass.'

'Kevin used to belong to the club, didn't he? But he was asked to leave because he was too old. Do you remember that?'

'Yes. Father O'Leary was furious, but in the end he went along with what the parents wanted.'

'When the parents complained, did they make any specific accusations against Kevin? Or was it just his age that they were worried about?'

'As far as I know it was just his age. That was what made Father O'Leary so angry. He couldn't see why it mattered.'

'Alright. Now, I know you won't like what I'm going to say next, but I do have to ask.' Jonah paused and looked Bannister in the eye. 'Were there ever any other complaints about the club? Did any of the boys – or their parents – ever suggest that anything untoward had gone on there?'

'No.'

Jonah said nothing. There was a lengthy silence.

Eventually Bannister felt obliged to add, 'nothing at all. I know people think that Catholic priests are all perverts preying on victims who don't dare speak out, but it's not true! Not in Father O'Leary's case anyway.'

'That's what everyone else says too,' Jonah told him. 'At least, everyone that is except Robert Lewis. Do you remember him? He was one of the boys who belonged to the club at the same time as Kevin Molyneux went missing.'

'Robert Lewis?' Bannister said slowly. 'No,' he shook his head. 'It doesn't ring any bells with me, I'm afraid.'

'He told his wife – this was years later – that Father O'Leary *had a lot to answer for*. Do you have any idea what he could have meant by that?'

'No. None at all,' Bannister said irritably. 'Why don't you ask him?'

'Because, unfortunately, he's dead. He became an alcoholic and died of liver failure. His wife blames it on his experiences at St Cyprian's.'

'Well, I'm afraid I can't help you. As I said, I don't remember the boy.'

'Do you remember Colin Kennedy? – or Timothy Norcott?'

'No – or at least, hang on! Kennedy sounds a bit

familiar. There *was* a family of that name, but I don't remember a boy. Why do you want to know?'

'We've heard that some boys, probably including Robert Lewis and Colin Kennedy, met Kevin the day he died and took him to play round the back of St Cyprian's. Lewis and Kennedy are both dead. Kennedy committed suicide and Lewis drank himself to death, which suggests that they were both troubled in their minds, doesn't it?'

'And the other boy? – Timothy something?'

'We still haven't managed to trace him.' Jonah hesitated. He was not sure how Bannister would take his next question. 'Now, please can you tell me why you left the priesthood?' he asked at last.

'What's that got to do with you?' As Jonah had expected, Bannister sounded hostile.

'I'm trying to get a picture of what it was like at St Cyprian's back then.' he explained patiently. 'So far, I have a young man who disappears and turns up murdered nearly forty years later, a boy who grew up to have nightmares about what went on, another boy who killed himself, a young man who ran away because a priest was taking too much of an interest in him, and a priest who -'

'That's a lie, for a start!' Bannister broke in angrily. 'What do you mean *too much of an interest*? Who are you talking about?'

'Leonard O'Connell? Do you remember him?'

'No.' Bannister looked puzzled.

'He was a young man with a troubled family life. Father O'Leary gave him a bed at the presbytery. In January 1980 – that's just two years after Kevin's disappearance – he ran away. We thought for a while that it might have been his body in the church, but he turned up alive and well and claiming that he went off to get away from Father O'Leary's over-zealous ministrations.'

'He's lying. He must be. Father Eamon wasn't like that at all. I'm sure he wasn't. He had a great relationship with all the boys. He was like a father to them – I don't mean just like a priest is supposed to be, like a real father. He …,' Bannister trailed off into a sigh. 'OK,' he said, after a long pause, 'OK. I admit, I was sometimes a bit concerned about how close he was to some of the boys; but I am *absolutely certain* that it wasn't sexual in any way. It was like they were his own kids. He'd do anything for them. And for some of them … well, some of them had dads who weren't that bothered with them or treated them badly, and Father Eamon was someone they could turn to. But you've got to believe me: he'd never harm any of them any more than he'd have hurt his own mother!'

Jonah smiled.

'You know, Mr Bannister, that is exactly what Leonard O'Connell told us. He ran away because Father O'Leary was acting like a father: giving him advice, trying to get him to go to college and make something of himself, suggesting he might be destined for the priesthood. He was starting to feel trapped and wanted his freedom back.'

'There you are then!' Bannister somehow managed to sound relieved, angry and triumphant all at once. 'If you knew that, why did you come here making all those vile insinuations about Father Eamon being a paedophile priest? Why couldn't you-?'

'I needed to hear your corroboration without me prompting you. Two independent witnesses are much more convincing than if I'd just asked you to confirm what O'Connell said. But you haven't answered my question. Why did you stop being a priest?'

'I just wasn't very good at it,' Bannister shrugged. 'When I was a priest, everyone used to expect me to have all the answers, and usually I was in at least as much of a fog as they were. And I thought I could do more good in other ways. I spent years studying so that I might at last be able to answer all the questions, and then, all of a sudden it struck me that it was all a waste of time when there were people out there like the men who come to this shelter, with no home and no job and no family – nothing!'

'I see. Thank you. Now, just one final thing: you never said whether you remembered Leonard O'Connell.'

'No. I don't. Did you say he stayed at the presbytery?'

'That's right. He was already there when your successor arrived in March 1979.'

'I left in September 1978. He must have come after that.'

'Which means that we can forget the hypothesis that O'Connell is our killer,' Jonah observed to Bernie a few minutes later, when they were back in the car. 'It looks as if he didn't even arrive until at least nine months after Kevin was already dead.'

'What about Father Bannister as a suspect?' Bernie asked. 'Do you think he's being straight with us?'

'Yes. I rather think I do. If he is the murderer, he isn't taking any opportunity to put us off the scent. He could easily have spun us a yarn that would have convinced us that Father O'Leary must be to blame, instead of being so keen to exonerate him.'

22 THERAPY

'Where next?' Bernie asked as they drove away from the homeless shelter. 'Back to the office?'

'No. Andy's got us an address for Colin Kennedy's mother. It's not too far. We'll go over there first and see what she has to say about Colin and his mates at the club.'

Bernie looked at her watch. Jonah's spinal injury made it important that he keep to regular mealtimes and took time out of his chair occasionally during the day.

'It's past our usual lunchtime. We ought to take a break first.'

'We can grab a sandwich on the way.' As usual, Jonah found it hard to pay attention to his own welfare while he was fired up to solve a case.

'On the way where?' Bernie asked suspiciously. 'Where exactly does Mrs Kennedy live?'

'Kingston Bagpuize.'

'Huh! I see you have re-defined the term *not far*. It must be twenty miles at least.'

'It'll only take a few minutes in the car.'

'And then another half hour to find the house. It'll be one of those quaint little villages with no names on the roads and no numbers on the houses. No,' Bernie said firmly. 'You've been sitting in that chair in one position for far too long already.'

'I've been using the tilting mechanism to shift my weight,' Jonah protested. 'I'll be fine.'

'It's not the same as changing your posture completely. I'm taking you back home first. Then you can have a proper break and a proper meal and I can look up where we're going on Street View so we don't get lost.'

Jonah sat in sullen silence in the back of the car as Bernie drove the short distance to their home in Headington. He knew that Bernie was right, but that only made him all the more annoyed with her for overriding his orders and resentful of the paralysis that made it possible for her to do so. He was also angry with himself for having needed her reminder that he must not push his body beyond its capabilities and conscious that he ought to be more gracious towards her and more appreciative of her concern for his welfare.

Bernie drove at the speed limit, intent on wasting as little time as possible, well aware that Jonah was counting the minutes. Luckily the traffic on the by-pass was light and they were soon turning in at the drive and pulling up outside their front door. Bernie turned off the engine and jumped out to set up the ramp and release Jonah from the straps that secured him.

Peter's car was parked on the drive, but there was no answer when Bernie called out as they entered the house. She looked around the hall.

'The buggy's gone. It looks as if Peter must've taken the kids out for a walk. I expect they've already had their lunch,' she added, looking at her watch. 'I'll rustle up something for us while you give yourself a quick physio session. Go in the bedroom; then I can get you out of the chair for a massage as well.'

Automatic doors, activated by a switch on his wheelchair, opened to allow Jonah through his study into the bedroom beyond. These rooms, together with his private bathroom, had been constructed out of the original dining and breakfast rooms when he came to live with Bernie and her family on the death of his wife. They contained an array of equipment necessary for his care.

Once inside the bedroom, Jonah manoeuvred his chair into the wide space between the bed and the wall. At a touch of a button, he made it recline, so that he was moved slowly into a lying position, relieving the pressure on his buttocks and thighs and redistributing his weight across the back of his body. Further manipulation of the controls caused the chair to tilt, first to the right and then to the left.

'Here you are!' Bernie returned with slices of pizza and two bananas. 'Now, if you're ready, I'll roll you on the bed and give you that massage to get your circulation going.'

She put down the food on the top of a chest of drawers while Jonah adjusted the height of his chair (which now resembled a hospital trolley) and brought it alongside the bed. Then Bernie rolled him from chair to bed and loosened his clothing ready for the massage.

'Do you think Bannister was telling the truth?' Jonah asked, as Bernie manipulated his calves to improve the flow of blood in his legs. 'I can't help wondering if he left the priesthood because of something he did – or something he saw – while he was at St Cyprian's.'

'If that was the reason, why didn't he do it right away?' Bernie argued. 'He went on to another parish, remember?'

'Sometimes these things take a while to sink in. And, if *he* was the guilty one, maybe he thought that he could make a fresh start and found that he couldn't.'

'You mean, if he was a paedophile, for example?'

'That sort of thing. It could even have been not really his choice. Isn't that part of the scandal of clergy abuse? Didn't the church often know about it and just move the perpetrators on instead of reporting them to the police? Perhaps the bishop, or whoever, tried moving him first and then told him he had to resign when he did it again in his new parish.'

'Except that there doesn't seem to be any evidence of anything untoward in his new place, whereas we have Leonard O'Connell for one apparently uncomfortable with being around Father O'Leary. If there was any clergy abuse going on, my money would be on him – except that everyone keeps telling us that he was the best priest they've ever known! Now let's get you back in your chair and we can have our lunch.'

Bernie carefully transferred Jonah back on to the chair and strapped his hand to the controls. Then Jonah brought it back up to a sitting position while Bernie took his urine bag to the adjacent bathroom to empty it. It was not long before they were sitting side-by-side, eating pizza and drinking Vimto[11].'

The meal over, they headed out to make the journey to the South Oxfordshire village of Kingston Bagpuize to interview Colin Kennedy's mother. In his haste, Jonah misjudged the speed of his wheelchair and collided with the hall-stand. There was a clatter as a small object fell on to the tiled floor. Bernie bent to pick it up.

'What's that?' Jonah asked as she replaced the string of black beads on the shiny wooden surface.

'Peter brought it back from St Cyprian's. Father Damien lent it to him – or gave it to him maybe; I'm not sure.'

'Prayer beads?'

'A rosary, yes.' Bernie led the way outside and busied herself with opening the car and setting up the ramp.

'I suppose that means that old Peter's going to be saying Hail Marys and all that stuff at home as well as in

---

[11] Vimto is a fruit-flavoured soft drink manufactured in Manchester. It is popular in the north of England. Jonah was first introduced to it by his wife, Margaret, who came from Horwich, near Bolton.

church,' Jonah muttered disagreeably, as Bernie strapped him in.

'Oh Jonah!' Bernie sighed, exasperated at her friend's sulky attitude towards Peter's conversion. 'Don't be like that. You know perfectly well that Peter never does anything to impose his beliefs on anyone else. It's not going to make any difference to you at all. Why can't you just leave him be?'

'I just don't understand,' Jonah answered, as Bernie climbed into the driver's seat and turned on the engine, 'how Peter, of all people, can go on about talking statues and praying to saints and mumbling the same words over and over again as if God – or those precious saints of his – only listen if you say things ten times over. It just doesn't make sense!'

'You're over-thinking everything,' Bernie contended. 'Why can't you ever just go with the flow? Why do you always have to understand the mechanics of everything, instead of just accepting that it works?'

'Because I've got a brain, that's why. It's about the only part of me that still works and I intend to use it. I don't hold with this blind faith stuff. I prefer my religion to be rational.'

'And you think Peter's isn't?' Bernie demanded indignantly.

'What's rational about claiming that a statue spoke to him?'

'Well, for a start, he never said that the statue spoke to him; he said that the Virgin Mary spoke to him, which is quite different.'

'But just as ridiculous. She's been dead two thousand years.'

'Will you shut up and listen for a change?'

'Sorry. Go on.'

'And secondly, you're taking it all too literally. You're as bad as the Young Earth Creationists who insist that we're all descended from a man who was moulded out of soil and a woman who was made out of one of his ribs!'

Jonah opened his mouth to protest, then thought better of it and closed it again. He could see that he had annoyed Bernie and did not want to provoke her further.

'People often talk about things speaking to them. They don't mean that they literally heard words coming out of them. When someone says that a picture – or a poem – or a piece of music – speaks to them, all they mean is that it conveys some sort of meaning to them; that they've learnt something from seeing it or reading it or hearing it.'

'I suppose so,' Jonah conceded reluctantly. 'But they don't usually talk back to the picture or the-'

'And it's the same when you talk about a person you've never met speaking to you,' Berne continued, ignoring his interruption. 'You might say, for example, that ... oh I don't know ... that Ghandi speaks to us about the power of peaceful protest. If you said that, you wouldn't mean that you could actually hear Ghandi speaking to you from beyond the grave, would you? You wouldn't even mean that you'd met him while he was alive and heard him speak or even that you'd read something that he'd written. What you'd mean is that his whole life is an illustration of how peaceful protest can be powerful. Do you see what I mean?'

'I suppose so,' Jonah mumbled grudgingly. 'But that still doesn't explain why Catholics pray to saints – or why they have to say everything ten times over!'

'I'm sure we've been through this before,' Bernie sighed. 'Asking saints to pray for us is just the same as asking people who are alive to pray for us. '

'Except that-'

'I know,' Bernie cut him off, 'except that they're dead and can't hear us. But that's only your opinion. Nobody actually knows. You say that the dead are in a state of unconsciousness, waiting for the last trump to sound. OK. That's fine, but it's no more *rational* than imagining them out there, watching over us.'

'But what's the point?' Jonah persisted. 'Why ask a saint – who may or may not be able to hear you – to pray for you, instead of going straight to God yourself?'

'If it makes you feel better, try thinking of the saints as just sort of … I don't know … aspects of God, if you like.' Bernie sighed. 'Like I said: don't try to rationalise it. Can't you just accept that it works for some people? It's like …,' Bernie strove to think of an illustration. 'It's like … you don't need to know how an internal combustion engine works to be able to drive a car.'

Theresa Kennedy's home in the village of Kingston Bagpuize turned out to be a modern bungalow on a small estate with neatly mown lawns and no boundary fences between the front gardens and the street. Bernie pressed the bell push and then stepped back, taking up an unobtrusive position behind Jonah's chair.

There was the muffled sound of a door closing somewhere inside the house. Then there was movement visible behind the frosted glass in the front door. Finally, it opened to reveal a large woman in a purple and green striped dress with blond hair cut in a bob and blue eyes behind ornate spectacles.

'Mrs Theresa Kennedy?' Jonah enquired. 'I'm Detective Inspector Jonah Porter. I rang earlier.'

'Yes – yes, of course – come in.' She opened the door wide and then turned to lead the way into a large L-shaped room, with easy chairs at one end, a fireplace in the inside corner of the L, and a dining table round the corner from the door. To the left of the dining table, another door, partly open, revealed a kitchen beyond. 'Sit down,' she urged Bernie, gesturing towards the chairs. 'Can I get you anything? A cup of tea, perhaps? Or coffee?'

No thank you,' Jonah answered, while Bernie busied herself with setting up her laptop computer. 'I hope this won't take long. We just wanted to talk to you about your son, Colin, and the Boys' Club at St Cyprian's church, which he used to belong to.'

'So you said, but I don't know that I can be much help.' Mrs Kennedy spoke calmly, looking round at them both with mild interest. 'What is it you want to know?'

'You know – I'm not completely sure about that myself,' Jonah said with a smile. 'At the moment, I'm just trying to build up a picture of what it was like for the boys back then; so I'll be interested in pretty much anything you can remember. But let's start with Colin: did he have any particular friends at the club?'

'It rather depends what you mean by *friends*,' Mrs Kennedy said darkly. 'There were a couple of the boys that he was always hanging around with, but they weren't my idea of friends.'

'Oh? Why's that?'

'They led him astray. They were real tearaways. We'd never had any trouble with Colin before he took up with them, but afterwards! First it was smoking – and bear in mind he was only eleven when it started – and then we found they'd been having secret drinking sessions in the shed at the bottom of Brendan Connolly's garden. The final straw was when we had the truancy officer around, saying he'd been skipping school. We were mortified – and so surprised. We couldn't think why he'd done it.'

'Brendan Connolly?' Jonah asked, taking advantage of a short pause while Mrs Kennedy shook her head and frowned in perplexity at the mystifying behaviour of the younger generation. 'You say he was one of the boys? Who was the other?'

'Robert Lewis. He should have known better, what with his father being a magistrate and his mother a leading light in the Women's Institute. She said to me, she couldn't understand it. She'd always been very strict with her children, and the girls all turned out fine … but Robert!' She sighed and shook her head again.

'So, Colin used to go round with Brendan and Robert,'

Jonah repeated. 'Were there any other boys in their set? Or was it just the three of them?'

'Those were the ones I knew about.'

'Someone else mentioned a Timothy Norcott. Do you remember him?'

'I remember Francesca Norcott. She had a boy who must have been about Colin's age, but they moved away.'

'What about Kevin Molyneux? Do you remember him?'

'That mentally-retarded boy that Mary and Norman Molyneux took in? Yes. I remember him, but he was much older than Colin. Colin never had anything to do with him.'

'He was older,' Jonah said gently, ignoring Mrs Kennedy's evident distaste at the thought of her son associating with someone with learning difficulties, 'but he was still going to the Boys' Club when Colin and the others joined.'

'Not for long, he wasn't. I soon put a stop to that. I went to Father O'Leary and I told him it wasn't right having someone of that sort mixing with young kids like Colin. It was unhygienic, apart from anything else, the way he used to drool all down his chin. So I talked to Father O'Leary and he told him he had to leave.'

'I see. And, on the subject of Father O'Leary, how did Colin get on with him? Did he like him?'

''I don't know about *like*. He respected him. And I'm very grateful to Father O'Leary for getting Colin back on track after the truanting. He took him in hand and got him to see that he wasn't doing himself any favours missing school and getting a reputation for being out of control. Colin got some good O' Levels and stayed on at school to do his A' levels – which was something we never thought he *would* do – and got a place at Nottingham University. We all thought he was going to ... that is until ... he must have been more cut up about losing his dad than we ever realised.'

Mrs Kennedy's composure suddenly vanished. Her voice faltered into silence and she blinked several times as if fighting back tears. She got up and walked across to a tall display cabinet behind the chair where Bernie was sitting. She picked up a photograph and brought it back to show to Jonah.

'This is the last picture we took of Colin with his dad,' she said, holding it out where both Jonah and Bernie could see. 'Brian died in 1982, just after Colin started in the sixth form[12]. Colin didn't seem that bothered about it, but it must've got to him more than we thought, because … because he …'

She turned away and went round behind Bernie to replace the photograph. 'It's alright, Mrs Kennedy,' Jonah said gently. 'We know about Colin killing himself. You don't have to go into the details.'

Mrs Kennedy sat back down in her chair, facing Jonah. She pulled out a dainty lace-edged handkerchief from her sleeve and dabbed her eyes. She took a few deep breaths to compose herself before lifting her face and smiling weakly towards him.

'The coroner's report said that he'd been suffering from depression for some time,' Jonah went on, speaking softly and keeping a wary eye on Mrs Kennedy for signs that she might be about to break down again. 'We thought that might have been to do with something that happened at the Boys' Club.'

'No, no,' Mrs Kennedy said quickly. 'That was all over and done with years before. No. I'm sure it was losing his dad and then going away from home and being on his own for the first time.'

'Father O'Leary died in 1982 too, didn't he? How did

---

[12] For historical reasons, in England, Wales and Northern Ireland the last two years of High School (from age 16 to 18) are known as the Sixth Form, with the first year being termed "Lower Sixth" and the second year "Upper Sixth".

Colin take that?'

'He was upset, naturally. We all were. Father O'Leary had been at St Cyprian's for a long time. Most of the younger people had never known any other Parish Priest. What are you suggesting?' she added, a note of suspicion entering her voice.

'Nothing,' Jonah assured her mildly. 'I'm just trying to build up a picture of what it was like at St Cyprian's back then. Some of the others have described Father O'Leary as being like a second dad to them. Was that how Colin saw him?'

'I don't know if he'd have put it that way, but he certainly owed Father O'Leary a lot.' Mrs Kennedy sat in silent thought for a moment or two. 'Maybe if he'd still been around, Colin wouldn't have killed himself.'

23 AMNESIA

There was good news waiting for them when they arrived back at the incident room.

'We've found Timothy Norcott,' Monica greeted Jonah almost before he was through the door. 'He's living in Norwich. I briefed the police there. They've talked to him at home and now they're bringing him in for questioning.'

'Good work,' Jonah congratulated her.

'I've organised a video-link, so that we can watch the interview,' Monica continued. 'They should be ready to start in ...' she glanced down at her watch, '... about half an hour.'

'Excellent!' Jonah said approvingly. 'That gives us just long enough for you to fill us all in on what you've found out about Norcott. Listen up everyone!' he continued, raising his voice to address the room in general. 'Monica's got news on one of our suspects.'

Blushing with pride, Monica related everything that she had found out about the boy who had teased Kevin Molyneux and then, after his disappearance, had been so solicitous towards his distraught parents.

'The Norcotts moved to Hastings in 1982 – four years

after Kevin's disappearance – and then to Colchester in 1983, when Tim was seventeen. The following year, he started a degree in Sociology at the University of East Anglia. While he was there, his family moved again, this time to Lincoln. His parents split up while he was in his final year and his mother took his two younger sisters to live with her parents in Grantham. Timothy stayed living with his father in Lincoln until he graduated and then he got a training post with Social Services in Norwich and moved into a flat there.'

She paused to consult her notes before continuing.

'He qualified as a Social Worker and has been working in Norwich ever since. The police there know him quite well, because he specialises in working with teenagers who exhibit anti-social behaviour. They told me that he does a good job.'

'Does he have any family?' Jonah asked.

'He's been married and divorced twice,' Monica told him. 'He's got two children with his first wife – both girls. She's re-married and moved up to Scotland with her new husband, and taken the kids with her.'

'And wife number two?'

'Is also a Social Worker in Norwich. She's got a teenage son of her own from a previous marriage. They married in 2014 and divorced by mutual consent two years later.'

A telephone rang on the desk at the front of the room. Bernie answered it.

'They're ready to interview Norcott now,' she reported.

'Good. Monica! Andy! Come with me, both of you,' Jonah said briskly, turning to go.

Bernie hastily jumped up to open the door for him. Within a matter of minutes, they were all seated in the video-conferencing suite gazing at a large screen, which gave them a bird's eye view of a police interview room. Jonah looked at the scene intently. Two men in suits were sitting with their backs to the camera. They must be the police officers who were to conduct the interview.

A door opened at the right and a uniformed officer entered. She stood to one side to allow a man wearing a green corduroy sports jacket over jeans to walk past her and sit down opposite the plain-clothes officers. One of those officers – distinguishable from his colleague only by his bald head and rather prominent ears – nodded to her and she went out again, closing the door.

'Thank you for coming in,' the bald officer said blandly. 'I'm DI Chris Parkes and I think you already know DS Gareth Simms.'

Timothy Norcott nodded nervously and moistened his lips with his tongue. He looked older than his forty-two years. His hair, which had appeared black in the Boys' Club photographs, was now grey, streaked with white. There were lines on his brow and around his mouth, and the skin beneath his jaw was sagging.

'For the record,' DI Parkes continued, 'please confirm that you are Mr Timothy Norcott, currently residing at 14B Concordia Place.'

'That's right,' Norcott answered in a husky voice, nodding again.

'We need you to answer some questions about your time in Oxford between 1976 and 1982. This is in connection with the abduction and death of Kevin Molyneux in 1978. Officers from Thames Valley Police, who are investigating that case, are watching this interview and they may wish to speak to you in person at a later date. Do you understand?'

'Yes.' Norcott nodded again.

'As you may have heard on the news, Kevin Molyneux's body has been found concealed within St Cyprian's Church. You used to be a member of the Boys' Club there, I understand?'

'That's right. We lived in Oxford until I was fourteen – nearly fifteen, in fact. My family all went to the church and I was in the Boys' Club. It was sort of expected of us.'

'Do you remember Kevin Molyneux?'

'Oh yes! He was quite a bit older than me, but he used to come to the club, even though he was really too old. He had a learning disability – only we called it *retarded* in those days, or *mentally handicapped* – and we teased him rather a lot, I'm afraid. He didn't seem to mind – or maybe he didn't realise that we were laughing at him.'

'*We* being?' Parkes asked.

'Me and some of the other boys.'

'Any boys in particular?'

'Not really. We were all a bit mean to him. Well, you know what boys are like. Anyway, as I say, Kevin didn't seem to mind. He still seemed to like knocking around with us boys. I heard he was upset when he was told he couldn't come any more.'

'And why was that?' Simms intervened sharply. 'Why was he asked to leave?'

'Only because he was too old,' Norcott shrugged. 'It was supposed to be for eleven to fifteen-year-olds and he was in his twenties, I suppose. I don't know much about it. I just overheard his mum talking to my mum about what a pity it was that he couldn't come any more.'

'Going back to the Boys' Club,' Parkes resumed, looking down at his notebook, where he had recorded key information that Monica Philipson had given to him. 'It was run by a priest, wasn't it?

'That's right – Father O'Leary. He'd been there since before I can remember – probably before I was born – and he'd been running the club for nearly as long, I think.'

'How was he with the boys?'

'What do you mean?' Norcott sounded suddenly defensive. 'He didn't abuse us, if that's what you're thinking. And he was very good with Kevin. He found him little jobs to do that took advantage of his height and physical strength – things like getting the table-tennis tables out of the store cupboard and putting up the Christmas decorations. And I remember one year, the church did a sort of passion play thing around the streets near the church on Good Friday and Kevin was Simon of Cyrene – the guy who's supposed to have carried the cross for Jesus – and he carried a big wooden cross all round the roads, while the choir walked behind him singing.'

'Do you remember the day Kevin went missing?' Parkes asked, changing the subject to avoid losing the goodwill of his witness. 'How did you hear about the incident?'

'Kevin's mum rang my mum asking if we'd seen him. I remember it, because that was the first thing mum said to me when I came in: *have you seen Kevin?*

'When you came in from where?'

'School. I was a bit late home, because I'd been sliding on the snow with some mates on the way back. So I think Mum was starting to get a bit anxious on my account as well, after hearing that Kev was missing.'

'I heard that some boys played truant that day, they were so excited about the snow,' Parkes said blandly. 'You weren't one of them, then?'

'No.'

'Do you know the names of any of the boys who did bunk off school that day?' Parkes asked, noticing that Norcott did not make eye contact as he gave this brief answer.

'No. I don't remember anything about it.' Norcott still did not look up.

'Do the names *Colin Kennedy*, *Robert Lewis* or *Brendan Connolly* mean anything to you?' Parkes pressed his advantage.

'They're all boys from the club. What about them?' Norcott muttered angrily, still apparently studying the surface of the table.

'It has been suggested that they – or perhaps just one or two of them, possibly with other boys from the club – could have met up with Kevin that morning and gone to play in the churchyard together.'

'That's nonsense!' Norcott looked up at last and glared

at Parkes. 'I suppose that whoever it was who *suggested* that also *suggested* that they killed him and hid his body in the boiler room? Why does it have to be anyone connected with the Boys' Club? Anyone could have hidden Kev's body in there. The church was always open. A tramp could've wandered in off the street or anything!'

'Right! That's it!' Jonah declared. 'We're bringing him in. Monica: get on to them to stop the interview and arrange for him to be cautioned and brought over here for questioning right away.'

'Yes sir.' Monica left the room to carry out his instructions. The others continued to watch the interview until it ended abruptly with the entry of a uniformed officer who informed DI Parkes that Thames Valley Police were requesting that the interview be suspended while they updated him on some new developments in the investigation. A few minutes later, the screen went blank.

'I take it you think Timothy Norcott was involved in killing Kevin Molyneux,' Bernie said to Jonah. 'What makes you so sure?'

'Why did he mention the boiler house specifically? There's nothing about that in the news reports.'

'And nothing in anything our investigation has turned up to suggest that it has anything to do with the case,' Bernie pointed out.

'Except that we have been trying to find somewhere hot and dry where the corpse could have been kept,' Andy put in eagerly. 'Is that your idea, sir? That Kevin's body was stored in there first and then moved to the vestry later – after it had mummified?'

'Precisely!' Jonah agreed. 'It all fits. The boys hide the body in the boiler house. It stays there for a few days – just long enough to dry out and mummify – and then Father O'Leary takes it through the interconnecting door to the vestry and hides it in amongst some old altar hangings that nobody ever uses anymore. Anyway, the main thing is that Timothy Norcott clearly knows a whole lot more than he's letting on – even if it's only things that he's heard from some of the other boys. If we can get him here and convince him that it's no good trying to cover it all up any longer, maybe he'll be able to tell us the whole story.'

'Talking of the other boys,' Andy added, 'I've been thinking about what Brendan Connolly told us. 'Did you notice the way he pointed the finger at Lewis and Kennedy, but only after you told him they were both dead?'

'Yes,' Jonah agreed. 'You're right. He probably knows more than he's telling too. He was clearly hoping that by pinning the blame on Lewis and Kennedy he might makes us think there was no one still alive who'd had a hand in the killing. Let's see what we can get out of Norcott and then we'll probably need to have Connolly back in again as well.'

'But why would Father O'Leary hide the body?' Peter asked when Jonah recounted the latest developments over tea that evening. 'Isn't it much more likely that the killer, or killers, hid it?'

'I don't know,' Jonah dismissed the objection, 'to preserve the seal of the confessional perhaps? I don't pretend to know why a Catholic priest would do anything. All I know is that whoever hid the body in the vestry must have been confident that nobody else would ever look in that chest. And who else could be so sure about that? Maybe Father O'Leary was responsible for Kevin's death and Norcott is covering up for him. That seems to be the big problem with this case,' he went on peevishly, 'those Catholics are all closing ranks and refusing to say anything that might throw a bad light on the church or on one of their priests. I'm convinced that half of them aren't telling us all they know. To hear most of them talk, you'd think Father O'Leary was some sort of saint!'

'Perhaps he was,' suggested Lucy innocently. 'There *are* some good people in the world, even if you mainly come across the bad ones.'

'Which is hardly surprising in your line of work,' Bernie added, smiling.

'Of course, you're all the same!' Jonah, unusually for him, missed the joke and continued with his complaint. '*You* were brought up as a Catholic-'

'Only half Catholic,' Bernie interjected. 'Don't forget, I was in the Salvation Army too!'

'You taught Lucy to be a Catholic,' Jonah continued, ignoring the interruption, 'Peter's determined to *become* a Catholic and Dominic's never been anything other than a Catholic. You're all there, reciting your Hail Marys and going along to confession – as if you can't have your sins forgiven without having a priest to wave his hand over you or whatever they do – and worshipping saints and statues and what-have-you, and-'

'Come on, Jonah,' Bernie cut in reproachfully. 'That's just a caricature and you know it. Catholics don't worship saints; they venerate them, which is something completely different – and probably a lot more healthy than the way some people idolise pop stars and footballers. And Confession isn't about the priest forgiving your sins, it's about admitting to having committed them and being given assurance of God's forgiveness.'

'And reciting Hail Marys over and over again? What's the point of that?'

'Tell him about your mantra theory, Dom,' Peter urged the young man.

'I'm not sure you can call it a theory exactly,' Dominic hedged, reluctant to share his thoughts in front of the whole family, and especially Jonah, who seemed , in his present mood, determined to misunderstand anything and everything to do with the Catholic faith. 'It's more just an idea I had to explain ...,' he paused and went rather red in the face as he realised that everyone was hanging on his words, 'well, to explain why saying the Rosary seems to – to … sort of *work*, even though logically it doesn't make a lot of sense.'

'Well there's something I can agree with you about at any rate!' Jonah said heartily; then in a tone of gentle mockery, 'Go on. This is fascinating.'

'I – I – I think the point is …,' Dominic began, now very flustered and feeling that the reputation of the entire Catholic Church depended on him, 'the point is that – that there isn't any point in praying to God in words. I mean, whatever words we use, He knows what we mean already. And anyway, praying isn't just about asking God for what we want, is it? It's about being in the right state of mind to – to – to hear what He's saying to us and – and – well, I told Peter that repeating the same prayers over and over again, in the Rosary for example, is just a way of stopping us thinking about other things and sort of … opening up the channel to God, if you like.'

'But then what's the point of using words at all?' Jonah objected, but sounding interested now rather than hostile. 'If it doesn't matter what they are? If they're just a tool to stop you thinking about other things?'

'I don't think it's quite that the words don't matter,' Dominic said slowly, thinking hard. 'In fact, probably the words do matter a lot, but not so much for communication as for … for creating an atmosphere, maybe.'

'*You* might get on better repeating the *Our Father* over and over,' Bernie suggested. 'Then you don't have to come to terms with the whole business of praying to Mary.'

'If it's all just about creating an atmosphere,' Jonah argued, 'why use words at all? Why not play some calming music or go for a walk in the countryside?'

'Or contemplate a religious picture?' Lucy teased, 'or a statue.'

'Yes, why not?' Dominic answered, more confidently now. 'That's the point I was trying to make. Different people find different things helpful, but one isn't better than another.'

'And I've been to a few prayer meetings in my time that have been every bit as repetitious as the Rosary,' Bernie remarked, determined not to allow Jonah to persist in any claim to intellectual superiority for his own brand of religion. 'There's always someone who insists that *we just want to thank you Lord,* and *we just want to lay before you Lord* …, and *we just bring into your presence Lord* …. And it just makes me think *Oh Lord!*'

'Yes,' Jonah laughed, remembering the lengthy extempore meanderings at the prayer meetings that his father had expected him to attend as a teenager, 'and then there were the ones who always *really, really* wanted to say everything. I suppose you're right, Dom. Each to his own.'

24 DIAGNOSIS

'I don't know why you've brought me here,' Timothy Norcott complained as he stirred sugar into the cup of tea, which Andy Lepage had put down in front of him on the table in the interview room. 'I've already told DI Parkes everything I can remember about Kevin Molyneux's disappearance.'

'But I'm afraid I don't believe you,' Jonah replied. 'I think that you know a whole lot more about what happened to Kevin – or at very least what happened to Kevin's body after he was dead. That is why you have been cautioned and brought here to answer our questions – or not, as is your right. Now, before we go on, are you still sure that you don't want to have a lawyer present? I can get the duty solicitor over here, if you don't have one of your own.'

'No. I don't have anything to hide, so why would I need a solicitor?'

'OK. If you're quite sure.' Jonah thought for a second or two. 'Let's start with your movements on Wednesday 11th January 1978. One of my officers has been trawling through the county archives and has found the attendance registers for your school. It turns out you weren't there that day. Do you want to change your statement at all in the light of that?'

'No.' Norcott looked surprised and flustered, but held his ground. 'I probably didn't get there until after registration. I often missed the bus and didn't get to school until everyone had gone down to assembly.'

'What about afternoon registration?' asked Andy. 'You were marked absent for that too.'

'Ah!' Norcott seemed more sure of himself now. 'Well, I'm afraid I often missed that too. There were a few of us used to go off out to the chip shop at lunch time – we weren't that keen on school dinners – and we often weren't back in time.' Seeing Jonah's sceptical expression, he went on, 'There was a newsagents next to the chip shop where they weren't averse to selling cigarettes to under age kids. There were about half a dozen of us who used to go there and then we'd hang around the bus shelter smoking.'

'I see,' Jonah said smoothly, looking at Norcott with an expression that left him in doubt as to whether or not he believed this explanation. 'And *is* that what you did that day? Or are you just speaking generally?'

'I'm afraid I can't remember. If the register says I wasn't there, then I suppose I must have done.'

'OK. We'll leave it at that for the time being. Tell me about the other boys who used to go with you. Can you remember their names? Were any of them members of the Boys' Club?'

'Yes. I remember Colin Kennedy and Robert Lewis.'

'Any others?' Jonah prompted. 'You said half a dozen. That's only three.'

'Brendan Connolly. He sometimes came. I – I'm sorry I can't remember any of the others.'

'And were any of them with you the day Kevin went missing?'

'I told you: I can't remember.'

'According to Brendan, Colin and Robert bunked off

school that day and went round the back of St Cyprian's church to play snowballs. Are you sure you didn't go with them?'

'Yes.'

'Brendan also says that they took Kevin with them. Do you know anything about that?'

'No.'

'Colin and Robert were your friends. Are you sure they didn't say anything to you afterwards about what they were doing that day?'

'Yes.'

'Please think back and try to remember,' Jonah urged gently. 'It's important that we find out what really happened, for Mrs Molyneux's sake. You liked her, didn't you? She told us all about how helpful you were after Kevin disappeared.'

'Yes ... well ... I was sorry for her – and for her old man. They were awfully cut up about Kevin.'

'And you did what you could to help then, didn't you? She said you used to do odd jobs around the house when her husband was ill and couldn't do them.'

'Like I said, I wanted to help.'

'And now maybe you can help her again,' Jonah persisted gently. 'What she needs now more than anything is to know what happened to Kevin. Is there anything at all that you can remember about it? Anything that Colin or Robert or Brendan said to you?'

Norcott shook his head in silence. Jonah waited.

'Have you talked to Rob and Colin about this?' Norcott asked at last, looking round distrustfully. 'What do they say?'

'Not a lot: they're both dead,' Jonah replied succinctly, 'which is why we are relying on you to tell us what happened.'

'You're kidding, right?' Norcott looked up with an expression of bewilderment on his face. 'They can't be dead. They were no older than me.'

'Accidents happen. People get ill. Lots of people are dead by the time they get to your age.' Jonah paused to let the news sink in. 'So now you can see why we're relying on you to tell us what happened that day. In your interview with DI Parkes, you said that anyone could have killed Kevin and hidden his body in the boiler room at the back of St Cyprian's. What made you pick on the boiler room specifically?'

'Because that's where-,' Norcott began. Then he stopped short and the colour drained from his cheeks. He swallowed twice and looked round at Jonah, Andy and Bernie in turn. 'Are – are you saying that isn't where you found him?'

'I'm saying that the press releases that we gave didn't mention exactly where the body was found, only that it was discovered inside St Cyprian's church.' Jonah told him. 'Now, will you answer my question, please? What made *you* think of the boiler house?'

'I – I – I don't know. I suppose it just seemed like the obvious place, seeing as it had a door from the outside that nobody could see from the church or the house.' Norcott floundered to a halt and sat there looking round nervously and moistening his lips with his tongue.

'Would you like me to ring for the duty solicitor now?' Andy asked helpfully.

'And maybe another cup of tea?' Bernie suggested.

Norcott looked round at them all again. Then he gave a little gulp and shook his head vigorously before leaning forward on the table and laying it down on his arms. The others waited patiently for him to recover himself. After about thirty seconds, he raised his head again and looked towards Jonah.

'You said Mary Molyneux needs to know what happened to Kev – what about Norman?'

'He's been dead for the past twenty years,' Andy told him.

'Kevin's mother is a widow,' Jonah added. 'She's living

221

with a nephew of hers. You may know him: Aidan O'Brien. He remembered you.'

'Yes. I remember Aidan.'

'He said that you and your friends used to bully Kevin. Is that true?'

'Yes,' Norcott answered regretfully. 'I'm afraid it is. We – we didn't understand about his disability. We just thought it was funny a grown man not being able to read or write and not understanding some of the things we said.' He paused and gave a sigh. 'And, I suppose we were a bit afraid of him at the same time. So we bullied him to prove to ourselves that we weren't. Does that make any sense to you?'

'Oh yes!' Jonah assured him. 'That makes perfect sense.'

'But that's all it was,' Norcott insisted. 'We never meant him any real harm. We just …'

'Carry on,' Jonah said quietly when Norcott's voice trailed off into silence. 'You just what?'

'We just teased him, that's all.'

'I think it went further than that. I think that, whatever you meant to do, somehow he died and one of you had the bright idea of hiding his body away in the boiler house. Isn't that what happened, Tim?' Jonah's voice contained a hint of menace in it now.

'No! I told you. I don't know anything about it.'

'Except that you did know about the boiler house. Did one of the others tell you about it? Why didn't you tell anyone else? Didn't you think about Kevin's parents? Didn't you think what it was like for them, not knowing if he was dead or alive? Do you know what his mother said to me the other day – before we were sure it was Kevin there in the church? She said that she hoped it was his body that we'd found because that would be better than thinking that he could be alive somewhere, being kept in dreadful conditions and maybe tortured or abused or forced to-'

'You mean she never knew he was dead?' Norcott burst out. He looked round wildly at each of them in turn, as if willing them to contradict this statement. 'All these years, she thought he might still be alive?'

'Yes, of course. Why would she think otherwise?'

'But didn't Father O'Leary-?' Norcott broke off in confusion and then buried his head in his arms again.

Jonah waited patiently. Andy looked towards him questioningly. Jonah shook his head almost imperceptibly to indicate that he too should remain silent. After several minutes, Norcott sat up again and looked round at them both.

'OK,' he sighed. 'I'll tell you what happened. Could I have a drink of water first?'

'I'll get it.' Bernie got up and left the room. The others waited in uneasy silence until she returned with a plastic cup, which she set down in front of Norcott and filled from a glass jug. He drank eagerly, draining the cup and putting it back down on the table. Bernie silently re-filled it. Norcott put out his hand and drew it closer to him.

'OK,' he said again. 'Here's how it was. Like you said, Colin, Rob and I all bunked off school that day. We'd been doing it on and off for months by then – especially on Wednesdays, because it was double games in the afternoon and the games master was a real sadist. We often used to go round behind St Cyprian's and hang out there. There were some big bushes round there where we could hide and no one would see us. We built a hide-out there.'

'Yes. One of my colleagues found it,' Jonah told him. 'He said you had some orange boxes and a tea chest for furniture.'

'That's right. It was too cold to sit in there that day, so, after we'd tried to build an igloo – which turned out to be more difficult than we thought – and thrown a few snowballs, we went inside the boiler house to keep warm.'

'And Kevin?' Andy prompted. 'Where did he come in?'

'We passed his house on the way to the church. He'd

just finished clearing the snow off the drive with a shovel and he was brushing up the last bits with a big broom. He called out to us as we went past and we stopped and had a chat. He told us that his work was closed because of the snow, so he was staying at home and helping his mum. Rob told him we were going round to the church to clear the snow for Father O'Leary. I don't know why he said that. Kevin said he'd like to come too. I can remember it so clearly …'

Norcott paused and wiped his hand across his face. Then he took a deep breath and continued his story.

'He said, "I'm good at clearing snow." He sounded really proud of himself about it. Rob said he could come with us if he liked, and Kevin said he'd have to tell his mum first; but then Colin said not to bother, because he'd already told her about him going with them to help Father O'Leary. Kev was a bit unsure at first, but Colin sounded so sure of himself that in the end he just stood the broom and the shovel in the porch and came along with us.'

'Why did Colin say that?' asked Andy. 'Why did he pretend that Mrs Molyneux knew about Kevin going with you?'

'I don't know,' Norcott shrugged. 'I suppose he was afraid that she'd realise we were skiving and tell his mum. They were great friends.'

'Alright,' Jonah said quietly. 'Now go on. What happened next?'

'Like I said before, we went round the back of the church and played in the snow; and then we got cold and went into the boiler house to warm up.'

'And that was you, Colin, Robert and Kevin?' Jonah asked. 'Nobody else? Brendan Connolly wasn't there, for instance?'

'No. It was just the three of us and Kevin.'

'So what happened?'

'There was a big pile of coke for the boiler. We started messing about on it, climbing up and sliding down on an old metal tray that Rob had brought for us to use as a toboggan – only we never found anywhere outside that was steep enough for it to slide. Kev got very excited at the idea of sliding down on the tray. We let him have a go and he pushed off hard and slid right down and across the room and the tray hit the wall.'

'Was he hurt?' Jonah asked.

'He banged his arm against the door frame. I don't know how bad it was, but Kev went very white and took hold of it with his other hand. The tray was all bent and buckled. Rob went ballistic when he saw it. He shouted at Kev that he'd broken it and his – that's Rob's – mum would go spare. I don't think she knew he'd borrowed it. We tried to straighten it back out again, but our efforts only made things worse. Kev said he'd pay for it, but Rob said, no, that wasn't good enough, Kev had to have a proper punishment.'

Norcott took another long draught from the plastic cup. Jonah waited in silence for him to continue.

'There was this long-handled shovel standing up against the wall. The caretaker used to use it to put coke into the furnace that heated the boiler. Rob got hold of it and started hitting Kevin with it. Then Colin went through the door into the vestry and got the candle snuffer – it was a brass one on the end of a wooden pole – and gave Kev a beating with that too. Kev didn't fight back; he just sat there whimpering and saying how sorry he was about the tray.'

'Which arm was it that Kevin hurt?' Jonah asked. 'Can you remember?'

'It was the right one,' Norcott answered surprisingly readily. 'I know that because, when Rob got bored with hitting him, he came up with the idea that he ought to make a proper confession and Kev tried to cross himself and he couldn't because of his arm.'

'That figures,' Andy murmured, looking across at Bernie, who had the post mortem report displayed on her computer screen. 'He'd fractured one of the bones in his arm. It must've been very painful for him to move it.'

'We didn't know that,' Norcott said quickly. 'Not that it would have made any difference, I don't suppose,' he added with a sigh, running his hand over his face, which had become very red and was moist with sweat. 'I don't know why we did it; I really don't.'

'What happened next?' asked Jonah, after a lengthy silence, during which Norcott continued to wipe his face with both hands.

'I'm not sure exactly. At least ... I can't remember exactly how it happened. The next I can remember was Kevin sitting right at the top of the coke pile hugging his arm to him and Colin and Rob standing over him laughing. Then the coke shifted and Rob fell down and slid to the bottom. I think Colin fell over too. And Kev ...'

'Yes?' prompted Jonah. 'What happened to Kevin?'

'Do you remember the long scarf that Dr Who used to wear back in the seventies?'

Andy looked blank, but Jonah nodded. He remembered the popular science-fiction television series well.

'Tom Baker, you mean?'

'That's right. Well, Kevin was a big fan of the doctor and his mum had knitted him a scarf like that one. It must've been twelve foot long at least. Kev had it on that day. It was wound round his neck two or three times and then it dangled down to his feet on either side. When the coke shifted ... when Kevin started to slide down ...' Norcott appeared reluctant to complete this sentence.

'Yes?' Jonah said encouragingly. 'What happened then?'

'I don't know exactly,' Norcott repeated. 'I suppose the scarf got caught on something. All I know is: the next thing we knew, there was Kevin slid halfway down the coke pile and his face was turning a funny blue colour. I – I'm afraid we thought it was funny at first. And then ... when he stopped thrashing about and lay still and his face started to look all sort of swollen and weird, we ...'

'Yes?' said Jonah again. 'What did you do then?'

'We started to get frightened and we tried to get the scarf off him, but we couldn't. It was pulled tight round his neck. Colin said we ought to push him back up the coke pile so it would go slack, but we couldn't shift him. In the end, Rob got a pair of scissors from the vestry and cut through the scarf and Kev rolled down to the bottom of the pile. We tried to wake him up, but he just lay there, all blue in the face.'

He stopped speaking and laid his head down on the table again, with his arms around it. In the silence that followed, they could hear the whirring of the machine recording the interview and the ticking of a clock on the wall.

'OK,' Jonah said in a matter-of-fact voice. 'Eventually you all realised that he was dead. What did you do then?'

'We didn't know what to do. Rob said we ought to go and get Father O'Leary and ask him to give Kev extreme unction. He said that's what his mum did when his gran died. But Colin said we mustn't tell anyone because then they'd see the bruises where we'd hit him and they'd think we killed him.'

Norcott paused and seemed to be picturing the scene in his mind. He ran his fingers through his hair and gazed up at the ceiling for a minute or more before going on.

'In the end, we looked round for somewhere to hide him. We found a sort of cubbyhole thing behind where the furnace was, and we somehow managed to get Kev's body into there. And we shovelled in some coke to cover it up. We stuffed his scarf inside the furnace, and then we found his coat lying on the floor where he'd taken it off when we came in, because it was quite hot in the boiler room. So we shoved that in too and pushed it into the middle of the fire with the shovel. We were hoping to stop anyone finding Kev for long enough that nobody would think about us being there when it happened. It never occurred to us that it would be thirty-odd years before he was found.'

'And when did Father O'Leary hear about what had happened?' Jonah asked.

'What do you mean?'

'At some point, Father O'Leary took Kevin's body out of where you'd put it, wrapped it in an altar cloth and hid it in a chest in the vestry,' Andy told him. 'Why would he do that?'

'I –I – I -,' Norcott looked round in disbelief. 'You're kidding me, right?'

'Wrong,' Jonah said firmly. 'And then, after Father O'Leary died, another priest found the body in among his things and hid it again. Can you throw any light on why they would do that?'

'Another priest? You're talking about Father Carey, right?'

'That's right,' Jonah confirmed.

'What does he say about it?'

'I'm asking the questions. When did you tell Father O'Leary what happened?'

Norcott sat in silence. Seconds passed, then minutes. Jonah waited patiently. He was about to repeat his question when Norcott took a deep breath and launched into his story.

'Colin made us both swear that we'd never tell *anyone* about what happened. For a day or two, I was too scared of him to say a word. But when the police came round asking about Kevin, and my mum kept on about how dreadful it must be for his mum and dad, and …,' he paused to drain his second cup of water. 'I went to Confession on the Saturday afternoon, and I told Father O'Leary all about it – except that I didn't say who the others were, just that they were some of the boys from the club. I expect he could guess within a couple of names though.'

'And what did he say?' Jonah asked.

'Why didn't he inform the police?' demanded Andy.

'He said that I'd committed a mortal sin and I must show my contrition by helping Kevin's mum and dad. I asked if that meant I had to tell them what we'd done, and he said no, they didn't need to know why I was doing it, I just had to be truly penitent and to act in charity towards them.'

'But what about telling the police?' Andy persisted.

'He said to leave everything to him and he'd see that it was all OK. I didn't know about him hiding the body. I just thought nobody must have looked round the back of the furnace. I assumed that was where you found him.'

'And what about Kevin's mum?' Andy demanded angrily. 'If it had been me, my mum would have been demented, worrying about what had happened. How could you all leave her like that, not knowing?'

'I – I thought Father O'Leary would have told her,' Norcott stammered. 'That's what I meant, when I said ... I mean, he told me he'd see to everything, and nobody need know who did it. I assumed that he'd have told her that Kev was dead but that he couldn't reveal who did it. I never knew ...'

Jonah leaned his head back and contemplated the ceiling, pursing his lips in thought. Then he looked towards Norcott again.

'Alright,' he said at last, 'I think we'll call it a day for now. Interview terminated at eleven forty-six.'

25 FAITH HEALING

'May we come in, Mary?' Father Damien asked, putting his head round the door of her sitting room and then advancing towards her without waiting for an answer. 'DCI Porter has some news for you.'

'Yes, of course. Make yourselves at home.' Mary Molyneux stuck her needle into the embroidery that she was working on and put it down on the low windowsill next to her chair. 'Aidan! Why don't you get us all some tea?'

'Right you are, Aunty!'

Her nephew went into the kitchen to do her bidding, while Jonah and Bernie followed Father Damien into the living room. Father Damien sat down in a chair close to Mary, facing her across the window. Jonah brought his wheelchair into a position where he could speak to her easily. Bernie took up an unobtrusive position some distance away on the sofa.

'Mrs Molyneux,' Jonah began. 'As the father says, we have some news. We think we know how Kevin died.'

'What do you know?' she asked eagerly. 'Did he suffer? Who …?'

'One of the boys who were there when it happened told us about it. We can't be sure that all the details are right, but what he said fitted in with what we already knew.'

'Boys? Was that why you were asking about the club? Was it some of them?'

'Yes. I'm afraid it was. The way he told it, they didn't mean to do him any serious harm – certainly not to kill him – but they did deliberately hit him about a bit and make fun of him.'

'And how did he …?'

'It looks as if the pathologist was right in saying that the crushed vertebrae suggested that he might have been strangled. Was he wearing a scarf that day, do you remember?'

'Yes. He had a long knitted scarf, all different colours. I made it for him. He was a great fan of Dr Who. Do you remember it? The doctor back then used to wear a long scarf and I made one like it for Kevin. Was that … was that what strangled him?'

'According to our witness, it got caught up on a hook on the wall of the boiler house, where they were playing on a big pile of coke, and when he slipped it went tight round his neck and they couldn't get it off.'

'So it was an accident?' There was relief in Mary Molyneux's voice.

'According to our witness, yes,' Jonah told her. He debated in his mind whether to mention his own suspicions that Timothy Norcott had been playing down both his own involvement in the incident and the intentions of the boys towards Kevin. Before he could decide how much to tell her, Mary was speaking again.

'And who was it?' she asked. 'Or aren't you allowed to tell me?'

'We've been speaking to Timothy Norcott, and he says that the others were Robert Lewis and Colin Kennedy. They're both dead, so they can't corroborate Norcott's story.'

'I told you Tim Norcott had it in for Kevin, didn't I?' said Aidan, coming in with the tea. 'He and Colin and Brendan were always bullying him.'

'He was very good to us,' Mary insisted. 'He used to come round every weekend and work in the garden while Norman was ill. And he used to do shopping for me, so that I didn't have to go out and leave him in the house on his own.'

'I think that was in remorse for what happened to Kevin,' Jonah told her. 'He felt guilty about it, even though he claims it wasn't deliberate.'

'If it was really an accident, why didn't they tell anyone about it?' Aidan demanded angrily. He had put the tea tray down on top of a glass-fronted cabinet that stood at the side of the room, and now stood in front of it looking towards Jonah. 'Why did they hide the body and pretend they didn't know anything about it? I remember it all, as if it was yesterday. Those three were all there – and Brendan too – pretending to be helping when we had everyone out searching the fields and woodland for him. Why did they let Aunt Mary and Uncle Norman carry on thinking he might be alive?'

'Hush Aidan!' his aunt reproved him gently. 'I expect they were frightened. They were only young boys, remember.'

'They were old enough to know better,' Aidan insisted. 'And I bet it was all their fault that Kevin died. They always had it in for him.'

'Whatever they intended, I think we can be fairly certain that they regretted what happened,' Father Damien interposed. 'Colin killed himself, remember? And Rob took to drink. I'm not saying that they weren't to blame or that they got justice, but it seems to me that they did suffer for what they'd done.'

'And what about Tim?' Aidan asked belligerently. 'Where's he now?'

'At this precise moment,' Jonah responded quickly, 'he's in one of our police cells, waiting to be charged with *prevention of the lawful and decent burial of a dead body*. He may also be charged with *assault and causing grievous bodily harm* and *perverting the course of justice*.'

'I meant, what's he been doing while we've all been left wondering what happened to Kevin?'

'He's been working with antisocial teenagers, trying to get them back on the straight and narrow.'

'There you are, Aidan!' Mary said with satisfaction in her voice. 'I always knew he was a good boy at heart.'

'That's all very well,' Aidan growled, still unconvinced, 'but that doesn't change what he did to Kevin – and to you and Uncle Norman. Uncle Norman died without ever knowing what happened. I don't care what he's done since; he should've told you that Kevin was dead and let you give him a decent burial, instead of hiding him away in the church like that and leaving you to imagine that Kev had been taken away to some sweatshop or – or ...'

'Well, I'm just glad we've heard the truth now,' his aunt said firmly, as Aidan trailed off into incoherence. 'And Norman may not have known before he died, but I'm sure he does now.' She turned to Jonah. 'Thank you for coming to tell me. I'm glad I found out now, before Good Friday and Easter.'

'I'll add Kevin's name to the intentions for the Easter Vigil,' Father Damien promised her. 'And Norman too.'

'Thank you.' Mary thought for a moment. 'And could you include those boys too – Tim and Colin and Robert?'

'What!' Aidan exploded. 'You must be joking Aunty. After what they did to Kev, they don't deserve-'

'I know what I want,' his aunt cut in gently but firmly. 'I'm going to be praying for the souls of Colin and Robert and for Tim. The worse their sins, the more they need our prayers, don't you see?'

'I'm not sure about naming the boys,' Father Damien said, looking towards Jonah a little anxiously. 'Their

233

involvement in Kevin's death isn't being made public yet and people might start drawing their own conclusions if they see them in a list with Kevin. Perhaps we could let them be included anonymously in the "parishioners' intentions" at the first mass on Easter Sunday morning?'

'Or how about just saying, "the boys from St Cyprian's who knew Kevin"?' suggested Bernie. 'Or "all those affected by his death"?'

'I suppose that will have to do,' Mary sounded reluctant. 'I'd like their names to be read out, but if that isn't allowed ...'

'Maybe later,' Father Damien suggested. 'Why not wait for a few weeks, until it's all in the public domain? It will make it more special for Kevin and Norman, won't it – if it's just them on Saturday?'

'I suppose so,' Mary still sounded disappointed. 'But I did want ... I would like to know that I've done all I can for those boys. I want to be sure that I've shown them proper Christian forgiveness. And Tim,' she turned suddenly from her musing to Father Damien and addressed Jonah. 'What will happen to him?'

'As I said, he'll be charged. Then he'll probably be released on bail while we continue our investigations. The Crown Prosecution Service will decide in the end which offences to try him for.'

'Can I see him?'

'Meet him, you mean?' Jonah asked.

'Yes. I'd like him to tell me himself what happened and I'd like him to know ... that I still appreciate what he did for us afterwards.'

'Aunty!' Aidan remonstrated. 'Get real, can't you? He's not a sweet little boy running errands for you anymore.'

'Inspector?' Mary looked at Jonah, waiting for a reply.

'I'm afraid that wouldn't be appropriate. Afterwards – when he's been tried and sentenced, then we can look into the Restorative Justice programme if you like.'

'Will he go to jail?'

'I honestly don't know,' Jonah shook his head. 'I've never come across a case like this before. If he'd been arrested at the time, all three boys would have ended up in youth custody. As it is ... well, I just don't know. He'll probably plead guilty to some, if not all, of the charges, which will be in his favour; and his exemplary behaviour over the last thirty-odd years will help him too. With a good lawyer, he may be able to convince the court that he was under the thumb of the other boys and was hardly more than an onlooker – and too scared to go to the police to report what happened.'

'But that's disgusting!' Aidan burst out indignantly. 'Are you telling us he may get away scot free?'

'No. I'm simply answering your aunt's question about whether or not he'll get a custodial sentence; and the short answer is: I don't know. He may be given a community sentence and he'll certainly end up with a criminal record, which will probably lose him his job, and possibly his pension as well, if they decide that he lied on his application.'

'It doesn't seem much, considering what he put us all through,' Aidan muttered angrily.

'Please Aidan, try to be more charitable,' his aunt urged him gently. 'They were only young boys, and it's our Christian duty to try to forgive. I'm sorry,' she turned to Jonah again. 'Thank you for coming, but I think it would be better if you went now. I'm sure you have a lot to do.'

'Yes. Of course.' Jonah turned to go. 'We can show ourselves out.'

Bernie, following his lead, got up and went to open the door for him.

'Would you like me to stay with you for a while?' asked Father Damien, rising from his chair too.

'No thank you Father. I think I'd rather have some time on my own; and I know you're very busy, with it being Easter.'

They walked down the garden path together and stopped on the pavement alongside Andy's car. Bernie had parked theirs at St Cyprian's when she and Jonah had called there to ask Father Damien to come with them to see Kevin's mother.

'I didn't tell Mrs Molyneux about Father O'Leary's involvement,' Jonah said to Father Damien, 'because I didn't want to distress her more than I had to. But I have to ask you: what would make a man of God conceal a young man's death and protect his tormentors? Why didn't he tell the police? And why did he hide the body?'

'I can't speak for Father O'Leary,' Father Damien began, speaking slowly but thinking very rapidly. 'I don't know the exact circumstances or what he may have been thinking. I suppose he felt that he couldn't tell anyone what Timothy Norcott had told him, because it was covered by the seal of confession.'

'But surely he could still have told the police where the body was – even if he gave the impression that he had just stumbled across it by chance?' Jonah insisted. 'If he'd told them right away, they might have been able to identify Kevin's attackers from forensic evidence. He wasn't just refusing to betray a confidence; he was actively covering up for the perpetrators of a crime.'

'And what about Kevin's mum and dad?' Andy demanded fiercely. He was very close to his own mother, who had brought him up single-handed after her unfortunate love affair with a postgraduate student from Nigeria, and he was enraged at the thought of Mary Molyneux being left in suspense for so long, unsure whether her son was dead or alive. 'How could anyone justify keeping it secret from them?'

'Andy's right,' Bernie agreed. 'That's the bit I can't understand. And he was always there at their house too! In Richard's diaries, every time he talks about going to see Mr and Mrs Molyneux, he says that the priest was there with them. How could he keep going along there like that after he knew where their son's body was and could have put them out of their misery by telling them?'

'I don't know,' Father Damien repeated. He was feeling extremely uncomfortable and conscious that his own faith and the reputation of the Church that he represented were being called into question. 'I suppose that he must have wanted to protect those boys, and his concern for them clouded his judgement.'

'But even Norcott thought he ought to have told Kevin's parents,' Bernie argued. 'Did you notice that, Jonah? Did you see how surprised he looked when you told him Mrs Molyneux still didn't know if Kevin was alive or dead? I'm sure he thought that Father O'Leary would have told them, in confidence, that he'd been killed.'

'I'm sorry,' Father Damien said, 'I really can't explain what he did. I can only think that he acted out of a misguided attempt to protect the boys. They *were* very young.'

'Old enough to know what they were doing,' Andy insisted uncompromisingly. 'I agree with Mrs Molyneux's nephew on that one.'

'But with their whole lives before them.' Father Damien felt obliged to make an effort to account for his predecessor's behaviour. 'I suppose he may have been afraid that they would spend the rest of their lives in jail for killing Kevin.'

'According to Norcott, they didn't kill him,' Jonah reminded him. 'They just roughed him up a bit and then weren't quick enough to cut him free when his scarf got caught and strangled him.'

'But that may not be the story he told his confessor,' Bernie said suddenly. 'Maybe he told Father O'Leary that they murdered Kevin. And maybe they did.'

'Surely that would make him more likely to want to hand them over to the police, not less, wouldn't it?' Andy asked in puzzlement. 'Wouldn't he want them locked up to stop them doing it to anyone else?'

'You might think so,' Father Damien answered, 'but I can see what Bernie's getting at. Father O'Leary knew those boys. He may have thought that he knew them well enough to be sure that they wouldn't do it again. I'm afraid that, back then, priests did have a tendency to believe that they knew best about a lot of things. I hope that we're a bit less arrogant now. I think I can imagine a priest of Father O'Leary's generation being convinced that he could deal with the boys better through the confessional than the police could through the criminal justice system.'

'It didn't work though, did it?' Andy argued belligerently. 'One of them killed himself, another became an alcoholic. They might just as well have been serving a life sentence, and Kevin's mum would have been saved all those years of not knowing.'

'I'm not saying he was justified in what he did. I'm just saying I think I can understand how it might have happened – back then, with the mind-set we used to have in those days.'

'And now you're going to say a few prayers for Kevin's soul and everything will be put right again?' Andy found himself saying in a sneering voice. Then, as soon as the words were out of his mouth, he regretted having allowed his feelings to impair his judgement. It was most improper for a police officer to appear to be mocking the beliefs of a member of the public.

'No. It's not like that at all.' Father Damien did not sound offended, more embarrassed, Andy thought. 'Mary Molyneux will undoubtedly gain comfort from knowing that our Easter Vigil Mass is being offered for the repose of Kevin's soul. And the congregation will be pleased that they are being given an opportunity to show their concern for her. And who knows what power God can release through her forgiveness of the boys who hurt her son. But no, everything won't be put right. I just hope it may help us all to live better with the consequences, that's all.'

'It's nearly the end of your shift, Andy,' Jonah said quietly. 'Why don't you get off home now? It's not worth going back to the station when you're so close. I'm taking the morning off tomorrow, because it's Good Friday, so can you bring the files up to date? And we'll try to get this case wrapped up tomorrow afternoon.'

'Yes sir.' Andy got into his car and drove off. The others watched him go and then set off on the short walk back to St Cyprian's church.

'So you don't really think that saying a mass for Kevin's soul will do anything more than comfort his mother?' Jonah asked as they made their way along the road. 'I thought you Catholics believed that you had to do those things to get people out of purgatory.'

'If I didn't believe that the Mass was more than just something comforting for old ladies, I wouldn't still be a priest,' Father Damien answered with a smile. 'I assumed that your sergeant was probably a modern young man with no time for religion and I tried to answer his question in a way that would be intelligible to him.'

'So, is Kevin in Purgatory? And will your prayers shorten his punishment?'

'It's not for us to know where Kevin's soul is at this moment in time – if, indeed, time is a meaningful concept in the context of eternity – and Purgatory isn't about punishment, it's about purification or purging, as the name suggests. It describes the necessary process that our souls go through to make them ready for heaven.'

'I was taught that that was all decided before we die – and then revealed on the Day of Judgement.'

'Decided perhaps, but just because you're welcome in heaven it doesn't mean you're ready for it. It's …,' Father Damien sought an example to illustrate what he wanted to say. 'It's like when you joined the police force. You did an interview or passed a test or whatever, and then you had to go on training courses to make you ready to do the job. Purgatory's a bit like that. It's getting your soul in trim so that it's fit to be in the presence of God.'

'Someone told me once that this idea of souls living on after we're dead was something that the church picked up from the Greek philosophers and that what Jesus taught was the resurrection of the body.'

'I don't think we can be sure exactly what Jesus thought about it. There's not a lot of evidence that he said much on the subject. Most likely, he followed the Jewish beliefs of the time, which, as you probably know, were varied – the Pharisees and the Sadducees, for example had differing opinions. I can only tell you what the Catholic Church believes – or at least how I interpret it – which is that human beings are a combination of a physical body and a spiritual soul. Death marks the separation of the two. After death, the body decays, but the soul is eternal. The Day of Judgement, as you call it, marks the point when all the souls are given new bodies – the "heavenly bodies" that St Paul speaks about to the Church in Corinth.'

'It's not just Catholics who believe in people having souls,' Bernie added. 'Plenty of Protestants do too. Charles Wesley, for example.' She began to sing, '*A charge to keep I have, a God to glorify, a never-dying soul to save and fit it for the sky.* Not one of his best, in my opinion. For a start, someone ought to have pointed out to him that "have" doesn't rhyme with "save". But you see what I mean? It's not just ignorant peasants who've swallowed the whole soul-and-body idea.'

They had reached the church by now and were standing in the car park next to their car. Bernie unlocked it and started setting up the ramp for Jonah to get in.

'And getting back to Father O'Leary,' Jonah said, turning to Father Damien again. 'Are you suggesting that he might have been more concerned for the welfare of those boys' souls than for the Molyneux family's peace of mind?'

'Not exactly.' Father Damien paused and let out a soft sigh. 'But, yes, I'm afraid there is something in what you say. I think that he may have seen himself as responsible for – for their spiritual welfare, I suppose, and not accountable to the secular authorities. And we don't know exactly what Norcott told him, do we? He may not have named the other boys. Father O'Leary may have wanted to wait, to give them a chance to confess to him too.'

'Yes. You're right about that,' Jonah agreed. 'Norcott only named them *after* he knew they were both dead. It makes me wonder whether there could have been any more of them involved that he *hasn't* named – Brendan Connolly, for example. Everyone seems to think that he was part of their gang too. I'm not at all sure that we are ever going to know what really happened.'

26 HEART OPERATION

When he entered the church, Father Damien found Peter waiting for him. He was sitting in his accustomed place near the statue of the Virgin and Child. On his lap lay a booklet entitled *Examination of conscience before confession: a guide for adults*. The priest hurried forward to greet him.

'I'm sorry, Peter; I completely forgot you were coming. I've been with the police to see Mary Molyneux. I suppose you know one of the boys who hid Kevin's body has confessed?'

'I knew they were bringing him over from somewhere in East Anglia in the hope that he might. What exactly has he confessed to? I mean – did he actually admit to killing Kevin?'

'No. Not quite. Apparently, he claims it was an accident – something to do with Kevin's scarf getting caught on something and pulling tight round his neck. But he did admit to hiding the body in the boiler house and to confessing to Father O'Leary a few days later.'

'He told Father O'Leary?' Peter exclaimed. 'Then why didn't Father O'Leary tell the police where to find the body?'

'That's exactly what Sergeant Lepage said – and DCI Porter. It looks like Father O'Leary then went on to move the body to a more secure hiding place in the vestry.'

'And then Father Carey moved it again when he found it,' Peter added thoughtfully. 'But why?'

'I don't know. That's what I've just been trying to explain to the police. I could only manage a rather feeble suggestion that times have changed and attitudes were very different then. I can only imagine that the two priests both thought that they were giving the boys a better chance of coming to repentance and a new life by keeping what happened secret, rather than putting them through a court of law.'

'But if it was an accident, what did they have to repent of? And what had they to fear from the law?'

'I gather they did beat Kevin up before he died. And they didn't do much to help him when his scarf got stuck.'

'Or maybe they did kill him – and admit as much to Father O'Leary – and the story about the scarf is just Norcott's last ditch attempt to get himself off the hook now he's been found out.'

'Yes. That's what Bernie said.'

'But then, wouldn't that be all the more reason to hand them over to the police and let justice be done?'

'I know.' Father Damien shook his head. '*I* can't justify what Father O'Leary did either. And I could see that Sergeant Lepage was very unimpressed at me trying. I'm afraid the reputation of the Catholic Church is at rock-bottom as far as he's concerned, at the moment. And I'm not sure that DCI Porter thinks much better of us either.'

'Jonah?' Peter laughed briefly; then he became suddenly serious. 'I'm afraid he's never had a lot of time for Catholicism. He thinks pictures and statues are graven images and veneration of saints is idolatry. His father was a Baptist minister, and he was brought up in a rather strict, puritanical household as far as I can make out. I've never seen it, but I imagine their church was one of those little four-square chapels, very austere with a big central pulpit, plain glass in the windows and Bible verses on the walls – probably the Ten Commandments.'

'And what would there be in that for someone like Kevin?' Father Damien asked. 'Someone who couldn't read or write or understand complicated sermons? And yet, your DCI Porter wouldn't question the need to install a wheelchair ramp at the door to help people with physical disabilities.'

'I'd never thought of that.' Peter considered this for a few moments. 'But that isn't why you – we – have pictures and statues, is it? They were there long before people started to think about accessibility and diversity and catering for people with learning disabilities.'

'They were put there when hardly anyone could read or write and when the services were in a language that they couldn't understand. In other words, when practically everyone was like Kevin as far as religion was concerned.'

'I suppose Jonah would say that a better answer was to have the services in the language that everyone spoke and to educate them to read and write.'

'Which is all well and good, but the danger is that a lot gets lost in the process – including having something for those who haven't learnt to read or aren't able to. Aren't lots of Protestant churches starting to see the value of visual aids, these days?'

'Yes. You're right. Our Methodist church has lots of banners, and there's one preacher who always brings a stock of candles for people to light during the prayers of intercession.'

'There you are then!'

'But the banners tend to be on biblical themes and they're often a bit abstract. I think they might still be a bit wary of pictures of saints. And that's what Jonah really can't understand. Although,' Peter laughed, 'come to think of it, there is a bust of John Wesley in the vestry!'

'I used to have a poster of Kevin Keegan[13] on my

bedroom wall when I was a kid.' Father Damien joined in the laughter. 'We all have our heroes. We just have to try not to let them become idols; that's all. Now, I'm sorry to rush you, but are you ready to start? I've got a few things that I need to do before the Mass of Our Lord's supper this evening.'

'I'm as ready as I'll ever be. And I need to get on too. I've left the kids with Bernie's cousin Dominic and I don't think he'll be best pleased if he's still saddled with them when Lucy gets home from school. He's staying with us for a few days, ostensibly to see me confirmed but really in the hope of spending some time with her, and he volunteered to look after them. He didn't seem to think it was appropriate to have them listening in on their grandfather's confession – although they're too young to take much notice.'

They crossed the side aisle and went into the larger of the two confessionals. One of Father Damien's first acts, when he took charge after Father Callaghan retired, had been to take out the screen separating priest and penitent to make a more modern confession room. It had comfortable seats, lighting that could be dim or bright according to need and a small table on which stood a crucifix, a candle and a vase of fresh flowers.

Peter sat down, feeling rather nervous and fiddling with the leaflet in his hand. Father Damien took a box of matches from a shelf that ran along the side of the room and lit the candle. He replaced the box and sat down facing Peter across the table. Peter looked down at his hands and hastily slipped the leaflet into his pocket.

'I'm not sure how to begin.'

'There's no right or wrong way, but if you're unsure you may find that following the usual form of words helps.

---

[13] Kevin Keegan was a football player and manager who played for several English clubs and in the national team during the seventies and eighties.

That's what liturgy is for – to help us when we don't know what to say. So we begin with the sign of the cross.'

They both crossed themselves – Peter still feeling rather awkward as he did so – and said together, 'In the Name of the Father and of the Son and of the Holy Spirit. Amen.'

'Good,' said Father Damien. 'And now you know the words to get you started, don't you?'

'Forgive me Father, for I have sinned,' Peter began. 'This is my first confession … and that's where I get stuck,' he admitted shamefaced. 'It was always the same in church, when they had prayers of confession at the beginning of the service. I was never much good at thinking of specific things I'd done. It was always more just a general feeling that I could have done better. Things like not giving as much to charity as I could have, or not getting round to volunteering at the Food Bank and then there was the whole *God* business. I used to feel guilty, when I was younger, about not reading the Bible or saying my prayers, but then I started to think God probably didn't exist anyway, so praying would have been hypocritical. If I'm confessing the sins of a lifetime, should it be my disbelief or not going through the motions that I ought to be concentrating on?'

'Let's go back a stage, shall we? You prepared for this by examining your conscience, didn't you? And by praying for guidance?'

'Ye-es,' Peter admitted hesitantly.

'And what sins did your conscience convict you of?'

'That's just it – I can't really think of that many, apart from just not doing as much to help other people as I could have done. I know that sounds arrogant, but … well that leaflet you gave me, wasn't really a big help. It took me through the Ten Commandments, but well … to be honest, all the examples it gave were either things I never do or things I find hard to think are really that bad – or both!'

'Can you give me an example?'

'Taking the Lord's name in vain. I don't swear, but that's only because it doesn't come naturally to me. I was brought up that way. It's no credit to me. But I've never been able to see the harm in it – except when it's done deliberately to offend people.'

'I see.' Father Damien thought for a moment or two. 'How about letting me help you to get started?'

'Yes please.'

'How are things between you and your mother?'

'My m-mother?' Peter stammered, taken aback at this sudden question.

'You were harbouring resentment against her.'

'Yes. The thing is …,' Peter paused, unsure how to go on. 'There's a bit more to it than I told you before. It's not just Valerie that's the problem – it's her daughter, Jane.'

'Your sister.'

'Yes, if you like,' Peter muttered irritably. Then he stopped short and smiled ruefully at Father Damien. 'I'm sorry. Yes. My sister Jane wrote to me only last week. That's what set me off thinking about them both. She's divorced – she has been for years, since long before I met her – and now she's planning to marry again.'

'And?'

'And she's asked me to give her away.'

'And?'

'My first reaction was to throw the letter in the bin without even reading it. We'd agreed, you see; we'd promised each other not to get in touch. Then when I found out what she wanted I …,' Peter sighed, 'I wanted to tell her to go way and get lost and stop persecuting me. But … I was afraid that I was just taking out my anger towards Valerie on her … so I wondered if maybe I *ought* to do it. But I don't see how I can without Eddie and Hannah finding out, and I don't want them to know what Valerie said about them.'

'Do they need to know? Even if you do tell them about

Valerie and Jane?'

'I'll have to give them some explanation for not letting them meet their grandmother before she died.'

'So, what did you say to your sister?'

'Nothing yet.'

'Have you decided if you'll do what she's asking?'

'No. Well, yes. I – I think I'll probably do it for her – if she still wants me.'

'You *think* you will?'

'Yes. I've decided really. I know I won't be able to live with myself if I refuse. I just can't quite bring myself to … well … I suppose I don't want to commit myself – to not be able to change my mind. But you're right. I shouldn't leave her in suspense any longer. I'll send her an email this evening.'

'Do it now.'

'What do you mean?'

'You've got your phone with you. Email her now – or send a text. Just a short note will do. You can follow it up with a proper message later.'

Peter got out his phone. Then he fumbled in his pocket for Jane's letter, which he was still carrying with him, to copy her email address into his *Contacts* list. Father Damien waited patiently while he typed a short message and sent it off into the ether.'

'Good. Now, tell me: have you forgiven your mother?'

'I'm working on it.'

'That's fine. Have you been keeping her in your prayers?'

'I've been dedicating one decade of the rosary each day to the repose of her soul.'

'And has that been helping – helping you, I mean?'

'Sometimes.' Peter paused, unsure whether to say more. 'Sometimes, I just get angry with her. I just can't understand how anyone could say the things she said.'

'Forgiving isn't about understanding. It's just *because* there is no excuse for her behaviour that you need to forgive.'

'I suppose it would be easier if she'd been at all sorry about it.'

'Did you give her any opportunity to be sorry?'

'No. I suppose not. Is that something else I have to confess to you?'

'You just did.'

27 APPOINTMENT CARD

'I'm sorry to disturb you so late,' Peter apologised as soon as Father Damien opened the presbytery door, 'but I just had to show you this!'

He held up his phone, turning it so that the priest could see that there was a photograph displayed on the screen.

'You'd better come in.' He stepped back, opening the door wide to admit his visitor.

'It won't take a minute,' Peter assured him. 'I wouldn't call at this sort of time normally, but I know you'll be busy tomorrow and all over the weekend, and I wanted you to see it.'

'Come into the study and sit down and tell me what this is all about.' Father Damien smiled at the excitement in Peter's voice, quite unlike his usual staid and steady manner.

Peter followed him into the study and they both sat down in their accustomed places around the table. Peter held out his phone again and this time Father Damien could see that the photograph was a head-and-shoulders picture of a dark-skinned man. His frizzy black hair had small traces of grey at the temples. His mouth was open in a smile, which showed off large white teeth. His deep brown eyes were shining.

'Jane sent me this when she got my email,' Peter explained. 'It's her fiancé, Jude Kimbugwe. His family were refugees from Idi Amin's Uganda, back in the '70s.' Peter swiped the screen and another picture appeared. It was of two young black women standing with their arms around each another's shoulders. 'These are his daughters Keziah and Dorcas. Keziah – the older one – is a Church of England vicar in Bradford. Dorcas is a Physics lecturer at Sheffield University, and she's married to another lecturer there. Jude is a primary school head teacher – like Jane. They met at a teachers' in-service training course.'

Father Damian gazed down at the screen for several seconds without speaking. He was trying to formulate some words that would express his pleasure that Peter's decision to accept Jane's invitation had produced such a satisfactory result, without any implied criticism of him for needing to be prompted to act.

'She said that she didn't tell me about Jude before, because she didn't want me to feel that I *had* to agree to give her away just because he was black,' Peter went on, apparently oblivious of Father Damien's lack of response. 'I showed the pictures to Eddie when he came to collect the kids this afternoon and I've forwarded them to Hannah as well. They both seem quite excited about the idea of having some new relatives.'

'And what have you told them about their grandmother?'

'Nothing yet – only that she and Jane's father are both dead, so I'm her only living relative. I haven't said anything about meeting Jane before. I've just allowed them to assume that she hunted me down in order to ask me to come to her wedding. I will tell them, but I'll need to pick a time when I can explain properly.'

'And how do *you* feel about your mother? Has this changed anything?'

'I don't know.' Peter paused to think. 'I suppose it's nice to know that she didn't pass on her odious views to her daughter. Maybe if I'd tried properly to explain to her – to get her to change – instead of just walking out like that …,' he sighed. 'I'm sorry. I'd like to be able to tell you that I've forgiven her and everything is OK now, but I just can't get out of my head the way she looked when she saw Hannah's photograph. And all that stuff about *couldn't I have found a nice white girl* …?'

'Don't beat yourself up about it. The important thing is the act of will – the decision to try to forgive – the feelings aren't yours to command. God will do that in His good time.'

'It makes me feel very inadequate, compared with the way Mrs Molyneux forgave those boys who tormented her son and were probably responsible for his death, even if they didn't do it deliberately.'

'She's an example to us all.'

They sat for several moments in silence. Then Peter got up to go.

'Well I'd better leave you to get some rest. I know you won't get much over the weekend.'

'Don't you worry about that. In fact, tomorrow is one of the few days that I don't have a morning Mass, because we celebrate the Lord's Passion in the afternoon instead. Will you be coming to that?'

'I don't know. There's a service at Cowley Road in the morning. If Jonah doesn't get called in to work, we'll probably all go to that.'

'That's OK. Don't feel you've got to be here for everything that goes on. There are a lot of my parishioners – very good people all of them – that I never see from one Easter to the next. So long as you don't forget to come to the vigil on Saturday, I'll be happy.'

He opened the front door and Peter looked out into the darkness.

'There's still a light on in the church,' he commented.

'Is that right?'

'Yes.' Father Damien grimaced. 'The Boswell's are just doing the last fine-tuning of the organ. They've promised me faithfully that it will all be in order in time for the afternoon service tomorrow – which probably means that we'll be lucky to have it working for the Vigil on Saturday evening.'

Peter stepped outside, stumbling as his foot caught on a soft obstacle in his path. It grunted and moved away. Looking down, he could just make out a hunched up figure sitting propped up against the wall. Then everything became suddenly brighter as a powerful light came on overhead. His movement had activated the security light on the wall above.

The man scrambled slowly to his feet and steadied himself with a hand against the wall. He looked at Peter and then at Father Damien, who was standing framed in the doorway.

'Father?' he said in a husky voice.

'Yes?' the priest stepped outside.

Peter, his experience in the police service making him instantly suspicious of the stranger, stood in silence, ready to step in if he were to threaten violence.

'I need to talk to you.' The man's speech was slurred and he seemed to find it difficult to remain upright. Peter studied him under the glare of the high-intensity light. He had an unkempt appearance with wispy grey hair standing up on end. The hand, with which he was supporting himself against the wall, had dirty, broken nails and brown tobacco stains on the fingers.

'Yes, of course,' Father Damien replied. 'But you look as if you could do with a good night's sleep first. Do you have somewhere to go? Or would you like me to-'

'No. I need to talk to you now!' the man insisted, lurching forward and taking the priest by the arm. Then he drew his hand back as if realising that this action was inappropriate. He leaned back against the wall and, with a shaky right hand, made the sign of the cross over his chest. 'Bless me Father for I have sinned,' he began, 'it is … years and years since my last confession …'

'I'll ring for someone to take him to one of the homeless shelters,' Peter volunteered as the man's voice tailed off into silence.

'No!' Suddenly the man was alert again. 'No. Don't let them take me away, father. I need you to hear my confession.'

'Of course,' Father Damien repeated. 'I'm always ready to hear confessions. But, don't you think it would be better to wait until tomorrow morning, when you're … less tired,' he finished diplomatically.

'No! It might be too late tomorrow. I'm in mortal sin. I might die in the night and then I'll go to Hell. You wouldn't want that on your conscience would you? You've got to hear my confession now.'

'Very well. Come inside with me.'

Father Damien took the man's arm and together they started along the path towards the door into the choir vestry, which was the nearest entrance to the church building. Peter hesitated and then took hold of the man's other arm. Together, they lurched and stumbled into the church.

'I'm Father Damien. I don't remember seeing you at St Cyprian's before. Are you new to the area?'

'No. I was born here. Used to come to Mass regular as clockwork when I was a kid. Long time ago now, though.'

'Ah! And what's your name? I always like to put a name to a face.'

'Brendan.'

Father Damien reached out one hand to open the door of the confessional room, still supporting the penitent with the other. They all went in. Peter helped to get Brendan settled in a chair and then went out, closing the door behind him. He sat down in his accustomed pew, gazing up at the Madonna and Child statue and trying not to strain his ears to hear what was being said in the room across the aisle. He did not trust Brendan and was determined not to leave Father Damien alone with him at night.

He need not have worried about eavesdropping on a confidential conversation: the organ tuning would easily have covered up any deficiency there might have been in the soundproofing of the confessional room. Eventually, the wheezing and blowing stopped. There was a brief pause and then the organ started up again. This time, Peter was treated to a short burst from a Bach fugue as Keith Boswell gave the organ its final check before declaring the job done.

Peter got out his phone and keyed in a number. After a few seconds, there was a reply.

'Peter?' came the slow, patient voice of PC Gavin Hughes. 'What can I do for you?'

'Hi Gavin. Are you on duty?'

'Just on my way off home.'

'Oh! Then never mind. I'll ask someone else.'

'What was it you wanted?'

'I've got a man here. He looks like one of your homeless people, and very much the worse for drink, or it could be drugs. I was hoping you might have been on duty to take him to one of the shelters.'

'No problem. I'll come over now.'

'I don't want to keep you from going home.'

'Don't worry about that. Chrissie will be in bed by now anyway. She knows better than to wait up for me when I'm on a late shift. Just tell me where to come.'

'If you're sure …? We're at St Cyprian's church in Headington.'

'Right you are. That should only take me a few minutes.'

Peter was grateful that Gavin did not ask what he was doing at the church. He had no desire to explain about his confirmation or his recent acquisition of a sister and incipient brother-in-law. Gavin's habitual lack of curiosity would have been a disadvantage to him had he aspired to becoming a detective, but it had proved valuable in his chosen role working with the homeless community, whose members had come to trust him more than they did most police officers.

'It's just, I'm afraid he'll manage to scrounge a bed for the night off the parish priest and I don't trust him not to take advantage.'

'Don't worry,' Gavin repeated. 'I'll be right over. Did he give a name?'

'Brendan.'

'Would that be Brendan Connolly?'

'I don't know. He didn't say.' Peter ended the call and sat back in the pew, wondering why that name sounded vaguely familiar.

'We'll be off now,' Keith Boswell called out as the two organ builders made their way to the door carrying bags of tools. 'Tell the Father that the organ's all ready for his big service, but we'll need to come back and tune it again after a few weeks – when it's had time to settle.'

'I'll do that,' Peter promised.

'And we'll put the invoice in the post.'

'OK. I'll let him know.'

The door closed behind them and the church fell silent. Then Peter became aware of a murmur of voices. The door of the confessional room opened and Father Damien came out looking rather shaken. He seemed relieved to see Peter.

'Could you give me a hand? He's not feeling too good and I told him I'd–' He broke off as the main door opened and the bulky figure of Gavin Hughes came in through it. Peter beckoned the police officer over.

'I called PC Hughes while you were hearing Brendan's confession,' he explained to Father Damien. 'He'll be able to find somewhere for him to sleep tonight.'

Peter and Gavin went into the confession room where

they found Brendan slumped down in one of the chairs. When he saw Gavin, he tried unsuccessfully to rise.

'Is that you Gav?' he asked indistinctly. 'Have you come for me?'

'That's right, Brendan. I've got the car outside. Now, let's get you up.'

Gavin took Brendan by one arm. Peter grasped him on the other side. Together they pulled him to his feet and helped him to stagger out through the church to the car park. Peter supported him while Gavin opened the door of the car and then they bundled him inside. Peter leaned in and fastened the seat belt before closing the door. He looked across at Gavin, who was getting into the driver's seat.

'Will you be OK? Would you like me to come with you?'

'No,' Gavin shook his head. 'He won't cause trouble. Brendan and I are old mates.'

'OK. Thanks for coming out. And see you get off home right away after you've dropped him off.'

28 DISCHARGE SUMMARY

They arrived early at the Easter Vigil and were surprised to find that the courtyard behind St Cyprian's Church was already busy with people making preparations. Two young men were engaged in laying a bonfire in the centre of the yard. There was a team of women unpacking candles from boxes and inserting them into cardboard guards, designed to protect those holding them from drops of hot wax, before laying them out on a long trestle table standing against the wall.

The Parish Centre, a low rectangular building across the courtyard from the church, was bright with lights and, as the daylight faded outside, figures could be seen moving around inside preparing food for the refreshments that would be served after the Vigil ended. The doors opened and a man emerged carrying a stack of plastic chairs, which he started to set out in a wide circle to provide seating for those who could not stand during the part of the service that took place out-of-doors.

A young altar server came out of the door from the church carrying a candle that seemed almost as tall as she was. Behind her came Father Damien bearing a sturdy wrought iron stand which he set up in a secluded corner. He checked that it was firmly in place before helping to settle the candle securely into it.

Jonah advanced across the courtyard and intercepted Father Damien as he headed towards the pile of wood in its centre to supervise the lighting of the fire.

'I'm sorry to interrupt,' he began apologetically, 'but I need to have a quick word with you. Is there somewhere private we can go? It won't take more than a couple of minutes.'

'Couldn't it wait until after the service?' The priest's voice was unusually tense. This was his biggest day of the year and he was intent on seeing that it went off without a hitch.

'I'm sorry,' Jonah repeated. 'I need to brief you on some new developments. And it does need to be before the service starts, because you may need to re-think any intercessory prayers that you had in mind for Kevin and the boys who were there when he died.'

Father Damien stopped in his tracks and looked keenly at Jonah.

'OK. We'd better go inside.'

He led the way inside the church. Jonah and Peter followed. Lucy was about to go too, but Bernie held her back.

'We'd better stay here,' she whispered. 'Perhaps we can make ourselves useful.'

She walked over to join the group preparing the candles. Lucy and Dominic followed. Soon they were busy helping to set up a second trestle table and spreading out the candles to make it easy for people to collect them as they arrived.

Peter and Father Damien sat down in the Welcome Area and waited for Jonah to speak.

'As I said, there have been developments. Brendan

Connolly has confessed to murdering Kevin Molyneux. But perhaps that won't be such a surprise to you, Father?' Jonah said, looking the priest directly in the eye.

'As I'm sure you know, I cannot comment on what any penitent says to me in the confessional.'

'Well that's what he told PC Hughes,' Peter confided. 'It seems that he thought Gavin was arresting him, when he came to get him the other night, and he came out with the whole story while they were in the car.'

'It took a good few iterations before we could get Brendan's story and Norcott's account to match up,' Jonah continued. 'They both seemed intent on keeping the other one out of it. However, in the end, they both agreed that all four boys – Connolly, Norcott, Kennedy and Lewis – were there in the boiler house with Kevin that day. Norcott is still insisting that Kevin's death was a complete accident. Brendan, on the other hand, says that they played a game of "execution", in which they strung Kevin up by his scarf from a beam in the roof of the boiler house. They didn't seriously intend to kill him, but it was a deliberate act rather than a pure accident.'

'And which version do you believe?' Father Damien asked.

'We'll probably never know what really happened,' Peter told him.

'Which is one reason that I'm asking you, in anything that you say about it, to emphasise the uncertainty rather than any other aspect,' Jonah added.

'Thanks. Yes. I'll be careful what I say. Have you told Mary Molyneux about this?'

'No.' Jonah shook his head. 'The interviews with Brendan and Norcott took all day, so there hasn't been time. And we're still not sure exactly what the implications are going to be. I'm only telling you because I didn't want you to give out misleading information during the service.'

'I see. OK.'

'And now we can let you get on with your

preparations.'

'Good.' Father Damien got to his feet. 'Will you be staying to the Vigil?'

'Of course! You don't think I'd allow old Peter to take a big step like that without me there to keep an eye on him, do you?'

'Dear friends in Christ,' Father Damien began, looking round at the assembled crowd clustered in the courtyard, which was lit only by the flickering flames of the fire. 'On this most holy night, when our Lord Jesus Christ passed from death to life ...'

Jonah listened to the alien and yet strangely familiar words, following them on his computer screen in the copy of the service that Bernie had downloaded for him. He watched as the priest blessed first the fire and then the Paschal candle, marking the candle with symbolic letters and the numbers $2 - 0 - 1 - 8$, the current year.

There was a murmur of anticipation as Father Damien stepped forward and lit the candle from the fire. Jonah looked round at the eager faces of the schoolchildren, some of whom were here for the first time, all gripping their candles and watching for the signal to come forward to light them from the Easter flame.

'May the light of Christ, rising in glory, dispel the darkness of our hearts and minds,' intoned Father Damien, holding the candle high and pausing briefly before leading the way to the door of the church, followed by the altar servers, who lit more candles from the large one and then stood on either side of the entrance.

There was a brief scuffle as ushers struggled to organise the procession. Jonah watched as the congregation filed past, lighting their candles from the Paschal candle and processing into the darkness of the church. Then it was his turn. Bernie had fixed a candle in a paper cup filled with sand and set it in the cup-holder attached to his wheelchair. When he reached the door, Lucy picked up the cup and lit both his candle and her own from the Easter flame.

By the time they got inside, the church was a sea of flickering candles. Peter led the way to the front, where there were seats reserved for him and his family. Jonah found himself at the end of the front pew, just across the aisle from the side chapel and confessionals, and close to the Virgin-and-Child statue. Looking round, he recognised Mary Molyneux, also on the front row, and her nephew on the row immediately behind.

The remaining people filed in and Father Damien led the altar servers in procession along the other aisle and into the sanctuary. He advanced to the altar and then turned to face the people.

'Christ our light,' he intoned.

'Thanks be to God,' came the answer from the congregation.

The lights came on and Jonah's eyes were drawn up to the sanctuary ceiling where blue changed to purple, pink and finally yellow giving the impression that the sun was rising above the altar.

Father Damien stepped forward and placed the Paschal candle in its stand next to the lectern. An altar server wafted a thurible across the candle and then over the large lectern Bible, sending a cloud of incense rising above them.

Peter had been allocated the second reading, which was the story of Abraham's offering of his son, Isaac. As Jonah listened to the familiar story, his eyes wandered around the church, now bright with electric light as well as the dozens of candle flames. They came to rest on the face of the Virgin, which was between him and Peter standing at the lectern.

'... because you have not refused me your son, your only son ...' Peter read.

That was odd! It must be a trick of the light – all those

flickering candle flames casting strange shadows – but it was almost as if the Virgin's expression had changed. Anyone would have thought that she was listening and that the words saddened her. Jonah hastily fixed his gaze on Peter and tried to concentrate on the remainder of the reading. It was funny the way your mind could play tricks on you sometimes.

By the time they reached the seventh reading, Jonah was beginning to think that he had been unfair, in his youth, in complaining at the length of some of his late father's services. He had to admit that these Catholics had stamina!

When it came to the renewal of baptismal vows and Peter's confirmation, a thought suddenly struck Jonah. 'Doesn't there have to be a bishop here to do the confirmation?' he whispered to Bernie.

'Not when it's done at the Easter Vigil,' she whispered back. 'Father Damien has been delegated by the bishop to do it. I suppose the bishop can't be everywhere at once.'

'I bet old Peter's glad about that. He never likes having a big fuss made about things.'

Jonah was surprised, when the service moved into its fourth phase, entitled on his screen as *Liturgy of the Eucharist*, that Peter got to his feet once more and went forward to carry the box of wafers and decanter of wine, from the small table where they stood, up to the altar. Then he noticed a footnote, which said that, at the Easter Vigil it was appropriate for the newly baptised to bring forward the bread and wine. Poor Peter! Father Damien was certainly making him work for his right to join the church.

After the Eucharistic prayers, which included prayers for the souls of Kevin and Norman Molyneux, and an appeal for God's blessing on the ongoing police investigation, the congregation lined up to receive communion. Peter, looking rather self-conscious, was at the head of the queue. Jonah, counting the communicants as they descended the shallow steps from the chancel, noted that Father Damien had been a little over-optimistic in his estimate of the congregation at a hundred.

After handing out the eighty-fourth wafer, the priest came down to give communion to the half dozen or so parishioners who were unable to make their way forward to receive it at the sanctuary steps. He worked his way along the front pew until he came to Jonah. Without hesitation, he picked up a wafer. Jonah opened his mouth to explain that he was not eligible, but before he could speak, Father Damien placed it on his tongue with the words, 'the body of Christ.'

There was nothing for it but to swallow, which Jonah did, with some difficulty because the wafer was dry and he was unprepared. He watched Father Damien as he walked back to the altar and set down the remaining wafers, covering them with a white cloth.

The priest turned to face the congregation.

'Before we end, I would just like to thank the ladies who have prepared refreshments for you all in the Parish Centre and to invite you all to join us there in just a few minutes.'

Then came a short prayer and words of dismissal, and Father Damien led the altar servers down the aisle to the door that led to the courtyard. Peter, looking embarrassed, but determined to do all that was expected of him, followed immediately behind them. He took up a position next to Father Damien ready to greet the people as they left, while the altar servers processed back up the other aisle and disappeared into the vestry, followed by the choir.

Jonah and the rest of the family remained in their seats until everyone else had reached the back of the church. Then they made their way to the door where Peter and Father Damien were waiting patiently.

'Well done!' Dominic said, shaking Peter vigorously by the hand.

'I don't know why people keep saying that,' Peter answered self-consciously. 'I can't see that I've done anything much.'

'I think you read beautifully,' Lucy declared, giving him a hug. 'And I think it was mean of Father Damien giving you such a long passage.'

'Now I know why I'm glad you aren't in my congregation every week,' the Father joked. 'It isn't good for my self-esteem to have such a critical audience.'

'I have to ask,' Jonah said, when the others had left for the Parish Centre and he was alone with Father Damien, 'why did you give me the bread? Weren't you breaking the rules?'

'That's between me and my confessor. I've always found that rules are best treated with a certain degree of flexibility. And now, I have a question for you too. What's going to happen to Timothy Norcott and Brendan Connolly?'

'I can't say for certain. Now that Brendan has admitted to having deliberately injured Kevin, I think the Crown Prosecution Service will probably feel obliged to try them both for murder – especially if the inquest comes up with an *unlawful killing* verdict. They may be able to argue for manslaughter or, if the outcome of the inquest is *accidental death* or *misadventure*, even for *unlawful wounding*. Whatever else, they are certainly guilty of concealing Kevin's death and preventing the lawful burial of his body – and they've both admitted to assaulting him.'

'But it's so long ago, and they were so young at the time,' Father Damien argued. 'Would there be any point in sending them to prison now?'

'Now *that* is why I don't envy the judge who has to pass sentence. If they had been prosecuted at the time, they would have been sent to a young offenders' institution and it would have been all about rehabilitating them and turning them into law-abiding citizens. Now, rehabilitation doesn't really come into it – especially as far as Norcott is concerned. So any punishment has to be for the sake of setting an example to deter others.'

'I'd say that Tim Norcott has more than paid back his debt to society through the work he's been doing.'

'You may say that,' Jonah countered, 'but you could argue it the other way. You could say that, while Connolly has clearly been badly damaged by the incident and has suffered as a consequence through his drug-addiction and homelessness, Norcott has been largely unaffected. He's got a degree and a good job with a salary and a pension to look forward too.'

'And what about Father Carey?' the priest asked cautiously. 'Will he be charged too?'

'I don't see how it can be avoided. He will presumably plead guilty to *prevention of the lawful and decent burial of a dead body* and he'll probably get a fine or a suspended prison sentence. He may well also be charged with *perverting the course of justice*, which is a more serious crime and could lead to him going to jail.'

'I see.' Father Damien sighed. 'Well, I suppose I ought to thank you for getting to the bottom of everything. And it could be worse. Father O'Leary was wrong and foolish, but at least St Cyprian's won't have to be investigated for historic child abuse.'

'And the organ was finished in time for Easter,' Jonah added with a grin. 'I have to say, it sounded splendid this evening!'

THANK YOU

Thank you for taking the time to read ORGAN FAILURE. If you enjoyed it, please consider telling your friends or posting a short review. Word of mouth is an author's best friend and much appreciated. Thank you,

Judy.

DISCLAIMER

This book is a work of fiction. Any references to real people, events, establishments, organisations or locales are intended only to provide a sense of authenticity and are used fictitiously. All of the characters and events are entirely invented by the author. Any resemblances to persons living or dead are purely coincidental.

Many of the locations and institutions that feature in this book are real. Their inhabitants and employees, however, are purely fictional. In particular,

- St Cyprian's church does not exist and it is not based on any church of any denomination anywhere;
- Cowley Road Methodist Church is real (and I have happy memories of attending it between 1977 and 1979), but any details mentioned in this book are fictitious;
- None of the police officers mentioned in this story are based on real members of Thames Valley Police or of any other police service.

MORE ABOUT BERNIE AND HER FRIENDS

There are now nine **Bernie Fazakerley Mysteries**. The other eight (in chronological order of the action) are:

- **Two Little Dickie Birds**: a murder mystery for DI Peter Johns and his Sergeant, Paul Godwin.
- **Murder of a Martian**: a double murder for Peter and Jonah to solve.
- **Grave Offence**: an assault and a suspicious death that Peter investigates, while Jonah is in rehab in the spinal injuries centre.
- **Awayday**: a traditional detective story set among the dons of an Oxford college.
- **Death on the Algarve:** a mystery for Bernie and her friends to tackle while on holiday in Portugal.
- **Sorrowful Mystery**: Jonah investigates a child abduction and Peter embarks on a new journey of faith.
- **Mystery over the Mersey**: a murder mystery set in Liverpool.
- **In my Liverpool Home**: Bernie and her friends return to Liverpool to investigate a suspicious death in Aunty Dot's Care Home.

Bernie also appears in two other novels:

- **Changing Scenes of Life**: Jonah Porter's life story, told through the medium of his favourite hymns.
- **Despise not your Mother**: the story of Bernie's quest to learn about her dead husband's past.

There is also a book of short stories, in which Peter narrates his side of the story:

- **My Life of Crime**: the collected memoirs of DI Peter Johns.

You can find them all on Judy Ford's Amazon Author page:
https://www.amazon.co.uk/-/e/B0193I5B1M

Read more about Bernie Fazakerley and her friends and family at https://sites.google.com/site/llanwrdafamily/

Visit the Bernie Fazakerley Publications Facebook page here:
https://www.facebook.com/Bernie.Fazakerley.Publications.

Follow Bernie on Twitter: https://twitter.com/BernieFaz.

LIST OF POLICE PERSONNEL

The following police officers recur in many of the Bernie Fazakerley Mysteries. This alphabetical list is provided to give some background to them and for reference.

- **Rupert Andrews** Detective Sergeant 2000, Detective Inspector 2012.

- **Malcolm Appleton** Police Constable 2007, Sergeant 2018.

- **Alison Brown** Detective Inspector 1989, DCI 2004, Chief Superintendent 2015.

- **Tracy Burton** Police Constable 1999, Sergeant 2005.

- **Anna Davenport** Detective Sergeant 2007, Inspector 2015. Married in 2001 to Philip Davenport. Separated in 2017. 3 children: Jessica (2001), Marcus (2002), Donna (2017). Archaeology and Anthropology graduate from Cambridge.

- **Pamela Gregson** Custody Sergeant.

- **Gavin Hughes** Police Constable 1988. Specialises in community policing and building bridges with rough-sleepers.

- **Peter Johns** Police Constable 1969, Detective Constable 1973, DS 1978, DI 1993, retired 2011. Married to Angie in 1978 and to Bernie in 2006. Father of Hannah (1980) and Eddie (1982). Stepfather to Lucy (2000).

- **Arshad Khan** Detective Sergeant 2002, Detective Inspector 2006, DCI 2014. Specialises in cases involving ethnic minority victims. Married to Anita.

- **Aaron King** Police Constable 2001, Sergeant 2009.

- **Andrew Lepage** Detective Constable 2007, Detective Sergeant 2015. Graduate in criminology (1st class) from Leicester University in 2005. Lives with his mother in Headington Quarry.

- **Monica Philipson** Detective Constable 2002, Detective Sergeant 2008. An ambitious police officer, who studied at Keble College, Oxford.

- **Richard Paige** Detective Constable 1960, Detective Sergeant 1967, DI 1973, DCI 1981, Detective Superintendent 1995, died 1999. Married to Bernie in 1997. Father of Lucy (2000).

- **Jonah Porter** Police Constable 1977, Detective Constable 1979, Detective Sergeant 1983, DI 1987, DCI 1996. Married to Margaret in 1982. Widowed in 2014.

- **Alice Ray** Detective Constable (2016)

ABOUT THE AUTHOR

Like her main character, Bernie Fazakerley, Judy Ford is an Oxford graduate and a mathematician. Unlike Bernie, Judy grew up in a middle-class family in the South London stockbroker belt. After moving to the North West and working in Liverpool, Judy fell in love with the Scouse people and created Bernie to reflect their unique qualities.

As a Methodist Local Preacher, Judy often tells her congregation, "I see my role as asking the questions and leaving you to think out your own answers." She carries this philosophy forward into her writing and she hopes that readers will find themselves challenged to think as well as being entertained.

Made in the USA
Columbia, SC
14 March 2018